STUCK RUBBER BABY

BY HOWARD CRUSE

STUCK RUBBER BABY

BY HOWARD CRUSE

HarperPerennial

A Division of HarperCollins*Publishers*

DC Comics

Jenette Kahn
president & editor-in-chief

Paul Levitz
executive vp & publisher

Andrew Helfer
group editor

Bronwyn Carlton Taggart
editor

Jim Higgins
assistant editor

Robbin Brosterman
art director

Bruce Bristow
vp-sales & marketing

Richard Bruning
vp-creative director

Patrick Caldon
vp-finance & operations

Terri Cunningham
vp-managing editor

Chantal d'Aulnis
vp-licensed publishing

Joel Ehrlich
senior vp-advertising & promotions

Lillian Laserson
vp & general counsel

Bob Rozakis
executive director - production

DEDICATION

FOR KIM,

FOR PAM,

AND

(AS ALWAYS)

FOR EDDIE

First HarperPerennial edition published 1996.

ISBN 0-06-097713-2

96 97 98 99 00 ❖/RRD 10 9 8 7 6 5 4 3 2 1

INTRODUCTION

by TONY KUSHNER

I first encountered book-length comic book art when I was ten or eleven years old, browsing the shelves of my synagogue library: a history of the Soviet Union, told in black and white drawings and word balloons. I remember neither its title nor its author, only that its pages teemed with burly, gap-toothed, Mongol-faced, furhatted greatcoated or butcher-aproned Ivans. This was a cold war history produced entirely from a right perspective, so the Ivans were invariably drawn steeped to their swollen upper biceps in blood — the blood rendered simply, and appropriately, in smears and swaths of black ink, slathered generously in practically every panel.

The effect was thrilling, alarming, faintly nauseating: in addition to the dark pools of gore it was meant to evoke, the flat black called to mind mud, excrement, and the burnt bones that are the source of a carbon soot pure enough for India ink. The technique more than successfully intimated sensational levels of depravity and bestiality. As I read the book I imagined its author in the grim ecstasy of graphically depicting the uncountable crimes of the Stalin era; with his oversoaked, ink-logged brushes dripping midnight, murder, and despair, the righteously aroused and enflamed cartoonist-historian-ideologue winds up as smudged and stained as the sadistically grinning commissars he is depicting, indicting. In this image there is a suggestion of some sort of disquieting complicity between the accuser and the accused: the accuser as creative artist, through the act of representing, having created the accused. I remember feeling extremely uncomfortable and impressed. The image of the inkstained artist, muddied up to his elbows with the grime he's busily, inexactly but passionately slinging about, will to this day flash through my mind on any occasion when I encounter a troubling, stirring example of the exuberant, complicitous outrage of the writers and the artists of the political right.

The cartoon history of the USSR, with its ardent, serious, political intentions, its screaming for justice and the world's attention, was similar to but also different from the super-hero comics I devoured monthly the instant they appeared on the local 7-Eleven magazine racks. Comic books were an important part of my transition to adulthood. My childhood, like most, was preoccupied with magic and enchantment, with day-dream versions of the world, in which the Terrors with which one would eventually come to terms were expressed in a guise sufficiently metaphorical to countenance unflinchingly. Comic books paved the path up to the portals of adulthood, offering sexy and dangerous fantasies in which the sex was present but still subliminal (muscular men in BVDs), the danger grand and improbable enough to be intensely gratifying and yet manageable for a neurotic, rather cowardly gay boy entering early adolescence. The super-heros were, like me, full of anxieties of being unmasked, rendered powerless, and destroyed. Unlike me they were beautiful and irresistibly strong, able to participate fearlessly in the violence that seemed increasingly to be the true language of the world.

My parents worried about the growing stacks of comic books in my room, believing that my addiction to pictures would keep me from becoming the adult reader I ought to become. I pointed out that the comic books I read were strewn with literary references, mostly unattributed quotes from the Bible, Shakespeare, Milton, and Coleridge; and the villains especially possessed an ambitious vocabulary — I remember learning "meretricious" and "invidious," among other useful words. My parents, unimpressed, continued to worry. Perhaps it was my unmistakable fascination for the muscular men in their BVDs.

I no longer remember when or even why I stopped reading comic books. I completed the transition they had helped me through, I suppose. Having found the nerve and the necessity, I turned to a literature that addressed sex and danger costumed as I was encountering them in real life, the drab drag of the quotidian.

But I never stopped adoring the drawing and word-balloon form. An adult now, free enough to indulge in all manner of parentally banned activities, I read the daily comic strips in the newspaper. I find that when the news is awful, as it almost always is, it's only the promise of the comic strips that keeps me wading through the pages of holocaust, catastrophe, psychosis, abuse, and chicanery that are, they tell me, the proper business of an adult.

Playwrights work within many of the same drastic economies of dialogue and image as comic book artists; both have to grapple, albeit in different ways, with severe limitations and pressures of time and space. So my admiration for the artists who produce good comic strips is unbounded, and yet I still detect in myself a certain furtiveness when I'm reading these strips out in the open, on the subway. Shame, an unavoidable residue of any successful transformation, attaches itself to the comics, as if reading them were age-inappropriate. The generic name, "comics" (or its earlier version, "funnies"), is no help in this regard.

My appetite for longer narratives in comic book form was left largely unsatisfied, and guiltily repressed, till the day I first purchased *The Advocate*. In the Pink Pages section at the back of the magazine, I discovered (along with many other forbidden delights) a picaresque novel, meted out in one-page installments in every issue. It was complicated, politically-minded, gently humorous and psychologically sophisticated. It was called *Wendel*, and for the next several years I followed its recountings of the lives of lesbians and gay men, while at the same time becoming acquainted with the previous work of its author, Howard Cruse, and with the author himself.

Howard Cruse is a pioneer in the field of lesbian and gay comics, an important participant in the underground comics movement, and in my opinion one of the most talented artists ever to work in the form. His short pieces are wonderful examples of narrative compression, politically and emotionally complex, provocative and moving. In short and longer works, like *Wendel*, Howard demonstrates a quicksilver intelligence and imagination that can shift, with lightning speed, from the hallucinatory and visionary to the gnarly and grotty, from the sexy and sublime to the downright revolting, from the comic to the tragic, and from one side of a political argument to the other. One part of this ability he owes to his region; such graceful, wry, apparently effortless chameleoning is a Southern virtue. The other part is attributable to sheer talent and a serious commitment to art that is unafraid of its usefulness in a political fight.

Howard was a body-and-soul participant in the '60s revolution, which made him an anarchist, or left-libertarian. His politics are the antithesis of doctrinaire; I find his opinions, as expressed in his work, irresistibly attractive, even when I disagree.

Howard told his friends a few years ago that he was stopping work on *Wendel* to devote himself to writing and drawing a graphic novel: the result of that labor you are holding in your hands.

It is ever the conundrum of the introducer of something really good that the thing itself needs no introduction, it needs only to be read. Its readers will surely find in *Stuck Rubber Baby* all manner of richness and depth and value, only one aspect of which is political. But as political art this book is timely. It articulates a crying need for solidarity, it performs the crucial function of remembering, for the queer community, how essential to the birth of our politics of liberation the civil rights movement was. The point, it seems to me, is not that one movement co-opts the energy or the nobility or the history of another; not that one people, rising to an angry knowledge of how it has been abused, competes for status of "most abused" with any other; but rather that we need to know the genealogies of our movements, and with that knowledge come to understand the interdependence of all liberation struggles. We must finally accept and practice what we've been saying for decades, for centuries: Freedom is only possible when it's everyone's freedom, and slavery anywhere means slavery everywhere.

To overcome the perils of the present moment will require all the human force and power and collective will we can bring to bear. Our political leaders these days seem more and more like the caricatures political cartoonists draw. Even a supremely gifted political cartoonist will have trouble exaggerating the malevolence of Gingrich, the manifest instability of Dole, the dithering and waffling of Clinton, the satanic flatulent eructations of Limbaugh. They're all bespattered with the inky muck of extremism, heartlessness, and criminality.

Here is a book drawn in a finer, more scrupled and scrupulous, more rigorous style. In the beauty of its details, in the subtlety of its narrative, its heart is manifest: Its author addresses his work to the labyrinthine internal politics one encounters in trying to be a good person in the world. This book is quiet, elegiac, and turned toward the past. In reconstructing a memory of a time when one struggle lit up the path for another, and an oppressed people gave instruction, through example, in the ways of resistance to the entire watching world, Howard Cruse offers us something deeply important and fortifying, something we need.

"The antonym of *forgetting*," says the Jewish historian Yosef Hayim Yerushalmi, "is not *remembering*, but *justice*."

*Tony Kushner is the author of **Angels in America: A Gay Fantasia on National Themes**, among other plays.*

STOCK RUBBER BABY

KEEP DIXIE WHITE

RACE MIXERS GO BACK NORTH

CLOSE MIXED SCHOOLS

LOOKING BACK, I DIDN'T SEE ALL **THAT** MANY DEAD BODIES WHEN I WAS A KID GROWING UP DOWN SOUTH...

...BUT THE ONES I **SAW** STUCK IN MY **MIND.**

AS A RULE, THE EXPERT HANDS OF OUR BEST **LOCAL MORTICIANS** HAD THE REMAINS **SPRUCED UP** BY THE TIME I GOT MY LOOK AT WHOEVER WAS LYING IN STATE...

...SO THERE WAS NEVER ANY **GORE** ON DISPLAY.

THE FIRST HUMAN CORPSE I SAW WAS **MISS VIOLET,** WHO'D BEEN MY **BABYSITTER.**

DADDY SAID SHE COLLAPSED IN A **DITCH.** IN HER **CASKET,** THOUGH, SHE DIDN'T LOOK THAT MUCH THE **WORSE FOR WEAR.**

WE HAD A PET **RABBIT** THAT GOT RUN OVER. NOW, **THAT** WAS A MESS!

AS A DUMB **KID**, THOUGH, I CONVINCED MYSELF THAT HUMAN BEINGS WERE **DIFFERENT** FROM ANIMALS.

THE **FUNERALS** I ATTENDED LEFT ME REASSURED THAT, WHATEVER TOLL GOT TAKEN ON MY **OTHER** BODY PARTS, MY **HEAD** WOULD SURVIVE DEATH **INTACT**.

THEN MY FRIEND BO WISED ME UP.

WANNA SEE SOMETHIN' **GROSS**, TOLAND?

SURE.

I FOUND A NIGGER MAGAZINE IN A TRASH CAN DOWNTOWN. LOOK AT THIS **PICTURE**....

IT WAS A CLOSE-UP PHOTOGRAPH OF A **DEAD BLACK PERSON** WHOSE **SKULL** WAS ALL CAVED IN.

SINCE THEN I'VE LEARNED THAT IT WAS **EMMETT TILL**, A FOURTEEN-YEAR-OLD BOY WHO GOT **BASHED, LYNCHED**, AND **DUMPED IN A RIVER** IN MISSISSIPPI BECAUSE HE SAID SOMETHING **FLIPPANT** TO A **WHITE WOMAN**.

SOMETHING IN MY BRAIN PERMANENTLY BLEW A **FUSE** WHEN I SAW THAT PICTURE.

I HAD **NIGHTMARES**.

I WAS WORRIED ABOUT MY **SKULL**.

DADDY, IS THERE ANY **DIFFERENCE** BETWEEN **NEGRO SKULLS** AND **WHITE PEOPLE'S SKULLS**?

HOW D'YA **MEAN**, SON?

ARE WHITE PEOPLE'S SKULLS **HARDER** THAN NEGRO SKULLS?

OH, I **DOUBT** IT, TOLAND. I DOUBT IT **SERIOUSLY**.

IF **ANYTHING**, NEGRO BONES ARE PROBABLY **TOUGHER**, SINCE COLORED FOLKS ARE CLOSER TO THE **ANIMAL STATE** THAN WE ARE AND HAVE GOTTEN **STRONGER** FROM HAVIN' TO GET BY IN THE **WILD**.

NOW, AS FAR AS **BRAINS** ARE CONCERNED, IT'S ANOTHER **MATTER.** WHITE PEOPLE'S BRAINS ARE MORE **DEVELOPED.** IT'S BEEN SCIENTIFICALLY **PROVEN.**

NOT THAT NEGROES AREN'T **SMART!**

THEY'RE **PLENTY** SMART! THEY'RE **SLOW,** BUT THE BRAINS THEY'VE **GOT** SERVE 'EM VERY **WELL.**

TAKE **STETSON,** THERE....

STETSON HAD COME ONCE A WEEK TO DO OUR YARD WORK FOR AS LONG AS I COULD REMEMBER.

STETSON'S ALWAYS ON **TOP** OF THINGS.

HAVE YOU EVER SEEN ME NEEDIN' TO **EXPLAIN** ANYTHING TO HIM MORE THAN **ONCE?**

NOPE.

ARE YOU TWO DISCUSSIN' THE **YARD MAN?**

YEP. DO YOU REMEMBER WHEN STETSON GOT THE OL' **FORD** RUNNIN', THE WEEKEND OF THE **ICE STORM?**

YES, I **DO.** IT'S A MIRACLE HIS **HANDS** DIDN'T FREEZE.

I DON'T THINK HE EVEN BROUGHT **GLOVES** WITH HIM THAT NIGHT.

DON'T EVER MAKE THE MISTAKE OF FAILIN' TO **RESPECT** THE **COLORED** MAN, SON.

TREATED WELL, HE'LL DO **BETTER** BY YOU THAN MANY A **WHITE.**

AND I DON'T **EVER** WANT TO HEAR YOU USE THE WORD **'NIGGER,'** THE WAY **SOME** FOLKS AROUND HERE DO.

IT'S A **HATEFUL** TERM, AND NO CREATURE OF GOD **DESERVES** IT.

I **WON'T.** I **NEVER** DO.

LATER I'D LOOK BACK **NOSTALGICALLY** AT THE WAY MY DAD ALWAYS TOOK TIME TO **EXPLAIN** STUFF TO ME IN HIS FUCKED-UP WAY.

I ASSUMED HE KNEW WHAT HE WAS TALKING ABOUT BECAUSE OF ALL THE **BOOKS** WE HAD IN THE HOUSE.

TRUCKLOADS OF 'EM!

THEY WERE JUST PART OF MY **CHILDHOOD** SCENERY.

I REMEMBER THE DAY MY SISTER AND I SPENT GOING **THROUGH** ALL THOSE GODDAMNED BOOKS, AFTER MAMA AND DADDY GOT **KILLED** IN A CAR WRECK.

THAT'S WHEN MELANIE SET ME **STRAIGHT.**

OH, TOLAND— DON'T **TELL** ME YOU THOUGHT THAT DADDY HAD ACTUALLY **READ** ALL OF THESE THINGS!

HE MIGHT'VE THUMBED THROUGH AN' LOOKED AT SOME **PICTURES**, BUT **YOU'VE** PROBABLY READ **TEN TIMES** AS MANY OF THESE AS **MAMA** OR **DADDY** DID.

I WATCHED 'EM GO SHOPPIN'. MAMA **MADE** DADDY SHELL OUT FOR BOOKS. I GUESS SHE FELT **EMBARRASSED** ABOUT HER AN' HIM HAVIN' QUIT **SCHOOL** SO EARLY.

I DON'T THINK SHE EVER **GAVE UP** ON MAKIN' A **READER** OUT OF 'IM.

I THINK THAT WAS GONNA BE HER PROJECT AFTER HE **RETIRED**.

SO MUCH FOR **THAT** PLAN, MAMA!

STETSON AND HIS WIFE CAME TO THE GRAVESIDE SERVICE. NOBODY **MINDED**, SINCE THEY STOOD WAY IN **BACK**.

I'M **SO** SORRY 'BOUT WHAT HAPPENED, MISTER TOLAND. IT JUS' BROKE MY **HEART** WHEN I HEARD.

I HOPE YOU AN' MISS MELANIE'LL BE **O.K.**

I THINK WE WILL, STETSON.

I FELT **GUILTY** FOR THE TIMES THAT I'D WATCHED STETSON WORKING IN THE GARDEN AND IMAGINED WHAT HE'D LOOK LIKE WITH HIS **SKULL CAVED IN**.

IT WASN'T ANYTHING **PERSONAL**. I JUST HAD A **FIXATION** ABOUT SKULLS.

4

FOR A TIME, EARLY IN MY LIFE, STETSON'S SON **BEN** WOULD COME OVER AND **PLAY** WITH ME IN THE **YARD** WHILE HIS DADDY PULLED **WEEDS.**

WE DID A LOT OF **WRESTLING,** WHICH I ENJOYED.

I WENT THROUGH A **PERIOD** OF LOOKING BACK AND **WONDERING** IF ALL THAT WRESTLING WITH **BEN** WAS WHAT MADE ME A **HOMO!**

SURE, TOLAND! ALSO WALKING ON A **SIDEWALK CRACK** WITH A **FULL MOON** OVERHEAD!

IT'S JUST ONE OF THE STUPID THINGS YOU WONDER WHEN YOU'RE **YOUNG** AND TRYING TO GET **USED** TO THE IDEA.

ANYWAY, MELANIE PUT AN **END** TO ME HAVING BEN OVER SO MUCH.

TOLAND, IT DOESN'T **LOOK** RIGHT FOR YOU TO PLAY WITH A **COLORED BOY** ALL THE TIME.

MY **FRIENDS** ARE STARTIN' TO MAKE **REMARKS.**

IT WOULD'VE BEEN **IMPOLITE** TO JUST TELL BEN TO **GO AWAY,** SO I DROVE HIM OFF BY BEING AGGRESSIVELY **BORING.**

WANNA PLAY **DETECTIVES?**

NAH.

WANNA THROW TH' **BALL?**

NAH.

WELL... WHATCHA WANNA **DO?**

I DUNNO. WHADDA **YOU** WANNA DO?

FINALLY HE **GAVE UP** ON ME AND STOPPED SHOWING UP.

THE **NEXT** TIME I SAW BEN WAS ABOUT A DOZEN YEARS **LATER.** HE WAS STANDING BY A **BUS** AT THE BIG **MARCH ON WASHINGTON** THAT **MARTIN LUTHER KING** GAVE HIS MOST FAMOUS **SPEECH** AT.

GINGER NOTICED ME **STARING.**

WHO'RE YOU **LOOKIN'** AT?

JUST SOMEBODY I USED TO **KNOW.**

I TOLD GINGER **WHO** BEN **WAS.** **SAMMY NOONE** OVERHEARD AND SAID I SHOULD GO OVER AND GIVE THE DUDE A BIG **HELLO.**

WHO **KNOWS?** THOSE MOMENTS HE SPENT **WRITHING** WITH YOU IN THE **DUST** MAY BE AMONG BEN'S MOST **CHERISHED MEMORIES!**

NOT TOO **LIKELY,** SAMMY!

I'D FEEL MORE **PLEASED** WITH MYSELF IF I COULD CLAIM THAT IT WAS PURE **SOCIAL CONSCIENCE** THAT GOT MY ASS OUT TO THE LINCOLN MEMORIAL THAT SUMMER, OR THE **MEMORY** OF HOW I HAD FELT ABOUT **EMMETT TILL...**

...BUT IN REALITY IT WAS MY ATTEMPTS TO COURT THE AFFECTIONS OF **GINGER RAINES** THAT NUDGED ME ONTO THE UNEXPECTED ROADS I ENDED UP TRAVELING.

AND BY THE WAY, IF YOU'RE **CONFUSED** BY THE FACT THAT I WAS COURTING A **GIRL** EVEN THOUGH I WAS A **FAGGOT**— WELL, YOU'RE NO MORE CONFUSED THAN **I** WAS WHILE I WAS **DOING** IT.

Tsk, tsk! BE A **GOOD** BOY AND SAY '**GAY,'** TOLAND, NOT '**FAGGOT.'**

I DIDN'T **FEEL** 'GAY' BACK THEN. I FELT LIKE A **FAGGOT!**

YOU'VE GOTTA BE AT LEAST A **LITTLE** BIT **UN-SCREWED-UP** TO BE '**GAY'!**

ANYWAY, MY **INTENTION** FOR QUITE SOME TIME WAS TO TURN MYSELF AROUND AND **NOT** BE GAY...

...WHICH I **KIDDED** MYSELF INTO VIEWING AS AN **OPTION.**

I SUBSCRIBED TO **PLAYBOY** AND HAD AN ABSOLUTE **RULE** THAT I WOULDN'T LET MYSELF **MASTURBATE** UNLESS I WAS LOOKING AT ONE OF THE **CENTERFOLD PLAYMATES** AT THE TIME.

Red Masque

I HELD TO THAT RULE FOR OVER **THREE YEARS,** WITH ONLY A **COUPLE** OF **LAPSES.**

WET DREAMS DIDN'T **COUNT.**

UNH-H-H-H...

IT WAS PLAYBOY THAT LED TO ME BEING FRIENDS WITH **RILEY WHEELER,** WHO I GOT TO KNOW AT CLAYFIELD'S MAIN **BOWLING ALLEY** SHORTLY BEFORE HE GOT **DRAFTED.**

RILEY COULD HOLD FORTH FOR **HOURS** ABOUT HUGH HEFNER'S **'PLAYBOY PHILOSOPHY'** ESSAYS.

HE HAD A **POINT.** THERE WAS DEFINITELY SOMETHING TO HEF'S **SOCIOLOGICAL VIEWS,** AND IT WAS OBVIOUS FROM THE **PHOTO SPREADS** THAT THEY WERE GETTING THE PUBLISHER A HELLUVA LOT OF **SEX!**

IRONICALLY, DESPITE RILEY'S ENTHUSIASM FOR THE WILD PLAYBOY LIFESTYLE, HE AND HIS GIRLFRIEND **MAVIS** SEEMED ABOUT AS **MONOGAMOUS** AS ANYBODY COULD **ASK.** I ONLY KNEW RILEY **ONCE** TO STRAY.

WHICH ISN'T TO SAY THEY LIVED BY STANDARD SOUTHERN **MORES.** THEY'D ALREADY BEGUN SHACKING UP WHILE THEY WERE IN **HIGH SCHOOL**—AND THEY HAD NO **APOLOGIES** FOR IT.

HEF WOULD'VE **LIKED** THAT.

AROUND A YEAR AFTER MY FOLKS DIED, RILEY INVITED ME TO MOVE INTO THE OLD **HOUSE** HE SHARED WITH MAVIS.

The Wheelery

SINCE RILEY'S NAME WAS **WHEELER,** WE CALLED THAT HOUSE **'THE WHEELERY.'**

UNTIL THEN I HAD LIVED WITH MY SISTER AND HER HUSBAND **ORLEY** IN THE HOUSE MELANIE AND I HAD BEEN **REARED** IN — WHICH WAS **ROOMIER** NOW, WITH ALL THE **BOOKCASES** TAKEN OUT.

Marshal Dillon! Marshal Dillon!

I HAD AN UNGLAMOROUS JOB AS A GAS STATION **PUMP JOCKEY.** MAMA WENT TO HER GRAVE ROYALLY **PISSED** THAT I WAS SPENDING MY TIME PUMPING **GAS** WHILE I WAS OF **COLLEGE** AGE.

BUT THAT'S JUST THE WAY IT WAS—AND THE WAY **I** WAS!

THERE WAS A LOT ABOUT THAT TIME THAT WAS **FUN,** ESPECIALLY **EARLY ON**— BEFORE THE **SHIT** HIT THE FAN.

NOT HAVING A GOOD HEAD FOR **DATES,** I JUST REMEMBER THE YEARS WHEN THIS STORY HAPPENED TO ME AS **'KENNEDY TIME.'**

Chapter 2

I SHOULD MENTION HOW I GOT BROUGHT OUT OF THE **CLOSET** BY THE UNITED STATES **ARMY.**

...AND HOW YOU BROKE ALL **RECORDS** TRYING TO SCRAMBLE BACK **IN!**

THAT WAS BACK WHEN MY **FOLKS** WERE STILL **ALIVE.** I HAD RECENTLY TURNED **EIGHTEEN**, AND **UNCLE SAM** WAS KEEPING **TRACK.**

SOMETHIN' FOR YOU FROM **SELECTIVE SERVICE.**

plop!

BEING ALREADY IN THE DOGHOUSE AT HOME FOR NOT GOING TO **COLLEGE**, I DIDN'T GET MUCH **SYMPATHY** WHEN MY **DRAFT NOTICE** ARRIVED.

MAYBE THE ARMY WILL HELP GIVE YOUR LIFE MORE **DIRECTION,** SON.

SURE, MA.

READY FOR A FEW **PUSH-UPS?**

I TOOK IT IN **STRIDE.** I VIEWED THE **MILITARY** BACK THEN AS A MODERATELY ANNOYING MIXTURE OF **CALISTHENICS** AND **HARASSMENT** THAT I WAS PROBABLY GONNA HAVE TO **PUT UP WITH** ONE WAY OR **ANOTHER.**

IT COULD EVEN BE **FUN,** JUDGING FROM 'SGT. BILKO' ON **TV.**

Hide, everybody! Colonel Hall's coming!

But we can't leave Pvt. Doberman dressed up like a pineapple!

Ha ha ha heh ha ha ha ha heh heh ha ha ha

I SHOWED UP AT THE **RECRUITMENT CENTER** AS INSTRUCTED AND GOT HAULED WITH THE OTHER DRAFTEES OFF TO MY **CENTRAL ARMORY** FOR MY **INDUCTION PHYSICAL.**

U.S. AR

MY MOMENT OF **TRUTH** CAME WHEN A COUPLA HUNDRED OF US, STILL ALL BUT **NAKED** FROM GETTING INSPECTED FOR **LICE** AND **HEMORRHOIDS**, GOT HERDED INTO A BIG, SWEATY HALL FULL OF **SCHOOLROOM CHAIRS** AND TOLD TO FILL OUT LONG MEDICAL-HISTORY **QUESTIONNAIRES...**

...WHEREUPON, THE KID SITTING **NEXT** TO ME, FOR REASONS KNOWN ONLY TO **HIM**, GOT A **HARD-ON.**

HEY, SARGE! WE'VE GOT A HOMO HERE!!!

THE **ZEST** THAT THE GUYS IN CHARGE BROUGHT TO MAKING SURE EVERYONE KNEW EXACTLY **WHO** AMONG US HAD 'CHECKED THE BOX' CAUGHT ME A LITTLE BY **SURPRISE.**

I HAD LOTS OF QUIET TIME TO **MULL** THINGS **OVER** DURING THE RIDE BACK **HOME,** SINCE NOBODY ELSE ON THE BUS WOULD SIT **NEXT** TO ME.

I KEPT THINKING DEPRESSING THOUGHTS ABOUT THE **DRAWBACKS** OF BEING A HOMO.

Bzz bzz bzz... *zz faggot bzz bzz...*

I THOUGHT ABOUT **EZRA GABLE,** WHO WAS PRESIDENT OF THE BIGGEST **BANK** IN CLAYFIELD FOR NEARLY **TWENTY YEARS...**

...UNTIL HE GOT **MURDERED** IN BACK OF THE **SAWMILL.**

SOME TEENAGERS ADMITTED **BLUDGEONING** HIM TO DEATH. THEY SAID THEY'D BEEN **TRAUMATIZED** BECAUSE HE'D **LOOKED** AT THEM 'IN A NASTY WAY.'

THE DISTRICT ATTORNEY SAID THEY WERE **GOOD BOYS** AT **HEART,** SO HE LET THE PROSECUTION **SLIDE.**

I THOUGHT ABOUT **ABBY BAXTER,** THE TOUGH **SCHOOL NURSE** WHO GAVE US OUR **POLIO SHOTS** AND WHO EVERYBODY **SNICKERED** ABOUT.

I WONDERED IF **ALEC** FROM **CAMP** HAD TURNED OUT MORE **NORMAL** THAN ME.

BY THE TIME **CLAYFIELD STADIUM** CAME INTO VIEW, I'D DECIDED THAT THIS **HOMO** STUFF HAD TO GET NIPPED **RIGHT** IN THE **BUD!**

SO I SET ABOUT DOING JUST **THAT.**

AND PRETTY **SUCCESSFULLY,** TOO, AS BEST I COULD **JUDGE.**

WHICH SHOWS WHAT A **LOUSY** JUDGE OF SUCH THINGS I COULD **BE!**

BUT HINDSIGHT **ASIDE,** NO-BODY'S EVER **SWEATED** MORE THAN **I** DID TO PERFECT ALL THE **MOVES** THAT COMMONLY PASS FOR **HETERO-SEXUAL BEHAVIOR.**

MAVIS, I FEEL **AWFUL** ABOUT THE WAY I ACTED LAST NIGHT.

DON'T **DWELL** ON IT, HON.

IF THERE WERE ANY **JUSTICE** IN THE WORLD, IT WOULD'VE BEEN **ME** WHO GOT KILLED, DRIVING HOME **DRUNK** THE WAY I DID THAT NIGHT.

BUT, **NO**... I HIT THE SACK **SAFE** AND **SOUND**.

MAMA AND **DADDY**, ON THE OTHER HAND, WERE **STONE COLD SOBER** WHEN THEY PULLED OUT OF OUR DRIVEWAY FOR THE LAST TIME THE NEXT MORNING.

THE MAN WHO SMASHED INTO THEM, HOWEVER, **WASN'T.**

HEY, LOOK AT **THIS** ONE, MELANIE. I TRIED **FOREVER** TO GET DADDY TO READ THIS BOOK.

I WANTED TO **TALK** TO HIM ABOUT IT. BUT HE NEVER **WOULD.**

AUNT IMOGENE SAID ONCE THAT DADDY ALWAYS HAD **TROUBLE READING**—BUT NOTHING COULD MAKE HIM **ADMIT** IT. YOU MUSTN'T TAKE IT **PERSONALLY**, HONEY.

I MUST'VE DRIVEN HIM **CRAZY**, NAGGIN' AT HIM THE WAY I DID.

IT'S WATER UNDER THE **BRIDGE.** YOU HAD NO WAY OF **KNOWING.**

THIS HOUSE IS GONNA BE SO **DIFFERENT** WITH ALL OF MAMA AN' DADDY'S **BOOKCASES** RIPPED OUT...

...BUT I'VE **GOTTA** CLEAR 'EM AWAY. THEY **SPOOK** ME.

THE HOUSE'D BE LESS **CROWDED** IF **I** WENT AHEAD AN' CLEARED OUT, **TOO**, Y'KNOW.

DON'T START UP!

NO, **REALLY!** WITH THE **INSURANCE MONEY** AN' WITH ME SELLIN' YOU 'N' ORLEY MY SHARE OF THE **HOUSE**, I'LL HAVE **PLENTY** ENOUGH TO SET UP HOUSEKEEPING ON MY OWN.

12

HUSH UP. **PLEASE.** IT'S GONNA BE BAD **ENOUGH** GETTIN' USED TO THIS HOUSE WITH **MAMA** AN' **DADDY** GONE.

HAVIN' **YOUR** BEDROOM EMPTY ALL OF A SUDDEN ON **TOP** OF THAT WOULD BE JUST **TOO MUCH!**

Thump thump

I KNOW YOU'LL BREAK AWAY **EVENTUALLY,** BUT DON'T DO IT **NOW.** SAVE THAT **MONEY** OF YOURS FOR A RAINY D—

Thumpa thumpa thumpa...

PSST! C'MERE. I WANT YOU TO SEE SOMETHIN' **ADORABLE.**

Thumpa thumpa thumpa thu

LOOK AT THAT LUG SHOOTIN' FANCY **HOOPS** TO IMPRESS THE **NINE-YEAR-OLD** NEXT DOOR. WHAT A **SHOW-OFF!**

OF COURSE, **SOME** FELLAS'D COME INSIDE AN' **HELP OUT** WITH THE **BOOK-SORTING,** BUT...

HEY! DONCHA WANNA COME **INSIDE,** ORLEY? PACKIN' UP THESE **BOOKS** FOR **STORAGE** IS TAKIN' TEN TIMES **LONGER** THAN WE **FIGURED!**

NOW, DON'T BE **SNOTTY** ABOUT MY **DEARLY BELOVED!**

I WANNA SHOW JOHNNY A COUPLE MORE **TRICKS** FIRST, MEL.

I THINK ORLEY'S GONNA BE A TERRIFIC **FATHER,** TOLAND.

YOU REALLY THINK ORLEY'S READY TO CHANGE **DIAPERS?** FAT CHANCE!

ONCE WE PUT A **BUN** IN THIS **OVEN,** I'LL START SHAPIN' HIM UP!

LEAVE MY **HUBBY** TO **ME,** BABY!

MAKIN' A **MAN** INTO A **HUSBAND** IS A MATTER OF **TRAINING.**

...BUT BEIN' A GOOD **DADDY**— I THINK THERE'S SOMETHIN' ABOUT **THAT** THAT'S **INBORN.**

Chapter 3

PUMPING **GAS** HAD NEVER BEEN **HIGH** ON MY LIST OF **PREFERRED OCCUPATIONS**. BUT THE **JOB** MARKET HAD BEEN **WORSE** THAN **PUNY** WHEN I FINISHED HIGH SCHOOL, THANKS TO A **BOYCOTT** BY LOCAL **BLACKS** OF ALL THE WHITE-OWNED DOWNTOWN **BUSINESSES**.

I'D LIKE TO **HELP** YOU, SON, BUT WE'RE **LETTIN' PEOPLE GO**, NOT **HIRIN'**.

ALTHOUGH CLAYFIELD'S BLACK FOLKS HAD BEEN **MAD** FOR A **LONG TIME** OVER THE WIDESPREAD **INJUSTICES** OF **RACIAL SEGREGATION**, AND ALTHOUGH VARIOUS **LEGAL CHALLENGES** WERE ALREADY IN THE **WORKS**, WHAT ACTUALLY **SPARKED** THE BOYCOTT WAS A RELATIVELY **PETTY** AGGRAVATION THAT TURNED OUT TO BE **ONE** PETTY AGGRAVATION TOO **MANY**!

HEY, DON'T GIMME **LIP**, BOY. AIN'T NO SHORTAGE OF PARKIN' FOR COLORED FOLKS OUT THERE ON THE **STREET**.

BUT I'M GON' HAVE SOME **BIG, HEAVY** PACKAGES TO BE PUTTIN' IN THE **TRUNK**....

THE **CARRYHOME DISCOUNT STORE** HAD SPENT MONTHS BALLYHOOING THE ROOMY NEW **PARKING DECK** IT WAS BUILDING FOR ITS CUSTOMERS. BUT WHEN IT OPENED, ONLY **WHITE** PEOPLE WERE ALLOWED TO **PARK** IN IT.

REVEREND HARLAND PEPPER TOLD HIS CONGREGATION AT THE **SMITH PARK BAPTIST CHURCH** HOW **FED UP** HE WAS WITH CARRYHOME. THEN HE CALLED FOR A **PROTEST RALLY**.

MISS MABEL, I WANT YOU TO **GRACE** THIS FLOCK WITH SOME **FERVENT MUSIC** NOW, 'CAUSE I WANT **EVERYBODY** AND HIS **COUSIN** OUT AND HOPPING AT THIS **RALLY** ON TUESDAY!

LEAVE 'EM TO **ME**, REV!

EVERYBODY THERE **KNEW** HOW MUCH MONEY GOT SPENT BY BLACKS EVERY DAY AT CARRYHOME. IT WASN'T **PEANUTS**!

AS TENSIONS ROSE, THE EVER-HELPFUL **SUTTON CHOPPER** SPOKE HIS MIND TO **REPORTERS** WHILE THE LEADERSHIP OF CLAYFIELD'S **DOWNTOWN MERCHANTS LEAGUE** NODDED ITS **APPROVAL**.

MY JOB AS **POLICE COMMISSIONER** IS TO **DEFEND** OUR CITY'S **FINE, TAXPAYING BUSINESSMEN** AGAINST THE IRRESPONSIBLE ACTIONS OF A BUNCH OF **UNRULY, MALODOROUS, COMMUNIST-INSPIRED NIGGER AGITATORS**!

IT WAS THE **STRAW** THAT BROKE THE **CAMEL'S BACK**.

OVERNIGHT, THE BEEF AGAINST CARRYHOME **MUSHROOMED** INTO A GENERALIZED FURY OVER **EVERYTHING** ABOUT THE WAY CLAYFIELD VIEWED ITS BLACK CITIZENS, AND THE **WHITE COMMERCIAL ESTABLISHMENT** DOWNTOWN FOUND ITSELF COLLECTIVELY TARGETED FOR AN EYE-OPENING LESSON IN **ECONOMICS**.

TIME PASSED, **HOPE** ESCALATED, **NEW ISSUES** GOT MIXED IN WITH THE **OLD** ONES—AND EVENTUALLY IT SEEMED LIKE YOU'D NEVER BE ABLE TO SET FOOT ON A **DOWNTOWN SIDEWALK** AGAIN WITHOUT HAVING SOMEBODY WITH **DARK SKIN** AND A **PICKET SIGN** SING A **FREEDOM SONG** AT YOU.

ON THE WHOLE, WHITE PEOPLE BEGAN FINDING IT TOO **STRESSFUL** TO SHOP DOWNTOWN, WHERE THEY WERE FORCED TO LOOK AT DISQUIETING SIGNS OF **SOCIAL TURMOIL**...

2 MILES TO GREEN LAWN MALL

...SO THEY CHANGED THEIR **SHOPPING HABITS**, PREFERRING LEISURELY DRIVES TO **STRESS-FREE MALLS** IN THE **SUBURBS**...

YOO-HOO! TOLAND!

GLENN'S GULF & TUNE-UP

...WHICH PUT EXTRA CASH IN THE TILLS OF **SERVICE STATIONS** ALONG THE **ROUTE**, SUCH AS THE ONE THAT CHOSE TO HIRE ME.

I MET **SAMMY NOONE** DURING THAT PERIOD AFTER MY **FOLKS** DIED, WHEN I WAS STILL LIVING WITH MY **SISTER** AND WHILE **RILEY** WAS IN THE **ARMY**.

COME ON OVER HERE.

Yip!

HI, MAVIS.

HIYA, LOCO.

I'VE GOT SOME **INTRODUCIN'** TO DO.

MAVIS DROVE INTO THE STATION ONE DAY WITH A **SAILOR** BESIDE HER AND RILEY'S DOG **LOCO** RIDING IN BACK.

I NEVER **KNEW** A DOG THAT LIKED RIDING AROUND IN **CARS** AS MUCH AS **LOCO** DID.

SAY HELLO TO **SAMMY NOONE**, TOLAND. HE AN' I WERE IN **GRADE SCHOOL** TOGETHER.

I'M PLEASED TO **MEETCHA**, SAMMY.

LIKEWISE.

SAMMY'S GONNA STAY AT THE **WHEELERY** FOR A FEW DAYS. HE'S JUST BACK FROM THE **NAVY** AN' GETTIN' **SITUATED**.

STOP BY ON YOUR WAY HOME FROM **WORK** TONIGHT— O.K.?

THAT NIGHT AT THE WHEELERY I FIGURED OUT THAT—MY **OWN** EXPERIENCE NOTWITHSTANDING—THE AMERICAN MILITARY WAS FALLING **SHORT** OF ITS GOAL OF MAINTAINING A **ONE-HUNDRED-PERCENT** HETEROSEXUAL FIGHTING FORCE.

SO, IF YOU'RE OUT OF THE **NAVY** NOW, HOW COME YOU'RE STILL WEARIN' YOUR **SAILORBOY BLUES**? ISN'T THAT AGAINST THE **RULES**?

SO MANY OF THE **BEST** THINGS IN LIFE **ARE**, TOLAND!

THAT'S FOR SURE!

ACTUALLY, IT'S SHEER **VANITY!** EVERBODY FINDS ME SO **SEXY** IN **UNIFORM**, I JUST CAN'T PEEL MYSELF **OUT** OF 'EM!

STILL, YOU'RE RIGHT—IT'S A HABIT I REALLY MUST **BREAK**. HAVE **YOU** BEEN IN THE SERVICE?

FLAT FEET?

NAH.. SOMETHIN' ABOUT MY **EYES**. SOME LONG WORD.

I GOT CALLED UP FOR MY **PHYSICAL** BUT ENDED UP **'4·F'.**

I'LL BET I CAN **GUESS**....

THEY'RE TOO **SOULFUL!** THEY DON'T HAVE THE SOLDIERLY **BRUTISHNESS** ONE LOOKS FOR IN THE **GROUND TROOPS**.

THE **NAVY**, ON THE OTHER HAND, PLACES A DEFINITE **PREMIUM** ON SOULFULNESS. **HEY!** LOOK WHAT'S **HERE!**

15

18

MAVIS HAD ALREADY **TOLD** ME THAT SAMMY'S FOLKS HAD BIG **BUCKS**, BUT THAT HE AND THEY DIDN'T HAVE MUCH **USE** FOR EACH OTHER.

WELL... PERHAPS **NOT**. *Cough!*

I HAVEN'T SEEN **YOU** SINCE THE **FUNERAL**, TOLAND.

YOU'RE LOOKING **WELL**.

WHY DON'T YOU EVER COME BY FOR ONE OF OUR **SERVICES**?

YOU AN' I HAVE **TALKED** ABOUT THAT, FATHER.

YOU **KNOW** I GOT **JESUS**-ED OUT AT AN **EARLY AGE**.

PEOPLE HAVE BEEN KNOWN TO **RECOVER** FROM THAT AFFLICTION. YOU DON'T MIND THAT I **CHECK** PERIODICALLY, DO YOU?

WATCH OUT HE DOESN'T **SNAG** YOUR **JACKET** AN' DRAG YOU DOWN TO PERDITION **WITH** HIM, FATHER.

SAMMY'S AN INCREDIBLE **ORGANIST**. WHY DON'T YOU JUST COME **WARM** A **PEW** AND LISTEN TO HIS **MUSIC** SOME SUNDAY?

SLAM!

YOU CAN DAYDREAM ABOUT **BASEBALL** DURING THE **HOMILY** IF YOU LIKE.

YOU'RE A SUCKER FOR **LOST CAUSES**, FATHER.

I'LL COME AN' HEAR SAMMY PLAY SOME-TIME, FATHER MORRIS.

I'M NOT AS **COMMITTED** TO MY HEATHENISM AS TOLAND.

I KEPT THINKING ABOUT RILEY'S **INVITATION** WHILE I WAS AT WORK LATER IN THE DAY.

FOR A SISTER AND BROTHER, MELANIE AND I DID BETTER THAN **AVERAGE** AT TOLERATING **FAMILY TOGETHERNESS**. BUT **ORLEY** COULD BE HARD TO **TAKE**, AND EVEN **SIS** GOT **INTENSE** SOMETIMES.

LIKE WHEN SHE'D GET ME ALONE AND START TALKING ABOUT THE **GHOSTS** IN HER BEDROOM.

IT'S **MAMA** AN' **DADDY**, I'M SURE.

THEY FLOAT NEAR THE **CEILING** AN' WATCH TO SEE IF ORLEY AN' I ARE **DOIN' IT** RIGHT.

MAMA'S GHOST IS ALWAYS PEEKIN' INSIDE MY HEAD TO SEE IF I **LOVE ORLEY** AS MUCH AS I'M **SUPPOSED** TO.

WELL... YOU **DO** LOVE HIM, DON'T YOU?

OF **COURSE** I DO.

IT'S JUST THAT, WHO KNOWS WHETHER, IF I WAS IN LOVE WITH SOMEBODY **ELSE**, I'D LOVE THE **OTHER** PERSON EVEN **MORE**?

I'VE GOT NO BASIS FOR **COMPARISON**.

YOU'LL MAKE SOME **GOOD** HUSBAND, TOLAND.

YOU'VE GOT **BRAINS**!

THAT'S GOOD TO KNOW!

MOST OF THE BOYS I HAD TO PICK FROM IN **HIGH SCHOOL**— WELL, YOU COULDN'T GET A GOOD **BRAIN** OUT OF 'EM IF YOU BOILED ALL THEIR **HEADS** TOGETHER IN ONE **POT**!

NO REFLECTION ON **ORLEY**. ORLEY CAN BE A **LIVELY TALKER**. BUT YOU'VE GOTTA PICK THE RIGHT **SUBJECT**.

ALSO, YOU HAD TO KNOW WHICH SUBJECTS TO STAY **AWAY** FROM.

DID YOU SEE WHERE THEY'VE DUG UP AN ACTUAL **PHOTO** OF MARTIN LUTHER KING ATTENDIN' A **SCHOOL** FOR **COMMUNISTS**?

UH... IS THAT **SO**, ORLEY?

YOU DIDN'T THROW AWAY NEARLY AS MANY OF THOSE OLD BOOKS AS YOU **THOUGHT** YOU WERE GOING TO, DID YOU?

NO. I HELD ON TO MORE THAN A **FEW**.

ALL I CAN SAY IS, I'M GLAD I'VE GOT PLENTY OF **BOOKS** TO READ!

I GUESS I HAD A SNEAKIN' **SUSPICION** I MIGHT NEED SOME **READIN' MATTER** TO PASS THE **TIME**...

...AT LEAST UNTIL I HAD A **BABY** TO TAKE CARE OF.

TOLAND, I REALLY THOUGHT I'D BE **PREGNANT** BY THIS TIME. I DON'T KNOW WHAT WE'RE DOIN' **WRONG.**

ORLEY AN' I HAVE SEX **MORNIN', NOON** AN' **NIGHT,** IT SEEMS LIKE.

AND I WON'T LET A **RUBBER** IN THE **HOUSE!**

THAT'S WHAT **YOU** THINK!

I'VE GOT ONE RIGHT HERE IN MY **BILLFOLD.**

HAVE YOU?! HAVE YOU **REALLY?!**

YOU DON'T **BELIEVE** ME?

LOOK AT **THAT!** *Sigh!* MY BABY BROTHER WITH A **RUBBER** AT THE **READY!**

WELL, YOU **SHOULD** BE PREPARED! YOU'RE A **BACHELOR!** YOU'RE NOT **TRYIN'** TO START A FAMILY!

IT'S **DIFFERENT** WITH US **MARRIED** PEOPLE.

I DIDN'T **TELL** MELANIE THAT THE VERY CONDOM I WAS **SHOWING** HER HAD BEEN TUCKED AWAY UNUSED IN MY **BILLFOLD** FOR WHAT MUST'VE BEEN **YEARS** BY THAT TIME...

...HOWEVER LONG IT HAD BEEN SINCE I **BOUGHT** IT OFF ONE OF MY WORLDLIER **FRIENDS** BACK IN **HIGH SCHOOL.**

HEY, THEY PRINTED MY **LETTER** IN THE **BANNER!**

NO KIDDING!

I **TOLD** YOU I WROTE ONE. AN' HERE IT **IS**—RIGHT **HERE**!

I WROTE IT 'CAUSE I WAS SICK OF ALL THE WHINING ABOUT 'POLICE BRUTALITY.'

PERSONALLY, I DON'T SEE HOW ANYBODY ON GOD'S GREEN **EARTH** CAN EXPECT A POLICE OFFICER TO KEEP HIS **TEMPER** WITH NIGGERS INSISTIN' ON **SINGIN'**, WAVIN' **SIGNS**, AN' CROWDIN' **EVERYBODY** WHO WASN'T BORN WITH **DARK SKIN** AN' A THOUSAND **COMPLAINTS** OFF THE **STREETS** AN' **SIDEWALKS** EVERY DAY—

ORLEY!!

The Clayfield Banner! SAY NO TO BLACKMAIL!

I KNOW, MELANIE, I **KNOW**! I **MEANT** TO SAY 'NEGROES.'

Tap, tap, tap!

SEE? **LOOK**! I SAID IT HERE IN THE PAPER—'**NEGROES**'—JUST LIKE I'M **SUPPOSED** TO.

OF COURSE, YOUR **BROTHER** PROBABLY THINKS IT'S VERY **SMALL-MINDED** OF WHITE FOLKS LIKE **ME** TO EXPECT FREE USE OF THE CITY **SIDEWALK** THAT WE PAY OUR **TAXES** TO **MAINTAIN**!

LAST **I** HEARD, THEY MAKE **NEGROES** PAY TAXES, **TOO**, ORLEY.

The Clayfield NO TO

EXCHANGES LIKE THAT ONE HELPED CONVINCE ME I WAS MAKING THE RIGHT **DECISION**.

YOU'RE **MOVIN' OUT**?

NOT INSTANTLY. BUT **SOON**. ONCE RILEY IS FINISHED WITH THE **ARMY**, WHICH WON'T BE **THAT** LONG.

YOU'RE TAKIN' THIS A LITTLE **HARD**, AREN'T YOU, MELANIE?

I'M **NOT** MOVIN' A **HUNDRED** MILES AWAY, Y'KNOW.

LOOK AT IT **THIS** WAY—YOU AN' ORLEY'LL BE ABLE TO SWITCH TO A **BEDROOM** THAT DOESN'T HAVE **MAMA** AN' **DADDY** ON THE CEILING!

DRIVING TO WORK THAT DAY, I MADE A RESOLUTION THAT IF **I** EVER GOT MARRIED, I'D PICK A GIRL WHOSE **COMPANY** I ENJOYED ENOUGH THAT I WOULDN'T NEED TO KEEP A **SIBLING** AROUND THE HOUSE FOR **RELIEF**!

Chapter 4

SAMMY WAS NEVER SHORT ON **SURPRISES**—LIKE WHEN HE TOLD MAVIS AND ME WE SHOULD COME TO A **PARTY** HE'D BEEN INVITED TO AT THE **MELODY MOTEL**.

THE **MELODY?!** DO THEY **LET** WHITE PEOPLE IN THERE?

IT'LL BE AN **INTEGRATED** PARTY, FULL OF **BEATNIKS**, **ANARCHISTS**, **HOMO-SEXUALS**, **NEGROES**, **VEGETARIANS**, **DRUNKS** AND **POETS!**

BULLSHIT! THERE AREN'T ANY **BEATNIKS** IN **CLAYFIELD!**

LET'S **DO IT**, TOLAND!

I MIGHT'VE HELD **BACK** IF MAVIS HADN'T SAID **YES** SO DAMN QUICK!

FOR THE AVERAGE WHITE PERSON IN CLAYFIELD, THE IDEA OF WHEELING UP TO THE FRONT GATE OF THE MELODY MOTEL WAS AN **INTIMIDATING PROSPECT**.

THEY MAY **LOOK** AT YOU A LITTLE CROSS-EYED BUT, HEY— IT'LL EXPAND YOUR **HORIZONS**.

THE MELODY STOOD AT THE EDGE OF **SMITH CITY**, A DEPRESSED BLACK NEIGHBORHOOD WITHIN **BLOCKS** OF THE HANDSOME DOWN-TOWN BUILDINGS WHERE CLAYFIELD'S **WHITE BUSINESS ELITE** WORKED.

AT SOME TIME IN THE **PAST** THE MOTEL MAY HAVE SERVED AS A SIMPLE WAY STATION FOR TIRED BLACK **TRAVELERS**, BUT BY THE TIME **I** CAME OF AGE IT HAD BECOME A FAMOUS SYMBOL OF TENACIOUS **POLITICAL ACTIVISM**.

THE MELODY WAS SECOND ONLY TO HARLAND PEPPER'S **SMITH CITY BAPTIST** (LOCATED *JUST DOWN THE STREET*) AS A SITE WHERE BOTH **HOMEGROWN INTEGRATIONISTS** AND **'OUTSIDE AGITATORS'** WERE WELCOME TO HUNKER DOWN AND CONCOCT THE **STRATEGIES** THEY HOPED WOULD **TRANSFORM** THE **SOUTH**.

FROM THE MELODY YOU HAD A CLEAR VIEW OF **RUSSELL PARK**, WHERE CROWDS OF **BLACKS**, JOINED BY A TINY SMATTERING OF **'TREASONOUS' WHITE SYMPATHIZERS**, CUSTOMARILY ASSEMBLED IN PREPARATION FOR THEIR **PROTEST MARCHES**.

THE MELODY HAD BEEN **BOMBED** MORE THAN ONCE IN ITS HISTORY. THE **KU KLUX KLAN** WAS **SUSPECTED**, BUT NOBODY EVER GOT **CHARGED**.

EXPLOSION AT NEGRO MOTEL

SECURITY GUARDS STAYED ON PERPETUAL **ALERT**.

SO WHEN MAVIS AND I DROVE UP, WE WERE GLAD TO KNOW WE'D ALREADY BEEN **VOUCHED FOR**.

CAN I **HELP** YOU?

UH...**SAMMY NOONE** SAID OUR **NAMES** WOULD GET **LEFT** WITH YOU— **TOLAND POLK** AN' **MAVIS GREEN**..?

OH, YEAH... LEMME LOOKIT THIS **LIST** HERE. POLK 'N GREEN... POLK 'N GREEN...

HERE WE GO. YEAH... YOU WANT **LES PEPPER'S** PARTY IN **SUITE TWO**.

SECOND DOOR FROM THE LEFT ON THAT **BALCONY.**

JUS' **PARK** AN' FOLLOW THE **MUSIC.**

...AN' HE DIDN'T EVEN **FRISK** US FOR **EXPLOSIVES** OR ANYTHING!

THIS IS SO **COOL!** NOW I'LL HAVE SOMETHIN' **INTERESTIN'** TO WRITE TO **RILEY** ABOUT.

THE PARTY WAS **LIVELY,** BUT I COULD SEE RIGHT AWAY THAT SAMMY HAD BEEN **PULLING** OUR **LEGS** WHEN HE LED US TO EXPECT SOMETHING **SCANDALOUS.**

♪ My mama told me, 'You better Shop Around!' ♪

HOORAY! YOU **CAME!**

MOST EVERYBODY THERE SEEMED FAIRLY **ORDINARY**...

LES! C'MERE A MINUTE, WILLYA?

I'M **COMIN'**, SAMMY—

OOPS!

HEY!

EASY, LESTER!...

...YOU'VE GONE AN' **DISARRANGED** MY **DÉCOLLETAGE!**

SORRY, ESMO.

...WITH A **FEW** EXCEPTIONS.

24

IN THE COURSE OF THE EVENING I MET **MARGE** AND **EFFIE,** A LESBIAN COUPLE WHO TOLD ME THEY RAN A **NIGHTCLUB** LOCATED ON THE CITY'S OUTSKIRTS. IT WAS MAINLY FOR **BLACKS,** BUT **ANYBODY FRIENDLY** WAS WELCOME.

YOU'LL HAFTA COME AN' **VISIT,** HONEY. WE **COOK** OUT THERE!

THERE AIN'T A **COLORED JAZZMAN** IN THE **WORLD** WHO'D **DARE** COME TO CLAYFIELD WITHOUT STOPPIN' OVER TO JAM AT **ALLEYSAX.**

ALL THE **DYKES** AN' **QUEENS** FROM THE RHOMBUS HAUL ASS OUT TO ALLEYSAX MOST SATURDAYS AFTER **CLOSIN' TIME.** I'M ASSUMIN' YOU'RE FAMILIAR WITH THE **RHOMBUS..?**

ACTUALLY, I'M **NOT.**

ACTUALLY, I DAMN WELL **WAS!**

EVEN US **HICK TEENAGERS** HAD BEEN HIP ENOUGH TO FIGURE OUT THAT THE RHOMBUS WAS A BAR THAT **'FAIRIES'** LIKED TO GO TO.

I HAD NEVER BEEN INSIDE OF IT **MYSELF,** THOUGH.

WHAT?!— ARE YOU **STRAIGHT??** I THOUGHT YOU CAME HERE WITH **SAMMY NOONE!**

NO, NO, MARGE! YOU GOT IT ALL **WRONG!** HE CAME WITH THAT SKINNY **REDHEADED** GIRL NAMED **MAVIS.**

WELL, HELL—EVEN **SO,** YOU OUGHTA CHECK OUT THE RHOMBUS AT LEAST **ONCE!**

IT AIN'T **ALLEYSAX,** BUT IT'S THE **ONLY** DOWNTOWN NIGHTSPOT THAT'S GOT ANY **LOOSENESS** TO IT.

EFFIE'S SISTER **MABEL** PLAYS THE **PIANO** THERE ON SATURDAY NIGHTS.

MABEL'S STRAIGHT, BUT THEY DECLARED HER AN **HONORARY DYKE!** THE QUEENS ALL **LOVE** HER 'CAUSE SHE **MOTHER-HENS** 'EM TO DEATH.

ANOTHER CONVERSATION FROM THAT PARTY THAT STICKS IN MY MIND WAS WITH A COUPLE NAMED **MACON** AND **ROSE** —PLUS A DUDE NAMED **RAEBURN,** WHO MADE ME **NERVOUS.**

NAW-w-w, I DON'T **HATE** THE CHOPPER. I **LOVE** THE CHOPPER!

SUTTON CHOPPER'S DONE **BETTER** BY US THAN THE MANGY CUSS'LL EVER **KNOW!**

AIN'T THAT **SO,** ROSE?

YOU **KNOW** IT IS, MACON!

IF THE CHOPPER'S **BULB** WASN'T SO FUCKIN' **DIM,** HE WOULDN'T GET US **NEARLY** AS MUCH GOOD **PRESS** AS HE DOES.

THE **TOUGHER** THAT OL' **BUZZARD** TRIES TO BE, THE BETTER HE MAKES **US** LOOK.

WHEN WE WANNA PLAN A **DEMONSTRATION,** WE JUS' SIT AROUN' AN' SAY, 'NOW WHAT CAN WE DO **THIS** WEEK TO MAKE THE CHOPPER PUT ON HIS **KLAN DANCE** FOR THE **TV NEWS?'**

Y'DON'T HAFTA DO MUCH MORE'N SLIDE YOUR **FEET** OUTA BED IN THE MORNIN' TO GET **THAT** CRACKER TO PLAY THE FOOL!

MACON, JUS' HOW MANY OF OUR **TRADE SECRETS'RE** YOU TWO **GIVIN' AWAY** TO THIS **STRANGER** HERE?

AN' HOW MANY OF J. EDGAR HOOVER'S **BUGS** D'YA THINK HE'S WEARIN' UNDER THAT **SHIRT?**

SAMMY, THERE'S SOMETHING YOU'VE REALLY GOTTA **UNDERSTAND**—

LET ME **GUESS.**

He ran 'til he came to a great big bin...

YOU'RE NOT **GAY,** AND YOU'D RATHER NOT GET **HUGGED** BY MEN WHO **ARE.**

The ducks and the geese were there put in...

DON'T TAKE IT **PERSONALLY...**

OH, I'M **INTENSELY** AWARE THAT YOU'RE NOT **GAY,** TOLAND. **ANYONE** CAN TAKE A LOOK AT YOU AND SEE...

He said, 'A couple of you are gonna grease my chin...'

...THAT YOU POSITIVELY **RA-A-A-A-A-ADIATE** HETEROSEXUALITY!

♪ *Before I leave this town oh'...*

AROUND THEN I DECIDED THAT—CHILLY AS IT WAS OUT ON THE BALCONY—I COULD DO WITH SOME **FRESH AIR.**

SHILOH, TELL LOTTIE I HOPE SHE FEELS **BETTER** SOON.

SURE THING, GINGER.

DO YOU AN' HIM HAVE AN **ACT?**

ME AN' **SHILOH?** Y'MEAN, DO WE SING FOR **MONEY?**

I **WISH!** MY FOLKS HAVE BEEN SINKIN' ENOUGH BUCKS INTO THE **VOICE TRAININ'** I'M GETTIN' AT THE **COLLEGE!**

BUT WHEN **SHILOH** AN' I SING TOGETHER, IT'S PURELY FOR **FUN.**

YOU TWO **DID** LOOK TO BE HAVIN' A **GOOD TIME.**

WE **WERE.** SHILOH'S **SERIOUS** ABOUT HIS MUSIC, THOUGH, MONEY OR **NO** MONEY.

HE DROPPED OUT OF A **MASTER'S** PROGRAM IN **CHORAL MUSIC** UP NORTH SO HE COULD COME TO CLAYFIELD AN' DO **MOVEMENT WORK.**

HE SAYS **MUSIC** IS WHAT CAN GIVE WORN-OUT PEOPLE THE **WILL** TO KEEP **STRUGGLIN'.**

28

MY FRIEND **SAMMY** SAYS YOU TOOK **GUITAR LESSONS** FROM HIM BEFORE HE JOINED THE **NAVY**.

OH, **THAT'S** WHERE I SAW YOU! YOU CAME WITH **SAMMY** TONIGHT, DIDN'T YOU?

DAMN! **EVERYBODY** THINKS THAT!

I DIDN'T COME 'WITH' HIM. SAMMY **TOLD** ME ABOUT THE PARTY AN' INVITED ME TO SHOW **UP**. ME AN' **MAVIS**, THAT IS. MAYBE YOU **SAW** HER..?

MAYBE I **DID**.

WELL, I'M GLAD YOU **STRAIGHTENED** ME **OUT** GOOD ON ALL **THAT**!

IT'S KINDA **COLD** OUT HERE—

MM-HMM. **THAT'S** GOOD TO KNOW.

I MEAN, MAVIS ISN'T MY **GIRL** OR ANYTHING. SHE AN' I JUST **CAME** HERE TOGETHER. HER BOYFRIEND **RILEY** IS IN THE **ARMY**, BUT HE'LL BE **HOME** SOON.

DO YOU EVER GO TO **BIRACIAL EQUALITY LEAGUE** MEETINGS? **MOST** PEOPLE I KNOW AT THE PARTY HERE ARE FROM THE EQUALITY LEAGUE....

UH...

I GUESS **NOT**.

NOW DON'T JUMP THE **GUN** ON ME LIKE THAT! IT'S **NOT** LIKE I DON'T KNOW WHAT YOU'RE **TALKIN'** ABOUT! THE EQUALITY LEAGUE IS **REV. PEPPER'S** GROUP — RIGHT?

IT'S NOT 'HIS' GROUP, BUT HE **IS** ONE OF THE **LEADERS**.

I GUESS Y'COULD SAY I'M NOT VERY **POLITICAL**.

NOT TO **PUT DOWN** THE EQUALITY LEAGUE OR ANYTHING...

...BUT THESE **MARCHES** AN' **DEMONSTRATIONS** COME **ONE** ON TOP OF THE **OTHER** FOR MONTHS ON END —AND WHAT REALLY GETS **ACCOMPLISHED?**

PEOPLE ARE JUST AS **SCREWED UP** AN' **HATEFUL** TO EACH OTHER AS THEY'VE **EVER** BEEN, AS FAR AS I CAN TELL.

OH. WELL, MAYBE WE OUGHT TO STOP **DOIN'** IT, THEN.

WE CAN LEAVE THINGS THE WAY THEY **ARE** AN' PUT OUR ENERGIES INTO SOMETHIN' **USEFUL.**

I'LL BRING THAT UP AT THE NEXT **MEETING.**

I'M **SLEEPY,** TOLAND. CAN YOU TAKE ME **HOME?**

I'LL BE READY IN JUST A **MINUTE,** MAVIS.

EXCUSE ME... I DON'T MEAN TO BE A **NUISANCE—**

—BUT IF YOU'RE NOT EVEN GONNA **ARGUE** WITH ME, WHAT'S THE POINT IN MY BOTHERIN' TO SAY SOMETHIN' **ASININE?**

Chapter 5

MAYBE YOU'D HAVE TO HAVE SEEN GINGER FOR THE FIRST TIME THE WAY *I* DID — MAKING *MUSIC* FOR THAT CROWD AT THE *MELODY MOTEL* — TO UNDERSTAND WHAT LED ME TO *SEIZE* ON HER THE WAY I DID, AND WHAT LED *HER* TO GET TANGLED UP IN MY *DREAMS* OF *STRAIGHTNESS.*

SHE STRUCK ME *RIGHT OFF* AS BEING IN A WHOLE DIFFERENT *CATEGORY* FROM THE GIRLS STONY AND I HAD BEEN PARTYING WITH AT THE *DIXIE STAR.*

When you wake, you will find...

...All the pretty little horses...

IT'S TRUE I'D FUCKED UP OUR FIRST ENCOUNTER, BUT I STARTED *MENDING FENCES* A DAY OR TWO LATER BY OFFERING TO DRIVE HER TO SOME *AUDITIONS* THAT SAMMY TOLD ME WERE COMING UP SOON IN *ATLANTA.*

THAT'S REAL *NICE,* SWEET-HEART!

SOME HOTSHOT HAD DECIDED THERE WAS A *FORTUNE* TO BE MADE BY SETTING UP A CHAIN OF SOUTHERN *COFFEE-HOUSES.* HE FIGURED HE COULD ORDER *ESPRESSO* IN *BULK* AND HIRE SOME *FOLK-SINGERS* FOR ATMOSPHERE.

HE SAID HIS *FIRST* IDEA HAD BEEN TO SCARE UP SOME *BEATNIK POETS,* BUT HIS WIFE INSISTED *BOHEMIANS* WERE *NEVER* GONNA CATCH ON BELOW THE *MASON-DIXON LINE.*

GINGER DIDN'T GET *HIRED,* BUT THE GUY TOLD HER SHE WAS GOOD AND SHOULD GET BACK IN *TOUCH* ONCE THE CHAIN HAD GOTTEN *LAUNCHED.*

CALL IT A PREMONITION, BUT I THINK I'M GONNA BE KNOWN SOMEDAY AS THE MAN THAT *DISCOVERED* GINGER RAINES!

THAT WAS THE LAST WE EVER HEARD ABOUT *HIM* OR HIS *COFFEEHOUSES.*

DRIVING HOME AFTERWARDS, GINGER WAS SO *HYPER* THERE WAS NO *DEALING* WITH HER.

DIDN'T YOU HEAR ME GO *FLAT* IN *'DEEP RIVER'*?

YOU *WEREN'T AWFUL!* YOU SOUNDED *GREAT!* YOU COULD PASS FOR *PROFESSIONAL* ALREADY!

IT REALLY ISN'T *HELPFUL* TO HAVE PEOPLE *PATRONIZE* ME. BE *HONEST.*

HOW COME YOU'RE ASSUMIN' I'M *DISHONEST*? MAYBE I'M JUST *TIN-EARED!* CAN'T YOU MAKE *ALLOWANCES* FOR THE *AFFLICTED*?

WHAT DO YOU *MEAN,* I SANG WELL?! I WAS *AWFUL!*

SHE GOT **CALMER** ALONG THE WAY, THANK GOD, AND WE WERE FINDING THINGS TO **LAUGH** ABOUT BY THE TIME I GOT HER BACK TO **WESTHILLS COLLEGE**, WHERE SHE WAS A **MUSIC MAJOR**.

...AN' ONCE I NOTICED THAT HIS **LIPS** LOOKED LIKE A **FRIED PIE**, I COULDN'T LOOK AT 'IM WITHOUT **CRACKIN' UP!**

YEAH, IT'S **HARD** TO **TALK POLITELY** TO A GUY WHILE YOU'RE TRYIN' TO STOP YOUR **EYES** FROM DRIFTIN' DOWN TO THE **BOTTOM** OF HIS **FACE!**

ALTHOUGH I'D BEEN THROUGH THE **GATES** ONLY A COUPLE OF TIMES IN MY LIFE, THE WESTHILLS **CAMPUS** WAS A FAMILIAR **SIGHT** TO ME, SINCE I DROVE PAST IT EVERY MORNING ON MY WAY TO **WORK**.

PARK FURTHER UP THE **STREET**. WE NEED TO SLIP IN BY A **BACK PATH**.

A **CAMPUS COP!** DUCK **DOWN!**

WE HAD TO SKULK AROUND LIKE **SNEAK THIEVES** ONCE WE GOT NEAR HER **DORM**, IT BEING AGAINST THE COLLEGE'S **RULES** FOR HER TO BE COMING IN SO **LATE**.

IT WAS ONLY THE **GIRLS** WHO HAD A CURFEW, OF COURSE. **BOYS** COULD ROAM FREE AT ALL **HOURS**.

THE GIRLS HAD SYSTEMS FOR BEATING THE CURFEW WHEN THEY **NEEDED** TO, THOUGH.

ALL CLEAR. LET'S **GO**.

UH... RIGHT.

Y'SEE THAT **WINDOW?** THAT'S MY **DORM ROOM**.

I JUST GRAB A **PEBBLE** AND...

PING!

THAT'S THE SIGNAL FOR **SHARON** TO COME DOWN AN' LET ME IN THE **BACK DOOR**.

SHARON'S MY **ROOMMATE**.

GOTCHA.

THANKS FOR TAKIN' ME TO THE **AUDITION**. IT WAS ALMOST **FUN**.

THANKS FOR THE DORM **PHONE NUMBER**. I'LL **CALL**.

I FELT PRETTY **CHEERY**, WALKING BACK TO THE **CAR**.

♪

GINGER WASN'T A HUNDRED PERCENT **EASY** TO GET **ALONG** WITH, BUT THE DAY HAD LEFT ME OPTIMISTIC THAT I HAD A **FAIR CHANCE** OF GETTING SOMETHING **GOING** WITH HER.

ON WEDNESDAY I TELEPHONED GINGER AND SUGGESTED WE GO **KITE-FLYING** THAT WEEKEND.

SOME GOOD **MARCH WINDS** WERE BEGINNING TO BLOW IN.

THEN, WITH SOME **NUDGING**, SHE GOT ME TO GO WITH HER TO A **BIRACIAL EQUALITY LEAGUE** MEETING ON ONE OF MY NIGHTS OFF.

...So then the Governor put his spoon down an' said 'If thass a honey wagon, y'all better have a talk with yo' bees!'

IT WAS INTERESTING. **HARLAND PEPPER** UP CLOSE WAS **FUNNIER** THAN YOU MIGHT EXPECT FROM SOMEONE ON A **MORAL CRUSADE.**

LES PEPPER, DRESSED UP IN **CONSERVATIVE** CLOTHES, WAS STILL AS **SEXY** AS HE'D BEEN AT THE **MELODY.**

AND I ADMIT I WAS **STARSTRUCK** AT FIRST AROUND LES'S MOTHER, **ANNA DELLYNE,** KNOWING SHE HAD ONCE BEEN **FAMOUS.**

GINGER THOUGHT IT WAS **NOVEL** THAT I WORKED AT A **GAS STATION.** SHE ASKED IF IT'D BE O.K. FOR HER TO LUG HER **NOTES** AND **BOOKS** OVER TO GLENN'S GULF & TUNE-UP OCCASIONALLY AND STUDY **THERE.**

STONY THOUGHT THAT WAS **WEIRD.**

MAVIS WARMED RIGHT UP TO GINGER, ONCE I'D INTRODUCED 'EM. THE WHEELERY WAS NEAR THE **COLLEGE BUS LINE,** SO SOMETIMES GINGER WOULD POP OVER BY HERSELF FOR SOME **'GIRL TALK'** AND MAYBE A SLICE OF **PIE** ON THE **PORCH.**

The Wheelery

PRETTY SOON THE TWO OF 'EM WERE LIKE OLD **PALS.**

GINGER HEARD SO MUCH ABOUT **RILEY** FROM MAVIS AND ME THAT SHE STARTED FEELING LIKE SHE **KNEW** HIM.

HEY, LET'S HEAR IT FOR THE **WHEELERY!** BEST LI'L HOUSE A MAN EVER **NAMED** AFTER HIMSELF!

SO SHE MADE A POINT OF BEING THERE AT THE WHEELERY **WITH** US THE DAY HE FINALLY CAME HOME FOR **GOOD.**

IT'S SO **COOL** T'SEE THIS PLACE AGAIN AN' KNOW I'M GONNA **STAY** HERE THIS TIME.

LET'S SHOW 'IM THE **HALL**.

HOT DAMN! IT'S A FUCKIN' **ART GALLERY!** THIS BEATS THE **LOUVRE!**

NOT THAT I'VE EVER **SEEN** THE LOUVRE!

IT'S ALL YOUR FAVORITE **PLAYBOY PLAYMATES.** REMEMBER ME **PUMPIN'** YOU FOR WHICH ONES YOU LIKED THE **BEST?**

THE THREE OF US **CHIPPED IN** ON THE CHEAP **FRAMES** AN' SPENT LAST **SATURDAY** PUTTIN' 'EM **UP.**

WE HAD TO **CHOOSE** BETWEEN FRAMIN' **THESE** AN' FRAMIN' SELECTED INSTALLMENTS OF 'THE **PLAYBOY** PHILOSOPHY.'

Y'MADE THE **RIGHT** CHOICE!

THE **LIGHT** HERE IN THE HALL IS **WAY** TOO **DIM** FOR SCHOLARLY **READIN'!**

BY THE WAY, GINGER, THIS IMPRESSION THESE TWO HAVE GIVEN YOU THAT I'M A **SEX PERVERT** IS ONLY **PARTLY** TRUE.

I'M ALSO **SENSITIVE** AN' **POETIC** AN' **DEEP.**

MY **DAD** SUBSCRIBES TO PLAYBOY. NUDES DON'T **BOTHER** ME.

MAN! HAVE I **MISSED** HAVIN' **WOODS** IN THE BACKYARD THAT YOU DON'T HAFTA LOOK AT THROUGH AN **ARMY FENCE!**

NOW I WANNA SEE THAT OL' **TREE HOUSE** OF OURS.

LET'S LET 'EM HAVE SOME TIME TO **THEMSELVES.**

GOOD IDEA.

I **LIKE** HIM.

I **TOLD** YOU YOU WOULD.

HE LIKES **YOU,** TOO. I CAN **TELL.**

WHEN DO YOU PLAN TO MOVE IN HERE **WITH** 'EM?

HEY, **YOU'RE** THE ONE REMINDIN' ME TO GIVE 'EM TIME TO **THEMSELVES.**

SOON. I **HOPE**.

DO YOU THINK YOU'LL **ENJOY** SLEEPIN' IN A BEDROOM THAT DOESN'T COME WITH A **SISTER** AN' **BROTHER-IN-LAW** NEXT DOOR?

DEFINITELY.

I JUST NEED AN **ALL-CLEAR** FROM RILEY.

'**SPECIALLY** IF RILEY AN' GINGER'LL LET ME INVITE A CERTAIN **FRIEND** TO SLEEP OVER. . . .

A KISS **HERE**. AN INNUENDO **THERE**.

LOVE **BLOOMS**.

IF **INNUENDOES** COULD MAKE YOU **PREGNANT**, GINGER AND I WOULD'VE HAD A **HEFTY BROOD** BY THE TIME **SPRING** AND **RILEY** CAME BACK TO CLAYFIELD.

FORTUNATELY, INNUENDO IS A **LOW-RISK ACTIVITY** IN A **LOT** OF WAYS.

MY KISSES WEREN'T **INSINCERE**. BY THEN I HAD WORKED UP A BONA FIDE, AUTHENTIC **CRUSH** ON GINGER.

I TOOK ITS MEASURE EVERY MORNING AND WATERED IT LIKE A **BEGONIA**.

STILL, IN LIGHT OF THE **PERSONALITY QUIRKS** I'VE ALREADY MENTIONED...

IT SEEMED BEST TO TAKE THINGS **SLOW** UNTIL, WELL...

TOLAND! GINGER! COME ON **OUT**! MAVIS AN' ME ARE GETTIN' A YEN FOR BARBEQUE!

IT'S GREAT TO **SEE YA** AGAIN, OL' BUDDY. AN' GINGER—HEY, **WELCOME** TO THE **GANG**!

IT'S GREAT TO SEE **YOU**, TOO, RILEY. WELCOME **HOME**!

...JUST **UNTIL**!

SAMMY HAD NEVER **MET** RILEY BUT HE WORKED UP A **WELCOME-HOME TREAT** FOR HIM **ANYWAY.**

HE PROMISED THAT, IF WE'D JUST GO TO THE MORNING SERVICE AT TRINITY AND LISTEN TO HIM **PLAY**, WE WOULDN'T BE **SORRY.**

I **RESISTED**, BUT GINGER AND MAVIS WERE SO **TAKEN** WITH THE IDEA THAT I **GAVE IN.**

THEN— **SURPRISE!** MY **SISTER**, WHO HAD GOTTEN WIND FROM MAVIS THAT HER WAYWARD **BROTHER** HAD BEEN ROPED INTO SITTING STILL FOR A **CHURCH SERVICE**, DECIDED THAT SHE AND ORLEY SHOULD **CRASH** THE **PARTY.**

WELL, LOOK WHO'S **HERE!**

SAMMY PLAYED **BEAUTIFULLY**—EVEN MY **'TIN EARS'** COULD TELL **THAT!** MEANWHILE, HIS PRIVATE JOKE TO **US** WAS THROWING IN FRAGMENTS OF **BOB DYLAN SONGS** DURING SUCH MUSICAL INTERLUDES AS ALLOWED FOR **IMPROVISATION.**

IT WASN'T AS **WICKED** AS IT SOUNDS IN THE **TELLING**, SINCE SAMMY WAS A MASTER AT **CHURCHING UP** HIS **ARRANGEMENTS.**

IS IT MY **IMAGINATION** OR AM I HEARIN' **'DON'T THINK TWICE'**...?

AS FAR AS **MOST** OF THE WORSHIPERS WERE CONCERNED HE COULD JUST AS WELL HAVE BEEN PLAYING SOME **BACH GOLDEN OLDIE!**

ORLEY **NEVER** CAUGHT ON.

WHAT TH' DINGDONG ARE ALL YOU PEOPLE **GIGGLIN'** ABOUT?

I'LL TELL YOU **LATER.**

I GUESS YOU'D HAVE TO CLASSIFY IT ALL AS **BAD BEHAVIOR.** STILL, THE CHURCH CAME OUT **AHEAD** ON THE DEAL, SINCE I ENDED UP PUTTING MORE IN THE **COLLECTION PLATE** THAN I PROBABLY WOULD HAVE IF I HADN'T FELT **GUILTY.**

FATHER MORRIS HAD ME **PEGGED**, THOUGH: AS SOON AS HE STARTED IN WITH THE **PREACHING**, I WAS OFF IN A **DAYDREAM.**

BUT NOT ABOUT **BASEBALL.** WHAT WAS ON MY MIND WAS A **BOOK** THAT HAD NAGGED AT ME EVER SINCE I CAME ACROSS IT YEARS BEFORE IN ONE OF MY PARENTS' **BOOKCASES.**

IT WAS CALLED **SEEING THROUGH THE LORD**, AND IT PURPORTED TO **PROVE**, WITH LOGIC AS **ELEGANT** AS Y'COULD **ASK** FOR, THAT GOD DIDN'T—AND **COULDN'T POSSIBLY**—EXIST.

I READ IT SEVERAL TIMES, TRYING TO FIND A **FLAW** IN THE **REASONING.** I COULDN'T.

WHAT CONFUSED MY ELEVEN-YEAR-OLD MIND WAS **THIS:**

IF SOMEBODY HAD **PROVED, ONCE** AND FOR **ALL** IN A THOROUGHGOING WAY, THAT THERE **WASN'T** ANY **GOD...**

...AND IF THAT SOMEBODY HAD **PUBLISHED** THE PROOF IN A **BOOK** FOR ALL TO **SEE...**

...THEN HOW COME ALL THE **CHURCHES** IN CLAYFIELD WERE PROCEEDING ON THEIR MERRY WAY EVERY SUNDAY WITHOUT MISSING A **BEAT?**

I DECIDED TO ASK MY **PARENTS** ABOUT IT.

MAMA, THIS BOOK SAYS THERE ISN'T ANY **GOD** AN' I WAS WONDERIN'—

I **BEG** YOUR PARDON?

UH... NEVER MIND!

YOU'D THINK I'D HAVE **LEARNED** BY THEN NOT TO TURN TO **MAMA** WITH THORNY META-PHYSICAL INQUIRIES.

DADDY HAD HIS **LIMITATIONS,** BUT AT LEAST HE WAS WILLING TO GO AROUND THE **TRACK** WITH ME A TIME OR TWO ON A DIFFICULT SUBJECT WITHOUT GETTING **BRISTLY.**

DADDY, I FOUND THIS BOOK THAT SAYS IT'S A **LOGICAL IMPOSSIBILITY** FOR THERE TO BE A **GOD.**

IT **DOES?** *Tsk tsk!* **THAT'S** A BOLD CLAIM FOR A BOOK TO MAKE!

IT'S NOT JUST A **CLAIM.** THE GUY **PROVES** IT.

HAVE **YOU** READ IT?

NO, I DON'T **THINK** SO, NOW THAT YOU'VE PUT IT TO ME **DIRECTLY.**

COULD BE **I'M** THE ONE THAT **BOUGHT** IT, BUT I CAN'T RECALL EVER FINDIN' THE TIME TO SIT **DOWN** WITH IT.

WOULD Y'MIND READIN' IT **SOON,** THEN, SO WE CAN **TALK** ABOUT IT?

WELL, **SURE,** SON, IF YOU'D **LIKE** ME TO.

GO PUT IT ON ONE OF THOSE **SHELVES** BY MY **BED** SO I'LL REMEMBER.

BUT PUT IT **UNDER** SOMETHING, NOT ON TOP OF SOME STACK WHERE IT'S **OBVIOUS.**

SOUNDS LIKE A BOOK THAT MIGHT **UPSET** YOUR MOTHER IF SHE NOTICED IT.

I SUPPOSE DADDY WASN'T **THINKING** TOO CLEARLY WHEN HE SUGGESTED I POKE AROUND IN THE PILE OF STUFF THAT WAS NEXT TO HIS BED...

...'CAUSE THAT WAS THE DAY I DISCOVERED MY DADDY'S **PORNOGRAPHY**.

tap tap!

Psst! **WAKE UP!** EVERYBODY'S **STANDING**.

OUR **PLAN** WAS THAT, AFTER THE SERVICE, WE'D ALL GO OVER TO SAMMY'S FOR **LUNCH**.

HIS APARTMENT WAS ALL BUT UNDER THE SAME ROOF AS THE **CHURCH**, IT HAVING BEEN BUILT ORIGINALLY TO HOUSE THE LIVE-IN **CUSTODIAL HELP**.

SINCE MELANIE AND ORLEY HAD SHOWN UP UNEXPECTEDLY, SAMMY INSISTED THAT THEY **JOIN** US.

IT WOULD'VE BEEN AWKWARD **NOT** TO...

...THOUGH NOT **HALF** AS AWKWARD AS WHAT ENDED UP **HAPPENING!**

SAMMY COULDN'T OFFER US MUCH TO **SIT** ON BEYOND HIS **COT**, SOME **PILLOWS** AND A COUPLE OF STRAIGHT-BACKED **CHAIRS**—BUT NOBODY **COMPLAINED**. WHILE SAMMY WARMED UP A **CASSEROLE** AND UNCORKED SOME **WINE**, MELANIE EXPLAINED TO ORLEY ABOUT THE **BOB DYLAN** SONGS.

WELL, I'M GLAD Y'ALL HAD SUCH A **JOLLY TIME** OF IT BACK THERE. IT SOUNDS KINDA **SACRILEGIOUS** TO **ME!**

OH, DON'T GET **STUFFY** ON US, ORLEY.

PERSONALLY, **I'D** VOTE FOR INSERTIN' A FEW MORE DITTIES LIKE '**BLOWIN' IN THE WIND**' IN THE LITURGY!

BOBBY DYLAN'S PROVIDED **ME** WITH MORE **MORAL INSPIRATION** LATELY THAN **BILLY GRAHAM** OR **NORMAN VINCENT PEALE** HAS!

DID YOU HEAR **THAT**, MELANIE? A DAMN **FOLK SINGER** IS MORE **MORAL** THAN THE **GREATEST PREACHERS** IN AMERICA!

I SWEAR I'VE JUST WANDERED INTO **TOPSY-TURVY LAND!**

YOU'LL **LOVE** IT, ORLEY. I'VE LIVED THERE ALL MY **LIFE!**

Snort! **THAT** I CAN BELIEVE!

ORLEY HADN'T BEEN **AROUND** SAMMY BEFORE THAT SUNDAY, AND IT WAS OBVIOUS HE DIDN'T KNOW WHAT TO **MAKE** OF HIM.

AT FIRST **RILEY** WASN'T ALL THAT COMFORTABLE WITH SAMMY, **EITHER**.

BUT SAMMY **CHATTED** HIM **UP** UNTIL HE RELAXED.

DO YOU HAVE A **JOB** LINED UP NOW THAT YOU'RE BACK HOME, RILEY?

YEP. TANNER APPLIANCES.

I THINK MY WIFE AN' I WILL BE **MOVIN' ALONG** NOW. I CAN SEE WE'RE NOT **LIBERAL** ENOUGH FOR THIS CROWD!

WAS IT SOMETHING I SAID?

ORLEY—

GET UP, MELANIE! I WANNA GO **HOME!**

ORLEY, NOBODY'S GONNA **MAKE** US GO TO THE RHOMBUS IF WE DON'T **WANT** TO. SIT DOWN AN' QUIT BEIN' **RUDE**.

YEAH, PAL—YOU'RE BEIN' **SILLY**.

RUDE?! SILLY?!

TOLAND, **RILEY'S** A **GROWN MAN** AN' DOESN'T NEED ANY **SHELTERIN'**, BUT HOW YOU CAN SUBJECT NICE GIRLS LIKE **GINGER** AN' **MAVIS** TO SOMEBODY LIKE **THAT** IS **BEYOND** ME!

SAMMY WAS MY FRIEND BEFORE TOLAND EVER **MET** HIM, ORLEY.

AND HE'S BEEN **MY** FRIEND EVEN LONGER THAN **THAT**.

WELL? ARE YOU GONNA GET IN THE CAR OR **NOT?**

DARN IT, ORLEY...I WAS HAVIN' **FUN**.

YOU AN' I DON'T **HAVE** ANY COLORFUL FRIENDS LIKE THAT.

AN' THANK THE LORD WE **DON'T!**

WHEN I THINK ABOUT SOMEBODY LIKE **THAT** BEIN' IN THE EMPLOY OF A **HOUSE** OF **GOD**, MELANIE—

LET'S JUST GET IN THE CAR AN' GO **HOME**.

DON'T MAKE ME **LISTEN** TO ANY **MORE**.

AN' FOR YOUR INFORMATION, I WAS **ENJOYIN'** THAT **CASSEROLE!**

SAMMY AND LES DRIFTED OFF TO **SHOOT** THE **BREEZE** AND LEFT THE REST OF US TO FEND FOR **OURSELVES** AWHILE.

I'M GETTIN' **NERVOUS.** THERE'S A GUY AT THE NEXT TABLE WHO'S **SMILED** AT ME **THREE TIMES.**

WELL, BY ALL MEANS, HAVE HIM **ARRESTED!**

TOLAND, HOW COME ALL THE **DANCIN'** IS OVER **THERE** AN' **WE'RE** SITTIN' **HERE?**

DON'T **TRY,** GINGER. YOU'LL **NEVER** GET POLK ONTO A **DANCE FLOOR.**

DIDN'T TOLAND EVER TELL YOU HOW HE WAS BROUGHT UP BY A **HEAVY-DUTY RELIGIOUS MAMA** WHO KEPT HIM FROM **DANCIN'** IN HIS **FORMATIVE YEARS** AN' LEFT HIM **INHIBITED** FOR **LIFE?**

SHIT, RILEY... THAT'S THE **LAST** TIME I'LL SHARE COMPLAINTS ABOUT MY UPBRINGING WITH **YOU!**

HOW ABOUT **YOU,** SMARTYPANTS? **YOUR** MAMA NEVER STOPPED **YOU** FROM LEARNIN' **ANYTHING!**

Y'THINK I'M GONNA GET OUT THERE AN' DANCE IN FRONT OF **EVERYBODY** WITH A MEMBER OF THE **OPPOSITE SEX?!** I'D FEEL **CONSPICUOUS!**

WHAT A PAIR OF **SLUGS!** O.K., GINGER, ON YOUR **FEET.** IT ONLY TAKES **TWO** TO **TANGO!**

I'M **GAME.**

WELL, **HELL! LOOK** AT THOSE **TWO!** THEY DON'T GIVE A DAMN WHAT **ANYBODY** THINKS!

AN' **NO,** I'M **NOT** READY TO GO OUT THERE AN' DANCE WITH **YOU** NOW, PUMP JOCKEY!

HEY, I'M NOT **ASKIN'!** HA HA HA!

Grumble... WELL, I THINK THE GUY AT THE NEXT TABLE MAY BE **ABOUT** TO.

I'M **GOIN'** TO THE BAR FOR ANOTHER **DRINK.**

tap tap tap..

THIS PLACE HAS SURE GONE **DOWNHILL** SINCE THEY STARTED LETTIN' SO MANY **NIGGERS** IN.

MY FIRST THOUGHT WAS: WHO WANTS TO HEAR BULL-SHIT LIKE **THAT**?

MY **NEXT** THOUGHT WAS: HOW COME I WASN'T HEARING IT **MORE**?

?

WAS I IN **DIXIE** OR **WASN'T** I?

THERE WAS **LES PEPPER**, GOSSIPING WITH **SAMMY**...

...AND **ESMERELDUS** (OUT OF DRAG TONIGHT) WAS CAMPING IT UP WITH **REX**, THE **BARTENDER**.

THERE WERE MORE **WHITES** THAN **BLACKS** THERE BY **FAR**, BUT YOU STILL COULDN'T CALL THE JOINT ANYTHING BUT **INTEGRATED**.

HOW COME NOBODY WAS FIGHTING ANY **RACE WARS** IN THE **RHOMBUS**?

DIDN'T THEY KNOW THAT 'HALLOWED SOUTHERN TRADITIONS' WERE IN DANGER OF **TOPPLING**?

WHERE WERE THE **REDNECKS**?

WHERE WERE THE **COPS**?

I WAS STROLLING OVER TO SHARE THESE MUSINGS WITH **RILEY**, WHO I SAW HAD STRUCK UP A **PIANOSIDE FRIENDSHIP** WITH **MABEL**...

...WHEN A **RED LIGHT** NEAR THE **CEILING** FLASHED ON...

...AND I GOT MY ANSWER ABOUT WHERE THE **COPS** WERE.

AS SOON AS THEY SAW THE **LIGHT** GO ON, EVERY-BODY ON THE DANCE FLOOR SWITCHED **PARTNERS**.

BEFORE THEY COULD TELL WHAT WAS **HAPPENING**, SHE AND MAVIS FOUND THEMSELVES DANCING WITH MEN THEY'D NEVER EVEN SAID **HELLO** TO.

HI, I'M **LOUIS**.

GINGER SAID AFTERWARDS THAT IT WAS LIKE BEING IN A GAME OF **MUSICAL CHAIRS** THAT NOBODY HAD **WARNED** YOU YOU WERE **PLAYING**.

I'M **BERNARD**.

WHAT'S **HAPPENIN'**?

COPS AT THE DOOR.

44

The theme from *DRAGNET*

DON'T LET YOUR **JAW** DANGLE, SONNY. THEY'RE JUST PLAYIN' THEIR **GAMES.**

I BETCHA AIN'T EVEN GOT **GAS** IN THE **PADDY WAGONS**, DO YOU, ED?

NEXT **ELECTIONS** ARE **THREE YEARS** OFF. AIN'T NO **ADVANTAGE** FOR THE **CHOPPER** IN A BUST RIGHT **NOW.**

BACK **OFF**, GRANNY.

MOVE ON, ED... 'FORE THEIR **CRABS** START HOPPIN' ON US.

~Snicker!~

LEAVIN' SO **SOON**, OFFICERS?

WHAT DO THEY **EXPECT** THEY'RE GONNA FIND IN HERE, **MABEL?** IT'S NO **SECRET** THE **RHOMBUS** IS A **GAY BAR.**

OH, THEY **KNOW** WHAT'S GOIN' ON!

BUT THE GOOD FOLKS DID PASS THEIR **LAW** SAYIN' **MEN** CAN'T DANCE WITH **MEN** AN' **LADIES** CAN'T DANCE WITH **LADIES**. THE **MAJORITY**, SHE **RULES.**

REX HERE BEHIND ME'S GOT A **MIRROR** ANGLED SO HE CAN SEE WHEN THERE'S **COPS** ABOUT TO COME IN.

REX HITS A SWITCH AN' THE **LIGHT** TELLS EVERYBODY TO PAIR UP THE **LEGAL** WAY.

NINE TIMES OUTA TEN THE COPS'LL **STRUT IN, SMIRK** AN' **SPLIT**... 'CEPT AT **ELECTION TIME** OR WHEN A **REVIVAL'S** IN TOWN.

AIN'T NO **POINT** TO IT AT **ALL**, EXCEPT TO KEEP THE **QUEERS NERVOUS**.

COME **ON**, MABEL—PLAY SOME **MUSIC**, DARLIN'?

HUSH UP, CLYDE! I'M **EXPLAININ'** STUFF! THESE CHILDREN ARE **NEW!**

I WAS IMPRESSED BY HOW **FAST** THE COLLECTIVE **MOOD** AT THE RHOMBUS BOUNCED **BACK** ONCE THE POLICE WERE GONE.

BY **CLOSING TIME** THE INTERRUPTION WAS ALL BUT **FORGOTTEN**. SPIRITS WERE **HIGH** AND MOST EVERYBODY WHO HADN'T PEELED OFF EARLIER FOR **SEX** OR **REST** SEEMED EAGER TO KEEP THE PARTY GOING INTO THE **WEE HOURS**.

SAMMY HERDED US INTO MY **MERCURY** AND I MANEUVERED US INTO THE **CARAVAN** OF CARS THAT WAS FORMING IN FRONT OF THE **BAR**.

LAST CALL FOR DRINKS!

ATTENTION, WHOEVER'S HEADIN' OUT TO THE **CLUB** NOW— TIME TO HOP IN YOUR **FAIRYMOBILES** AN' FOLLOW BERNARD!

LET'S **SCURRY**, MY LOVELIES, BEFORE NAUGHTY **REX** TURNS ON THE **BRIGHT LIGHTS** AND EXPOSES OUR **CROW'S FEET!**

SOON MINE WERE AMONG AN EERIE TRAIN OF **HEADLIGHTS** THAT SNAKED THROUGH THE BACK ROADS OF CLAYFIELD TOWARD **ALLEYSAX**.

I THOUGHT ABOUT THE **REGULAR PEOPLE** SLEEPING PEACEFULLY IN THE DARK **HOUSES** WE WERE PASSING, AND WONDERED WHAT THEY'D HAVE **THOUGHT** IF THEY'D KNOWN WE WERE PASSING BY.

EFFIE! MARGE! BREAK OPEN THE CHAMPAGNE! ESMERELDUS IS HERE!

WHEN WE ARRIVED, ESMO HIT THE GROUND **RUNNING**.

ALLEY SAX

TRY TO KEEP YOUR **SCREAMIN'** DOWN TO THE **EAR-SPLITTIN'** LEVEL, GIRL.

WE'VE GOT SOME GOOD **MUSIC** HAPPENIN' INSIDE.

ALLEYSAX WAS **CROWDED** AND **LOUD**, BUT THE **LIVE JAZZ** CUT RIGHT THROUGH THE **DIN**.

OH, **LOOK**, TOLAND! OVER THERE IN THE **SHADOWS**.

WHAT? WHERE?

IT'S **ANNA DELLYNE**.

DOES ANNA DELLYNE EVER GET UP ON THE STAGE AN' SING HER OLD **SONGS**, SAMMY?

NOPE.

FREEDOM SONGS AN' **CHURCH SONGS** ARE ALL SHE'LL SING IN **PUBLIC** THESE DAYS, AN' SHE WON'T GO **SOLO** ON **THOSE**!

OL' **ESMERELDUS** HASN'T **GIVEN UP** ON HER! **THIS** QUEEN'S GONNA HEAR 'SECRET IN THE AIR' FROM THE LADY'S LIPS **ONE MORE TIME** OR DIE TRYIN'!

SHE SAYS SHE'S **FINISHED** WITH IT.

SHE **CLAIMS** NOT TO **MISS** IT, BUT **LES** THINKS SHE'S **BULL-SHITTING**.

I DO, **TOO**.

JUST LOOK AT THOSE **EYES**.

LATER ON I FOUND MYSELF STANDING BEHIND LES IN THE **BATHROOM LINE**.

WHAT'S YOUR **STORY** ANYWAY, POLK? TO SEE YOU AN' **GINGER BILLIN'** AN' **COOIN'** AROUND THE **EQUALITY LEAGUE**, I DIDN'T FIGURE YOU'D BE PUTTIN' IN APPEARANCES AT THE **RHOMBUS**!

BLAME **SAMMY NOONE**.

Flush!

HE SAYS HE'S GIVIN' US A TOUR OF CLAYFIELD'S **SEEDY UNDERBELLY**.

Snicker! IT'S **YOUR** DAMN UNDERBELLY HE'D LIKE A **TOUR** OF, PROBABLY!

WELL, YOU'RE ALWAYS **WELCOME** AT THE **RHOMBUS**. US HOMOS JUS' **LOVE** HAVIN' **STRAIGHT PEOPLE** AROUND. Y'ALL ARE SO **WITTY** AN' **WELL-GROOMED**!

MM-HMM.

UH...'SCUSE ME FOR ASKIN' A **PERSONAL QUESTION**, LES, BUT I CAN'T HELP BEIN' **CURIOUS**.

I SEE YOUR **MOTHER** STANDIN' THERE ACROSS THE ROOM.

SHE **HAD** TO OF BEEN **WATCHIN'** WHEN YOU TROOPED IN WITH THE CROWD FROM THE **RHOMBUS**.

SO THAT MUST MEAN YOUR FOLKS **KNOW** YOU'RE **GAY** —RIGHT?

MAMA KNOWS. IT'S COOL. SHE'S **ALWAYS** HAD 'SISSYBOY' FRIENDS.

AN' **PAPA** KNOWS.

—WHICH AIN'T TO SAY HE'S EVER SAID THE FIRST **WORD** ABOUT KNOWIN'.

HE USED TO PUSH ME TO GET **MARRIED**, BUT HE'S LEARNED **THAT** AIN'T IN THE **CARDS**.

PAPA'S THE **PREACHER** IN THE FAMILY AN' **I'M** THE **FAGGOT**.

MARTIN LUTHER KING **HIMSELF** COULD WALK UP AN' SAY TO ME, 'LES, YOU GOTTA **QUIT** BEIN' **GAY!'**...

...AN' I'D SAY TO HIM, '**SURE THING,** DR. KING—

Flush!

'—JUST AS SOON AS **YOU** STOP BEIN' **NEGRO!'**

Flush!

I BEG YOUR PARDON... IF **YOU'RE** NOT READY TO USE THE **ROOM** THERE, I THINK MAYBE I'D LIKE TO.

OH. SORRY.

WELCOME BACK FROM THE **ARMY,** HON.

Chapter 7

THE DAY I MOVED INTO THE WHEELERY, ORLEY LAID SOME **ADVICE** ON ME THAT HE HAD OBVIOUSLY BEEN CHEWING ON SINCE HIS **TANTRUM** AT TRINITY.

THERE'S A **SAYING**, TOLAND: A MAN IS **KNOWN** BY THE **COMPANY** HE KEEPS.

A WORD TO THE **WISE!**

HMM. THANKS, ORLEY. I'LL **REMEMBER** THAT.

WHAT'S ORLEY **GOT** AGAINST **SAMMY NOONE?** HE'S ONLY **MET** HIM **ONCE**...FOR AN HOUR.

SODA, BOYS?

IT'S **YOU** ORLEY'S **THINKIN'** ABOUT. HE DOESN'T WANT YOU TO FALL PREY TO '**SINFUL INFLUENCES.**'

DID SAMMY TAKE Y'ALL TO THAT '**RHOMBUS**' PLACE LIKE HE **SAID** HE WAS GONNA DO?

HE SURE **DID.**

IT WAS **INTERESTIN'.**

YOU SHOULD **GO** SOMETIME.

ME IN A **GAY BAR?!** NOT **QUITE!**

THINGS WERE **BACK** ON **TRACK** BETWEEN ME AND GINGER BY THEN.

THERE HAD BEEN SOME MILDLY **TROUBLED WATERS** THAT NEEDED CALMING RIGHT AFTER OUR VISIT TO THE RHOMBUS AND ALLEYSAX.

YOU BARELY ACTED LIKE I WAS **ALONG**, TOLAND. **THINK** ABOUT IT!

YOU SPENT SO MUCH TIME **STROLLIN' AROUND** AN' TALKIN' TO **OTHER PEOPLE....**

I WAS **DISTRACTED.**

I WAS **SEEIN'** A LOT OF STUFF FOR THE **FIRST TIME.**

BESIDES, **YOU** RAN OFF DANCIN' WITH **MAVIS.**

I'D OF BEEN **GRAY** BY THE TIME I GOT AN INVITATION FROM **YOU!**

THERE WAS SOMETHING ABOUT THAT EXCHANGE THAT **SCARED** ME.

I MADE A RESOLUTION TO START BEING **EXTRA-ATTENTIVE** TO GINGER.

AND I **DID** DO **BETTER.**

I BEGAN SWINGING BY THE COLLEGE CAFETERIA AND HAVING **BREAKFAST** WITH HER MOST EVERY MORNING BEFORE GOING TO **WORK.**

WE TALKED ABOUT **PHILOSOPHY** AND **POLITICS** AND **BERGMAN MOVIES** AND WHICH **COURSES** SHE HATED AND WHETHER KHRUSHCHEV WAS LIKELY TO DROP AN H-BOMB ON US BEFORE SHE GOT HER CHANCE TO BE A 'REAL' SINGER.

I WAS DRIVING TO THE COLLEGE FOR ONE OF THOSE BREAKFAST DATES, IN FACT, WHEN I LEARNED THAT **SLEDGE RANKIN** WAS DEAD.

SOME GODDAM **JERKS** FOLLOWED GINGER AN' HER FRIEND ALL THE WAY FROM **FRANK'S BEND.**

WHOEVER THEY WERE, THEY'RE **GONE** NOW—AN' I WANNA ENCOURAGE 'EM TO **STAY** GONE!

HI.

YOU'RE O.K.?

INSIDE THE **HOUSE,** AFTER GINGER AND I HAD HAD A CHANCE TO **HUG** FOR A MINUTE...

YEAH.

...I GOT TOLD MORE ABOUT THE **CAR** THAT HAD FOLLOWED THEM BACK TO CLAYFIELD.

IT HAD **TAILGATED** THEM FOR THE WHOLE **EIGHTY-FIVE MILES,** ITS HEADLIGHTS ON **BRIGHT...**

...SO THAT SHILOH WAS **HALF-BLINDED** BY THE **REFLECTION** IN THE **REARVIEW MIRROR.**

ALL I COULD THINK OF WAS HOW **STUPID** WE WERE—A '**NIGGER AGITATOR**' FROM UP **NORTH** AN' A **WHITE SOUTHERN FEMALE,** DRIVIN' MILE AFTER MILE THROUGH DIXIE FARMLAND AT NIGHT WITH THE **KLAN** ON OUR TAILS!

YOU DIDN'T THINK ABOUT IT BEIN' **DANGEROUS** WHEN YOU **SET OUT?**

WE WEREN'T USIN' OUR **HEADS.**

SHEER FOOL RECKLESSNESS IS WHAT IT **WAS!** WE WERE SO LOST IN THOUGHTS ABOUT **SLEDGE,** WE IGNORED THE **OBVIOUS!**

THERE WAS A FAIR AMOUNT OF **TRAFFIC** ON THE ROAD. THAT MIGHT'VE DISCOURAGED 'EM FROM GETTIN' ANY **NASTIER** WITH THE TWO OF **US.**

GUNS! DAMN!

DID RILEY TELL YOU HOW THEY PARKED OUT IN FRONT OF THE **HOUSE** FOR A TIME, TOLAND? THAT'S WHY RILEY'S OUT ON THE **PORCH** WITH HIS **GUN.**

THEY STILL MIGHT HAVE A **TEACHIN' SPOT** FOR YOU BACK AT THAT **CONSERVATORY** IN **BOSTON,** SHILOH.

DON'T THINK LOTTIE AN' I DON'T **THINK** ABOUT THAT EVERY MORNIN' WHEN WE POUR OUR **CORN FLAKES,** MISS GINGER.

I KEPT WAITING FOR GINGER TO LET DOWN AND **CRY** ON MY **SHOULDER** LIKE SHE'D **SAID** SHE MIGHT. BUT HER FACE STAYED **NUMB** AND **DISTANT.**

OCCASIONALLY SHILOH WOULD REACH OVER AND SQUEEZE HER **FOOT.**

I DON'T KNOW HOW TO **TALK** ABOUT WHAT HAPPENED TO SLEDGE....

YOU DON'T HAVE TO TELL US **NOW,** GINGER, IF IT **HURTS** TOO MUCH.

Chapter 8

CHURCHES!! THERE'S NO GODDAMN **ESCAPE** FROM THEM DOWN SOUTH!

And before I'll be a slave...

...I'll be buried in my grave...

I'VE GOTTA **ADMIT**, THOUGH, THAT AT THE **BIRACIAL EQUALITY LEAGUE** MEETINGS AT **SMITH CITY BAPTIST**...

...WHEN **REV. PEPPER** WOULD PREACH ABOUT **JUSTICE**...

...AND WHEN **SHILOH** WOULD FILL THE ROOM WITH SONGS ABOUT **HOPE** AND **FREEDOM**...

...I COULD ALMOST **FORGET** HOW **OPPRESSED** THOSE BUILDINGS WITH THE STEEPLES COULD MAKE ME **FEEL.**

OF COURSE, I COULD PRETTY WELL COUNT ON ANY **WHITE PREACHER** ON MY **CAR RADIO** TO REMIND ME.

Oh Lord, help us know that Thou art a Prince of Peace, not Strife...

...and that Thou dost not protest noisily in the street, but rather whispereth sweet psalms of salvation in the heart....

GINGER AND I HASHED OVER **RELIGION** AND **MORALITY** A **LOT** DURING OUR BREAKFASTS AT THE COLLEGE.

SUPPOSE YOU WERE AN **ATHEIST**...

...DO YOU THINK YOU'D FEEL **FUNNY** ABOUT ALL THE **HYMNS** AN' **PRAYERS** AT REV. PEPPER'S RALLIES?

I DOUBT THAT DISBELIEVIN' IN **GOD** WOULD MAKE ME SKEPTICAL ABOUT THE THINGS THOSE SONGS AN' PRAYERS ARE REALLY **ABOUT.**

AN ATHEIST IS STILL GONNA CARE THAT **SLEDGE RANKIN** GOT **MURDERED**, ISN'T HE?

I'M AN ATHEIST, **YOU** KNOW THAT.

SO? TAKE YOURSELF AS AN **EXAMPLE.**

OF **COURSE** I CARE ABOUT SLEDGE.

AS MUCH AS A PERSON **CAN** CARE ABOUT SOMEBODY HE NEVER **KNEW.**

BUT TO BE **HONEST,** I'M NOT SURE HOW MUCH OF WHAT I FEEL THESE DAYS COMES FROM THE FACT THAT I KNOW **YOU** AN' TEND TO PICK UP ON WHAT **YOU** FEEL.

LET'S **FACE** IT—NEGROES'VE BEEN GETTIN' LYNCHED THE WAY **SLEDGE** GOT LYNCHED SINCE A LONG TIME BEFORE **I** ARRIVED ON THE SCENE.

I'D HEAR THE **STORIES**, BUT IT WASN'T LIKE THEY HAD ANYTHING TO DO WITH **ME**. **I** WASN'T OUT THERE BURNIN' CROSSES.

MAYBE I'M **JADED**.

IT'S NOT A CHARACTER TRAIT TO BE **PROUD** OF, BUT—I DUNNO, SOMETIMES IT SEEMS LIKE I WAS **BORN** WITH IT!

PEOPLE AREN'T **BORN** WITH CHARACTER TRAITS.

YOU CARE. **YOU'VE** TOLD ME HOW THAT PICTURE OF EMMETT TILL GOT TO YOU.

SURE! THAT PHOTOGRAPH SCARED THE **SHIT** OUT OF ME!

IT DON'T TAKE MUCH **SOCIAL CONSCIENCE** TO GET THE SHIVERS FROM A **HORROR MOVIE!**

R-R RING!..

WE'RE NOT TALKIN' ABOUT **MOVIES**, TOLAND. I CAN'T **FATHOM** PEOPLE BEIN' JADED ABOUT THINGS THAT'RE **REAL** AN' **TRAGIC**.

HEY, BABY, DON'T HOLD ME TO ANYTHING I SAY THIS **EARLY** IN THE **MORNIN'?**

ANYWAY, **HALF** OF MY **BULL-SHIT** COMES FROM WANTIN' TO GET SOME KINDA **UPPER HAND** ON YOU.

THE FACT IS, **YOU** SCARE ME, **TOO**.

IT'S **ALWAYS** SCARED ME TO **ADMIRE** SOME-BODY. IT'S **FRAUGHT** WITH **PERIL!**

BREAK IT **UP**, LOVE-BIRDS! ♪

HI, SHARON.

DIDN'T YOU HEAR THE **BELL** RING, CHILDREN? IT'S TIME FOR **STUDENT ASSEMBLY**.

ARE YOU STILL GONNA **DO** WHAT YOU **SAID** YOU WERE GONNA DO TODAY, GINGER?

SURE **AM**.

G'BYE, Y'ALL.

THIS I'VE GOTTA **SEE!** *Chortle!*

DON'T **GO** YET, TOLAND. COME **WATCH**.

WELL-L-L I'VE GOTTA LEAVE FOR WORK BY **TEN**...

...BUT MAYBE IF YOU CAN GET UP TO THE MIKE REAL **QUICK**...

GINGER HAD SIGNED UP TO MAKE AN **ANNOUNCE-MENT** THAT MORNING AT THE **STUDENT ASSEMBLY**.

SHE HAD SAID IT WAS GOING TO BE ABOUT SOME **PLANS** FOR WHAT COULD BE THE **BIGGEST** SADIE HAWKINS DAY PARTY **EVER**.

O.K., BEFORE WE START THE **PROGRAM**...

...A PRETTY LADY NAMED...UMM...**GINGER RAINES** HAS A FEW WORDS TO SAY ABOUT SOMETHIN' I BET WE'LL **ALL** WANNA PARTICIPATE IN.

SHE HAD **LIED**.

IF YOU'VE BEEN READIN' THE **PAPERS**, YOU KNOW THAT OUR BELOVED **CITY FATHERS** VOTED THIS WEEK TO CLOSE DOWN **RUSSELL PARK**—SUPPOSEDLY 'FOR **RENOVATIONS**.'

AND IF YOU'VE PAID ATTENTION TO RECENT SOUTHERN **HISTORY**, YOU KNOW EXACTLY **WHY** THE MAYOR AND POLICE COMMISSIONER CHOPPER **WANT** THAT PARK CLOSED!

IT'S BECAUSE **RUSSELL PARK** IS WHERE CLAYFIELD'S **NEGRO CITIZENS** HAVE ALWAYS GATHERED TO DEMONSTRATE AGAINST **RACIAL SEGREGATION**!

UH... 'SCUSE ME, GINGER...

BARRY...?

THE GUY WHO HAD TURNED THE MIKE OVER TO GINGER LOOKED LIKE HE WAS ABOUT TO **PEE** IN HIS **CHINOS**.

WHICH THEY HAVE A **CONSTITUTIONAL RIGHT** TO **DO**!

NOW, FOR THE LAST **YEAR** I'VE BEEN A MEMBER OF THE **BIRACIAL EQUALITY LEAGUE** HERE IN CLAY-FIELD—

GINGER, YOU **KNOW** THE COLLEGE HAS **RULES** AGAINST GIVIN' **POLITICAL SPEECHES** THAT AREN'T ON THE **SCHEDULE**.

IT WAS **STARTLING** TO SEE GINGER TURN INTO SUCH A **LIVE WIRE** ONCE SHE WAS UP IN FRONT OF A **CROWD**.

IT BROUGHT BACK THE QUALITY ABOUT HER THAT HAD **FASCINATED** ME THE NIGHT I FIRST **SAW** HER SINGING WITH **SHILOH** AT THE **MELODY MOTEL**.

BARRY, I'LL BE DONE A LOT **QUICKER** IF YOU'LL STOP BREAKIN' MY TRAIN OF **THOUGHT**.

WHOA, GIRL!

I'D HAD SO MANY **QUIET** TIMES WITH HER SINCE THEN THAT I'D LET THE **OTHER** SIDE OF HER SLIP MY **MIND**, ALMOST.

IT WAS A REAL **SEXY** SIDE.

WE'D ALL LIKE TO TO ASK YA REAL **NICELY** TO **SIT DOWN** AN' LET US GET ON WITH THE **PROGRAM**.

DON'T YOU HAVE A **PLEDGE SWAP** OR SOMETHIN' Y'CAN GO TO? THIS IS **IMPORTANT**!

FROM MY OBSERVATION POST BESIDE THE DOOR I COULD VIEW A **FAIR PERCENTAGE** OF THE **FACES** IN THE ROOM.

GINGER—

MY **POINT**, IF BARRY'LL QUIT **INTERRUPTIN'**, IS THAT IT'S TIME FOR US WESTHILLS COLLEGE STUDENTS TO DO OUR **PART** TO KEEP RUSSELL PARK **OPEN**!

GINGER... **SERIOUSLY**, NOW—

SOME **GRINNED** AND APPEARED TO THINK THE COMMOTION WAS **FUN**.

I **AM** SERIOUS! WE'VE GOTTA PROVE THAT **YOUNG WHITE PEOPLE** IN THE SOUTH **CARE** ABOUT **JUSTICE**!

GINGER!

IF Y'THINK SHE'S A SPITFIRE UP **THERE**, YOU SHOULD TAKE **CONTEMPORARY SOCIOLOGY** WITH 'ER.

OTHERS NARROWED THEIR EYES AND LOOKED **HOSTILE**.

I WANT US TO START A WESTHILLS COLLEGE **CHAPTER** OF THE **EQUALITY LEAGUE**!

I STARTED HEARING **HISSES**...

...AND I **BRACED** MYSELF FOR THE **HECKLERS**.

WINE?

ALL MY **INSTINCTS** WERE TELLING ME THAT GINGER FELT THE SAME WAY **I** DID.

TONIGHT WAS THE **NIGHT.**

YOU WERE PURE **DYNAMITE** AT THAT **ASSEMBLY** TODAY.

Wurf!

DID YOU GET ANY OF YOUR FELLOW **STUDENTS** SIGNED UP FOR THE **EQUALITY LEAGUE?**

A FEW SAID THEY **WISHED** THEY COULD HELP, BUT THEY'RE **SCARED.**

Whimper!

THERE'S PRESSURE ON THE SCHOOL TO **SUSPEND** ANY-BODY WHO GETS INVOLVED IN **SOCIAL UNREST!**

I'D LIKELY BE LONG GONE **MYSELF** IF THE DEAN'S **COUSIN** WASN'T A **BUSINESS PARTNER** OF MY **DAD'S** UP IN **OHIO.**

AREN'T COLLEGE STUDENTS SUPPOSED TO HAVE FREEDOM OF **SPEECH** AN' FREEDOM OF **ASSEMBLY** AN'—

TOLAND, THIS IS THE **SOUTH!** WHERE DO YOU THINK YOU **ARE,** ANY-WAY—IN **AMERICA?!**

POLITICAL TALK. NOT SO **EROTIC.**

IT CAN BE **TOUGH** TO SWITCH **GEARS.**

WINE HELPS.

BY THE WAY...

SO IT JUST PERCHED THERE LIKE A **RAINCAP** ON THE END OF YOUR **THINGIE,** ALL **GUMMED UP** AND **USELESS.**

YEP, AND WITH ALL THE **CLUMSINESS** AND **EMBARRASSMENT,** YOU CAN BET I WENT **LIMP** AS A **RAG.**

AT WHICH POINT EVERY **DOUBT** I'D EVER **HAD** ABOUT MY TENUOUS CLAIM TO **STRAIGHTNESS** CAME BARRELING OUT OF THE **WOODWORK!**

FROM THE WAY I BLEW MY **COOL,** YOU'D HAVE THOUGHT I WAS THE FIRST POOR FUCKER WHO EVER LOST HIS **BONER** UNDER **FIRE!**

BASICALLY I **PANICKED!**

I POURED **EVERYTHING** OUT TO GINGER, EXPLAINING HOW—IN ALL **PROBABILITY** AND DESPITE MY BEST **INTENTIONS**— I WAS A **QUEER.**

Tsk, tsk!

POOR **BABY!**

WELL, WHAT FOLLOWED WAS ONE **KILLER CONVERSATION...** THE KIND THAT'S **CALM** AND **SOULFUL** ON THE **SURFACE,** BUT THAT'LL LEAVE YOUR **STOMACH** TIED UP IN KNOTS FOR A **WEEK.**

WHEN **ENERGY** FLAGGED, WE TIPTOED INTO THE **KITCHEN,** MADE SOME **COCOA...**

...AND TALKED SOME **MORE.**

OCCASIONALLY OUR VOICES WOULD DROP AWAY TO **NOTHING** FOR A WHILE, AND WE'D SIT LISTENING TO THE **GEARS** IN THE **KITCHEN CLOCK** WHIR.

THE SILENCES WERE **PAINFUL,** AND SO WAS **NINETY PERCENT** OF WHAT GOT **SAID.**

I STILL **SQUIRM** WHEN I REMEMBER SOME OF THE **SELF-PITYING GARBAGE** I DUMPED ON GINGER THAT NIGHT...

...LIKE THE **ABSOLUTE CONVICTION** I'D PICKED UP SOMEWHERE IN MY **TRAVELS,** THAT HOMO-SEXUALS WEREN'T **CAPABLE** OF **LOVING** EACH OTHER THE WAY HETEROSEXUALS COULD.

The spring I finished high school, they held a **picnic** in honor of the seniors. It was the same every year...

Half the class, it seemed, was **paired off**: boy, girl, boy, girl....

Some of 'em were in **love**, or **felt** like they were.

A fair number knew they'd be **separated** soon, what with **college** or goin' into the **military**.

They sat around on the **grass**, some of 'em holdin' **hands**, a few practically **neckin'** right there in front of **everybody**.

The chaperons were careful to see that nothin' got out of **hand**, but even **so**, they kept castin' **tender, indulgent glances** at all the young couples...

...Like it was so fuckin' **wonderful** that the **plan** of **nature** was bein' **fulfilled** by these sweet, straight teenagers, all moon-eyed an' **horny**...

...An' I felt like **shit**, 'cause I knew in my **gut** —as much as I worked at not puttin' anything into **words**— that I'd **never** be part of that **picture**.

GINGER...

I'd been born **different**—an' nobody was **ever** gonna look at **me** an' think it was wonderful that **I** was in love.

WOULD YA MIND NOT **TELLIN'** ANY OF OUR FRIENDS ABOUT ME? IT'D JUST **COMPLICATE** AN' **CONFUSE** THINGS.

Y'SEE, I DEFINITELY PLAN ON BEIN' **STRAIGHT** IN THE **LONG RUN**.

I THINK, IF I'M **DETERMINED** TO, I CAN **DO** IT.

I'VE BEEN DOIN' PRETTY **GOOD**. O.K.—I SCREWED UP **TONIGHT**, BUT, IN GENERAL, I'VE REALLY BEEN FEELIN' LIKE I WAS IN **LOVE** WITH YOU.

TOLAND, YOU NEED TO **THINK** THINGS **THROUGH**.

I MEAN, I **AM** IN LOVE WITH YOU.

I'VE BEEN GETTIN' THAT WAY MORE AN' MORE EVERY **DAY**...

...AN' FROM WHAT I COULD TELL, **YOU'VE** BEEN IN LOVE WITH **ME**, TOO.

HAVEN'T YOU?

I GUESS I SHOULDN'T EXPECT YOU TO SAY ANY-THING ABOUT THAT RIGHT **NOW**.

I'M **WORN OUT** AN' MY **HEAD'S** THROBBIN' AN' I DON'T KNOW WHAT SOMEBODY IN MY SHOES IS **SUPPOSED** TO SAY.

GINGER, YOU'RE THE ONLY GIRL I'VE EVER BEEN CONVINCED I **COULD** BE IN LOVE WITH. YOU'RE MY **LIFELINE**.

I'M **NOT** YOUR 'LIFELINE.' I DIDN'T SIGN UP TO BE **ANYBODY'S** LIFELINE!

EVENTUALLY GINGER ASKED ME TO DRIVE HER BACK TO THE **DORM, LATE** AS IT **WAS**.

WE KISSED GOODNIGHT IN THE **USUAL** WAY...

...ACTING LIKE NOTHING OF ANY IMPORTANCE HAD **CHANGED**. MEANWHILE, SOMETHING INSIDE OF ME STOOD **APART** FROM IT ALL AND **WATCHED**...

...STOOD APART WHILE THE **WORDS** SHE'D SAID TO ME CIRCLED 'ROUND AND 'ROUND IN MY **HEAD**.

Chapter 9

THE NEXT MORNING...

YOU AN' GINGER WERE UP **LATE** ENOUGH LAST NIGHT.

DID GINGER GO BACK TO THE **CAMPUS** OR IS SHE STILL IN THERE **SNOOZIN'**?

SHE WENT **BACK**.

DAMN, I WOKE UP **TIRED**! GLAD I'VE GOT TODAY AN' TOMORROW **OFF**.

BEST THING GOD EVER **INVENTED** WAS DAYS OFF.

...This is Chauncey Blake reporting from Russell Park...

Y'DIDN'T BOTHER **ME**.

SORRY IF WE KEPT YOU **AWAKE**.

SAY, GUYS—ACCORDIN' TO THE **RADIO**, THERE'S A BIG **STIR** BUILDIN' UP DOWNTOWN RIGHT NOW.

SNOOKY LANS... LOOKS BAC...

Y'KNOW THE **TALK** THAT'S BEEN IN THE AIR ABOUT THE CITY CLOSIN' DOWN **RUSSELL PARK?** WELL...

...SINCE **SUNUP** THE COPS'VE BEEN ALL **OVER** THE PARK, AN' IT APPEARS THEY AIM TO START RUNNIN' THE NEGROES OUT **TODAY**.

CAN THEY GET **AWAY** WITH THAT?

I THOUGHT THERE WAS AN **INJUNCTION** IN FORCE TO **PREVENT** THAT KIND OF STUNT.

THE **CHOPPER** CAN'T BULLDOZE RIGHT OVER THE **FEDERAL COURTS**.

ARE YOU A HUNDRED PERCENT SURE HE **KNOWS** HE CAN'T?

I WONDER IF **GINGER'S** HEARD ABOUT THIS....

I GOT **SHARON** ON THE HALL PHONE AT THE **DORM**. GINGER HAD LEFT THE ROOM **EARLY**, SHARON SAID.

SHE GOT A **CALL** ABOUT SOMETHIN' HAPPENIN' AT THE **PARK** AN' **LIT OUT**, TOLAND.

Please, Girls!! REMEMBER THE 10-MINUTE RULE...

YOU TWO DON'T PUT MUCH STOCK IN LONG HOURS OF **SLEEP** THESE DAYS, **DO** YOU!

MAVIS AN' I ARE GONNA DRIVE DOWNTOWN AN' WATCH SOME OF THE **EXCITEMENT**. WANNA **COME**?

SURE. WHY **NOT**?

JUST LEMME FIND SOME **EATS** TO TAKE ALONG. Y'ALL HAVE HAD BREAKFAST; I HAVEN'T.

No, No, **Loco**!...YOU CAN'T RIDE IN THE CAR **THIS** TIME. CIVIL UNREST MAKES YOU **NERVOUS**.

LET'S **GO**! LET'S **GO**!

GRAB THE **DONUTS**. THEY'RE **PORTABLE**.

Wurf!

WE PILED INTO RILEY'S **CAR** AND HEADED **DOWNTOWN**.

WHATEVER WAS COOKING AT THE PARK, IT HAD **ACTIVISTS**, **COPS**, AND **RUBBERNECKERS** STREAMING IN FROM ALL SIDES LIKE **ANTS** AT A PICNIC.

HEY, NEIGHBORS!

Honk!

Beep!

Honk!

WHERE'D Y'ALL HAFTA PARK **YOUR** JALOPY— SOMEWHERE IN OKLAHOMA?

PRACTICALLY! OURS IS PARKED BACK AT THE **TRAIN YARD**. THIS IS SOME **CROWD** THAT'S GATHERIN', **ISN'T** IT?

YOU REMEMBER WHO THOSE LADIES **ARE**, DONCHA, RILEY?

AREN'T **TWO** OF 'EM THE WOMEN WHO RUN THE **NEGRO NIGHTCLUB** SAMMY TOOK US TO?

AN' THE **THIRD** ONE'S **MABEL**, THE **PIANO PLAYER** AT THE **RHOMBUS**.

RIGHT.

MABEL'S **COOL**. SHE AN' I TALKED UP A **STORM** THAT NIGHT.

THE POLICE HAD OBVIOUSLY **UNDER-ESTIMATED** HOW MANY CITIZENS WOULD TAKE AN **INTEREST** IN THE DAY'S GAMBIT. THEIR **BARRICADES** WEREN'T KEEPING ANYONE **OUT** WHO WANTED **IN**.

LOOK AT THE PEOPLE STILL POURIN' **IN**!

DO YOU THINK IT'S **SAFE** FOR US TO BE HERE?

♪ Woke up this mornin' with my mind... ♪

THE **MOVEMENT** PEOPLE I'VE MET ARE **SERIOUS** ABOUT **NON-VIOLENCE**.

♪ ..stayed on free- dom... ♪

I DON'T THINK ANYBODY'S GONNA **RIOT** OR ANY-THING.

A GLANCE AROUND CONVINCED ME THAT FINDING **GINGER** ANYTIME SOON WAS GONNA BE A MATTER OF **BLIND LUCK** AT **BEST**—ASSUMING SHE WAS **THERE**.

THE CROWD IN RUSSELL PARK WAS **SWELLING** BY THE **MINUTE**, AND AS BEST WE COULD **TELL** SOME KIND OF **DEMONSTRATION** WAS UNDER WAY.

♪ Woke up this mornin' with my mind... ♪

BUT THINGS WERE **CONFUSED** AND IT WAS HARD TO TELL WHAT WAS **WHAT**.

WE **EAVESDROPPED** 'TIL WE CAUGHT THE DRIFT OF WHAT HAD **GONE ON** UP TO THEN.

THE **COPS** HAD BEEN THERE SINCE **DAWN**, FOLKS WERE SAYING.

THEN CITY **WORK CREWS** HAD BEGUN WHEELING UP TO THE PARK IN THEIR BIG **TRUCKS**, THEIR CLEAR **INTENTION** BEING TO ERECT A TALL **FENCE** AROUND THE SITE.

THEY'D GOTTEN A FEW **POLES** STUCK IN THE GROUND AND HAD BEGUN UNLOADING ROLLS OF **CHAIN LINK** WHEN THE TROUBLE **BEGAN.**

REALIZING WHAT THE CITY WAS **UP** TO, SEVERAL DOZEN NEIGHBORHOOD **RESIDENTS** SURGED SPONTANEOUSLY FORWARD AND THREW THEMSELVES ONTO THE **GRASS** ALONG THE PARK'S **PERIMETER** WHERE THE NEW FENCE WAS SLATED TO **GO.**

AS WORD **SPREAD,** RUSSELL PARK WAS QUICKLY FILLED WITH ALARMED **SPECTATORS,** MANY OF WHOM **JOINED** IN THE PROTEST ONCE THEY'D SIZED UP THE **SITUATION.**

HUNDREDS **MORE** CHOSE TO STAND WARILY ON THE **FRINGES** OF THE SIT-IN AND OFFER TENSE **SUPPORT.**

YOU **COLORED** PEOPLE ARE **ILLEGALLY INTERFERING** WITH THE WORK OF **CLAYFIELD'S PARK MAINTENANCE DEPARTMENT!**

IN THE THICK OF THE ACTION WE COULD SEE **SHILOH REED** LEADING THE PEOPLE AROUND HIM IN A SPIRITED **SING-ALONG.**

♪ ...Stayed on freedom! Hallelu!... ♪

I ORDER YOU TO **CLEAR** THE AREA **PEACEFULLY** AND **IMMEDIATELY** OR YOU WILL BE **FORCIBLY REMOVED!**

STAND BACK!

MOVE ASIDE!

WE GOT SOME **OBSTRUCTIN'** O' THE **LAW** TO DO!

C'MON, CHILDREN!

GRAB A **SEAT!**

UH...

RILEY, IT LOOKS **DANGEROUS.**

WE JUST CAME TO **WATCH,** MA'AM—

TRAITORS! WHITE NIGGERS!

??! THEY'RE TALKIN' TO **US,** BABY!

WELL, SCREW **THEM!**

UH...

MOVE **OVER,** MABEL!

COMMENTARY FROM A PACK OF SNOTNOSED **HECKLERS** ON THE **SIDELINES** HELPED MAKE UP OUR **MINDS** FOR US:

POLICE LINE

BEFORE I KNEW IT I WAS ON THE GROUND GIVING THE **POLICE** AND **FENCE-BUILDING CREW** A HARD TIME LIKE EVERYBODY **ELSE**.

OF COURSE, AS SOON AS I WAS **DOWN** THERE AND **COMMITTED**, I STARTED WONDERING WHAT I HAD GOTTEN MYSELF **INTO**.

MARGE, **LOOK!** HERE COMES TH' **REVEREND**.

AN' THERE'S **LES** AN' **RAEBURN** HELPIN' OUT.

POLICE LI

LISTEN **UP**, EVER'BODY— WHO HERE AIN'T HAD THE **EQUALITY LEAGUE'S CIVIL DISOBEDIENCE** TRAININ'? LEMME SEE **HANDS**.

LES!

'LO, TOLAND. SAY-YY! LOOKS LIKE THE **GANG'S ALL HERE!**

WHADDAYA THINK'S GONNA **HAPPEN?**

O.K., IF YOU **AIN'T** BEEN TO THE WORKSHOPS, **FORGET** ANY NOTIONS Y'GOT ABOUT REFUSIN' TO **DO** WHAT THE MAN **SAYS** IF A COP LOOKS STRAIGHT **AT** YOU AN' TELLS YOU TO **MOVE**.

WELL, TOLE, THERE'S **ONE** THING OPERATIN' IN OUR FAVOR: THE **CHOPPER** AIN'T ON THE SCENE SO FAR.

LOTS OF FOLKS OUT HERE HAVE ALREADY BEEN **TRAINED** IN PASSIVE RESISTANCE IF IT **COMES TO** THAT. LET **THEM** CARRY THE BALL.

THE COPS'RE **EDGY**, BUT PAPA'S HAD PAST **DEALINGS** WITH MOST OF THE **KEY** ONES I'VE SEEN HERE.

IT DON'T **PAY** TO TRY AN' MAKE THIS SHIT **UP** AS YOU GO **ALONG**, BELIEVE ME! AN' REMEMBER 'BOUT KEEPIN' THINGS **NON-VIOLENT**. NOW I NEED THE **NAMES** OF ANYBODY WHO'S

Tell the Chopper, we shall not be moved...

HE'S BETTIN' HE CAN CONVINCE 'EM TO **HOLD OFF** FOR NOW AN' SEE WHAT THE **FEDERAL JUDGE** HAS TO SAY ABOUT THEM CLOSIN' THE PARK DOWN.

...We shall not be moved...

AROUND THEN WE NOTICED THAT THE **BACKGROUND MUSIC** WAS COMING FROM A **SMALLER** SET OF **VOICES**.

Tell the...

WHO'RE THE **KIDS** THAT'RE SINGIN'?

...Chop-per...

THAT'S SHILOH'S **FREEDOM CHORUS**.

THEY ALL GREW UP **HARMONIZIN'** FOR **FUN**.

WHEN HE GOT TO **TOWN**, SHILOH MADE A **PROJECT** OF TEACHIN' 'EM ALL THE **FREEDOM SONGS** HE KNOWS.

HE'S ABOUT GOT 'EM READY TO DO **CONCERTS**, SHILOH SAYS.

ARE YOU **ALL RIGHT**, SAMMY?

Groan! THE BASTARD HIT MY **HAND**! AN' HE **KNOWS** HOW I EARN MY **LIVIN'**!

DAMN COP BETTER NOT SWING AT **ME** OR I'LL KNOCK HIS **BUTT** CLEAR TO **BILOXI**!

DON'T TALK LIKE **THAT**, MABEL! **THAT** AIN'T THE **SPIRIT**!

Y'WANNA GO TO A **DOCTOR**, PAL?

DON'T WANNA GO **ANYWHERE** RIGHT NOW. JUST LEMME BE **STILL** HERE 'TIL IT STOPS **THROBBIN'**.

IF ASKED, I'D HAVE TOLD YOU A **RIOT** WAS GONNA BREAK OUT ONCE THE **KICKING** STARTED. BUT SOMEHOW **TEMPERS** GOT HELD.

COME MID-AFTERNOON, OUR ASSES WERE STILL RIGHT **THERE** ON THE **GRASS**.

IT WAS A HELL OF A WAY TO SPEND A **SATURDAY**.

IT WAS HARD TO GET A FIX ON WHAT WAS **HAPPENING**, WITH THE **NOISE** AND SOMEBODY'S **HEAD** ALWAYS BLOCKING YOUR LINE OF **VISION**.

EVERY TIME SOME POLICEMAN WOULD **SHOUT** SOMETHING **OUT** OR JUST START **RUNNING**, YOU COULD FEEL THE WHOLE CROWD **STRAIGHTEN** AND **BRACE** ITSELF.

REV. PEPPER KEPT TALKING WITH MEN WHO LOOKED TO BE **BRASS**, WHILE **SIXTY RUMORS** A **MINUTE** CIRCULATED AS TO **SUTTON CHOPPER'S** WHEREABOUTS.

YOU'D HEAR SOME **BARKING** SOMEWHERE AND WONDER, ALONG WITH SEVERAL HUNDRED **OTHERS**, WHETHER IT WAS NEIGHBORHOOD **STRAYS** CHASING A **CAT** OR POLICE DOGS GETTING TRUCKED IN FOR **CROWD CONTROL**.

BEING **WHITE**, I'D NEVER LOOKED A CLAYFIELD **POLICE** DOG IN THE **EYE**, BUT PLENTY OF THE FOLKS **AROUND** ME CLEARLY **HAD**.

THEY BETTER NOT SIC NO **DOGS** ON ME, **NEITHER**.

COONS WARE!

AND THERE, TO GRATE ON **EVERYBODY'S** NERVES, WERE CARS FULL OF COCKY WHITE **TEENAGERS** THAT KEPT CIRCLING THE BLOCK WITH REBEL **FLAGS** FLAPPING FROM THEIR **RADIO ANTENNAS**.

MABEL, DO YOUR **EYES** FOR MAVIS AN' TOLAND.

AW, **HELL**, RILEY... I CAN'T JUST DO MY **EYES** AT THE DROP OF A **HAT**. I'VE GOTTA BE IN THE **MOOD**.

C'MON, **YOU** CAN DO IT. I WANT 'EM TO HEAR YOUR 'CRAZY NIGGER' STORY.

LORD! YOU BEEN TELLIN' THAT STORY **AGAIN**, SISTER?

WELL... O.K.

YOU **ASKED** FOR IT.

HERE GOES.

YIKES!

THERE! Y'SATISFIED, RILEY?

I WILL BE WHEN YOU TELL MAVIS AN' TOLAND THE STORY.

TELL US, MABEL.

HE'S GOT US CURIOUS NOW.

THE STORY I TOLD RILEY WHEN Y'ALL WAS AT THE RHOMBUS WAS 'BOUT HOW, BACK IN THE 'THIRTIES WHEN I LIVED IN PARTS OF THE SOUTH MORE BACKWARDS EVEN THAN CLAYFIELD...

Nossir! In fact, I usually sat right up in **front** by the **driver.**

...I **never** used to let 'em put me in the **back** of a **bus.**

DIDN'T THEY HAVE THE BUS LAWS BACK THEN?

OH, INDEED THEY DID!

JIM CROW WAS KING O' THE HILL!

COLORED FOLKS GOT BEAT UP OR TOSSED OFF THE BUS ALL THE TIME FOR NOT STEPPIN' FAST ENOUGH WHEN A DRIVER TOLD 'EM TO MOVE ON BACK.

NOW ASK 'ER HOW SHE GOT AWAY WITH IT EVEN SO.

I had a job **housekeepin'** in the next **county,** an' most of the time I was ridin' the **same** bus at the **same** times of the **day...**

...So the drivers got to **know** me.

But even when I was on a **different** bus with a **different** driver from **usual,** I pulled the **same** stunt.

YOU BE THE BUS DRIVER, EFFIE.

SEE, THE DRIVER, HE'D SWING 'ROUND TO SISTER LIKE THIS AN' SAY:

'YOU GOTTA MOVE— Y'HEAR? LAW SAYS COLORED PEOPLE GOTTA BE BACK OF THAT THERE MARKER!'

NOW SHOW 'EM WHAT YOU'D DO, MABEL.

I'D GO: →

WHUH- WHUH- WHUH- WHUH'D JOO SAY?

Well, he'd say it **again:**

YOU GOTTA MOVE BACK THERE... Y'HEAR??

WHUH- WHUH'D JOO SAY?

AN' THEY'D GO BACK AN' FORTH, 'ROUND AN' 'ROUND.

AN' AS MANY TIMES AS HE'D TELL 'ER TO MOVE, SHE'D GIVE 'IM BACK THAT SPOOKY LOOK, LIKE SHE DIDN'T HAVE A CLUE WHAT HE WAS TALKIN' 'BOUT.

I LEARNED I COULD DO THAT THING WITH MY EYES WHEN I WAS A BABY. cackle!

MOST PEOPLE CAN'T DO IT! I'M GONNA GET A PATENT ON IT, I THINK!

Heh heh! I **SWEAR** I COULD GIVE THE WILLIES TO **ANY** WHITE BUS DRIVER I RAN **INTO!**

Chortle!

I'D GIVE 'EM MY **LOOK** AN' THE **STARCH'D** GO RIGHT OUTA THEIR **SPINES!**

ALL THE **OTHER** NIGGERS'D BE IN THE **BACK** LIKE ANYBODY WITH GOOD **SENSE** WOULDA BEEN...

...But young an' sassy as I **was**, I'd park myself right up **front** every **time.**

...An' sooner or later some cracker would gen'rally yell up to the **driver** an' say:

HEY, **DRIVER!** HOW COME YO'RE LETTIN' THAT **NIGGER** SIT UP THERE IN THE **FRONT** LIKE THAT?

...An' he'd answer back:

JUS' KEEP **QUIET** AN' LEAVE 'ER **BE,** MISTER. THAT THERE'S A **CRAZY** NIGGER.

A 'crazy nigger'! **That's** what I was!

...AN' **THAT'S** HOW I GOT TO SIT IN THE **FRONT** OF THE **BUS** IN THE 'THIRTIES.

HEY THERE, ANNA DELLYNE!

HOW'S **SAMMY** DOIN'? SOMEBODY SAID HE GOT **HIT.**

HIS **HAND** GOT SLAMMED.

I'M O.K., ANNA DELLYNE.

I DON'T THINK YOU'RE O.K., SAMMY. LOOK HOW THAT HAND'S ALL **SWOLLEN.**

I'M GONNA FIND SOMEBODY WHO'LL GET YOU TO A **DOCTOR,** SUGAR.

ANNA DELLYNE TOOK OFF WITH SAMMY IN **TOW.** THE **REST** OF US MADE A MEAL OF THE **DONUTS** I'D BROUGHT FROM THE **WHEELERY.**

THE STANDOFF WITH THE COPS DRUG ON AND **ON.** THE SUN GOT **HOT.**

I SLIPPED OFF TO SEE IF I COULD FIND **GINGER** IN THE CROWD.

Which side are you on? Which side are you on?...

EVENTUALLY I **SPOTTED** HER.

WALKING BACK TO WHERE I'D LEFT MY **FRIENDS**, MY MIND WAS HUNG UP ON THE IMAGE OF GINGER **LOOKING** AT ME BUT NOT **SMILING**...

...'TIL IT HIT ME THAT THE **SONGS** HAD SUDDENLY **STOPPED** A FEW SECONDS BEFORE.

I'D BARELY HAD TIME TO WONDER **WHY** WHEN THE COLLECTIVE **PITCH** OF ALL THE **VOICES** IN THE PARK SHOT UP LIKE AN **AMBULANCE SIREN**...

...AND I **HEARD** THE **DOGS** BARKING.

WHAT'S GOIN' **ON?**

THE **CHOPPER'S** HERE.

FROM THEN ON IT WAS ALL BUT **IMPOSSIBLE** TO KEEP MY **BEARINGS**.

'SCUSE ME.

BEG PARDON.

'SCUSE ME....

PEOPLE ON THE **GROUND** STARTED JUMPING **UP** AND PEOPLE WHO'D BEEN **STANDING UP** STARTED **RUNNING**.

THEN I **SAW** SUTTON CHOPPER... AND THE **DOGS**.

THIS IS YOUR **LAST WARNING!** THE CITY HAS VOTED TO **CLOSE DOWN** RUSSELL PARK AS OF **TODAY** FOR PURPOSES OF **RENOVATION** AND **BEAUTIFICATION!**

THOSE WHO REFUSE TO **WALK PEACEFULLY** OUT OF THE PARK WILL BE IN VIOLATION OF THE **LAW** AND WILL BE **EJECTED** FROM THESE GROUNDS BY **WHATEVER MEANS** ARE **NECESSARY**.

DON'T **WORRY**, FOLKS...THE **COURTS** ARE GONNA TAKE **OUR** SIDE IN THE **END**.

NOW LET'S KEEP OUR **WITS** ABOUT US AN' KEEP THE **MUSIC** GOIN' WHILE WE MOVE BACK REAL **SLOW**....

We are not afraid... We are not afraid...

BUT SOME WERE **PARALYZED** AT THE SIGHT OF THE DOGS.

MOST OF THE DEMONSTRATORS TOOK THEIR CUE FROM **SHILOH** AND EASED SLOWLY **BACK**, SINGING **FREEDOM SONGS** TO KEEP **CALM**.

Growl! Snarl!

SEVERAL COPS MADE A GAME OF SEEING HOW **CLOSE** THEY COULD LET THE DOGS GET TO THE PROTESTERS WITHOUT ACTUALLY MAKING **CONTACT**.

Snap! Grrr!

THEN ONE OF THEM **MISCALCULATED**.

A DOG CAUGHT A LADY'S **SHAWL**.

SHE LOST HER **FOOTING**... SHRIEKED FOR **HELP**...

... AND THE CROWD CAME **UNHINGED**.

DON'T BE DISHEARTENED! OUR LAWYERS ARE ON THE JOB AND THE HOLY FORCE OF **JUSTICE** IS ON OUR SIDE!

ANYBODY BUT **GINGER**, THAT IS! WHEN I'D URGED MAVIS AND RILEY TO HEAD BACK TO THE WHEELERY **WITHOUT** ME, I'D BEEN IMAGINING THAT, IF I **FOUND** HER, SHE'D WANNA SPEND **TIME** WITH ME.

I WAS ALL GEARED UP TO BE **STRONG** AND **COMFORTING.**

BY THEN THE ACTION HAD SHIFTED TO **SMITH CITY BAPTIST**, WHERE MOST OF THE DEMONSTRATORS HAD REASSEMBLED ONCE THE **COPS** AND **DOGS** HAD SUCCEEDED IN DRIVING THEM OUT OF THE **PARK.**

I RAN INTO **ROSE**, WHO TOLD ME SHE'D JUST SEEN GINGER TALKING TO **SHILOH.**

LOOK!

THERE'S ONE!

SCREEEEECH!

HEY! WHATCHA DOIN' IN **NIGGERTOWN**, SONNYBOY?

COME OVER **HERE!**

WE WANNA **TALK** TO YA!

WHEN I GOT ON THE BUS, MY **INTENTION** WAS TO TRANSFER AT EIGHTEENTH STREET TO THE **COLLEGE LINE**, WHICH WOULD HAVE TAKEN ME DIRECTLY OUT TO THE **WHEELERY**.

BUT I NEVER **TRANSFERRED**.

INSTEAD I RODE ON TO **NINTH STREET**.

YOU **HAVEN'T** EATEN A **BURGER** UNTIL YOU'VE EATEN A **DONBURGER**

DID YOU KNOW ABOUT THESE **DIXIE PATRIOTS** BEIN' STACKED THERE BY THE DOOR?

OH, **THOSE** THINGS! AREN'T THEY **AWFUL?**

SOME MAN **INSISTS** ON COMIN' AN' PUTTIN' **PILES** OF THOSE PAPERS OUT FRONT. MY **BOSS** LETS HIM DO IT. NOBODY ASKS **ME!**

THE PEOPLE THAT PUT THAT OUT **SAY** THEY'RE **CHRISTIANS**, BUT I DON'T THINK THEY **ACT** VERY CHRISTIAN... DO **YOU?**

THEY **SAY** THINGS ABOUT PEOPLE THAT DON'T SEEM CHRISTIAN TO **ME** AT **ALL!**

OF COURSE, I **DO** THINK THEY HAVE A **POINT** WHEN THEY SAY IT'S PROBABLY THE **COMMUNISTS** WHO'RE CONVINCIN' THE NEGROES THAT THEY'RE SO **DISSATISFIED**.

BUT IT'S THE UGLY **WAY** THEY SAY IT! **UHN-UH!!**

IT'S **WAY** TOO UNCHRISTIAN FOR **ME!**

AFTER MY **MEAL**...

I STOOD, THEN STOOD SOME **MORE**. THEN FINALLY I WENT **IN**.

IT WAS MY FIRST TIME TO SET **FOOT** IN THE RHOMBUS ALL BY **MYSELF.** FRANKLY, I'D FORGOTTEN HOW **DEAD** A DAMN BAR COULD **BE** THAT EARLY IN THE EVENING.

BUT THAT WAS O.K. IT GAVE ME TIME TO GET A FEW **DRINKS** UNDER MY BELT BEFORE THE **SATURDAY NIGHT CROWD** POURED IN.

BY THE TIME THE ROOM FILLED UP, I WAS HAVING **NO** TROUBLE AT **ALL** STRIKING UP **ACQUAINTANCES.**

...SO MY FATHER, HE THREW A **FIT** AN' SAID THAT, AFTER ALL HE'D BEEN THROUGH WITH MY **BROTHER,** THERE WAS NO **WAY** HE WAS GONNA GIVE HIS BLESSIN' TO ME LEAVIN' THE FAMILY BUSINESS AN' BOY...

MM-HMM.

MM-HMM.

WANNA COME OVER TO MY **HOUSE** FOR A WHILE TONIGHT?

Y'CAN **SLEEP OVER** AN' I'LL DRIVE YOU HOME **TOMORROW.** I KNOW YOU SAID Y'DIDN'T HAVE YOUR **CAR** WITH YOU....

♪ UH... ♪

AW, **GOSH,** CHIP— I DIDN'T MEAN TO **MISLEAD** YOU. I'M NOT **GAY.**

I WAS JUST ENJOYIN' **TALKIN'** TO YOU. **SHIT,** I'M **SORRY** FOR LEADIN' YOU **ON!**

IF YOU'RE NOT **GAY,** WHAT'RE YOU DOIN' IN A GAY **BAR?**

I'M A FRIEND OF **MABEL'S.**

♪ Many a tear has to fall... ♪

I ENJOY COMIN' **DOWNTOWN** AN' HEARIN' HER **PLAY.**

POLICE DOGS OR **NO** POLICE DOGS, MABEL HAD REPORTED FOR **PIANO DUTY** AROUND **NINE.**

♪ ...But it's all in the game... ♪

THAT'S **COOL.** Y'GONNA GO OUT TO **ALLEYSAX** TONIGHT? GOOD MUSIC **THERE, TOO.**

I HAVEN'T GIVEN IT ANY **THOUGHT.**

WELL, IF YOU WANNA **GO** AN' Y'NEED A **RIDE,** YOU CAN COME IN **MY** CAR.

HE SOUNDED SWEET **SAYIN'** IT, BUT IT TURNED OUT TO BE AN **EMPTY PROMISE...**

...AS I FOUND OUT **LATER** WHILE I WAS CHATTING WITH A LESBIAN NAMED **IRENE.**

SAY, WHO ARE YOU **CRUISIN'** OVER MY **SHOULDER?**

DID **MR. UNIVERSE** JUST WALK IN?

IT'S **NOTHIN'**.

ONE OF THOSE FELLAS WHO'RE WALKIN' OUT THE **DOOR** TOGETHER RIGHT NOW TOLD ME **EARLIER** TONIGHT THAT I COULD HITCH A **RIDE** WITH HIM TO **ALLEYSAX**.

HELL, **I'LL** BE GOIN' TO ALLEYSAX FOR **SURE.** YOU CAN RIDE WITH M—

OH, **LOOK,** IT'S **IRE-E-ENE!** MY FAVORITE **DYKE** IN THE **WOR-R-RLD!**

I WAS **DESPERATE** TO **MARRY** THIS WOMAN UNTIL I FOUND OUT HER **DOWRY** WAS FOR SHIT!

YEP. **I** GOT NO **DOWRY** AN' **BERNARD'S** GOT NO **CUNT!**

?

IF **THAT** AIN'T 'STAR-CROSSED LOVERS' FOR YOU, I DUNNO WHAT **IS!** BERNARD, THIS IS **TOLAND.**

IT'S SO **CHARMING** TO **MEET** YOU, TOLAND. I THINK I SAW YOU COME IN WITH **SAMMY NOONE** A FEW WEEKS AGO.

I **TOLD** MISS NOONE HOW **CUTE** I THOUGHT YOU WERE, BUT I SUPPOSE THAT DIZZY QUEEN FORGOT TO **RELAY** MY **MESSAGE.**

I STAYED PUT AND LET BERNARD BAT HIS **EYES** AT ME FOR A WHILE, NOT WANTING TO SEEM **UNFRIENDLY.**

THEN I **EXCUSED** MYSELF AND WORKED MY WAY ACROSS THE ROOM TO WHERE **MABEL** WAS ABOUT TO CLOSE UP **SHOP.**

SHE AND I HAD SWAPPED **NODS** FROM A **DISTANCE,** BUT I HADN'T **SPOKEN** TO HER ALL **NIGHT.**

I SURE DIDN'T THINK I'D SEE **YOU** PLAYIN' HERE TONIGHT.

IT'S MY **JOB.**

NOBODY PAYS ME TO LIE 'ROUND AN' **LICK** MY **WOUNDS.**

WOUNDS? DID YOU GET **HURT?**

OH, I'M JUS' **TALKIN'** DRAMATIC, HONEY.

I TWISTED MY **BACK** SOME. GOT SOME **SCRATCHES...**

CHIGGERS TOOK MORE BITES OUTA ME THAN THAT OL' **RIN-TIN-TIN** DID. I **SWEAR,** THOUGH, TOLAND...

...I'M GETTIN' KINDA **OLD** FOR THAT **SATURDAY-AFTERNOON-CHAPTER-PICTURE** STUFF!

STILL, I'M LIKE **EFFIE:** SISTER SAYS THE DAY WON'T **DAWN** WHEN SHE'LL LET THE CHOPPER SEE HER SITTIN' OUT A **SIT-IN!**

LAST CALL FOR DRINKS!

C'MON, SPORT— IF YOU STILL WANNA GO TO **ALLEYSAX** WITH ME, BETTER HOP IN THE **JAGUAR.**

THANK **GOD** FULL THE MOON ISN'T TONIGHT! I GET SUCH **UNSEEMLY NOCTURNAL DESIRES** WHEN MOONS ARE FULL!

AS IF MISS ESMERELDUS WASN'T IN HEAT **365 DAYS** A YEAR!

YOU DELIGHTFUL YOUNG GENTLEMEN ARE COMING WITH US TO **ALLEYSAX**, AREN'T YOU?

TO ALLEY **WHAT?**

WE DON'T KNOW WHERE IT **IS.**

JUST FOLLOW ALL THE **CARS.** THE **MORE** THE **MERRIER!**

A MILE OR SO SHORT OF ALLEYSAX, IRENE SPOTTED ONE OF THE RARE **STORES** IN THAT NEIGHBORHOOD TO KEEP **ALL-NIGHT HOURS.**

I GOTTA **STOP** FOR JUST A MINUTE, SPORT. I'M ALL OUTA **CIGARETTES.**

I WAITED IN THE **JAGUAR** WITH MY **BRAIN** ON **IDLE,** WATCHING THE **MIDNIGHT PARADE** GO BY.

ONE OF THE CARS HAD A **BUMPER STICKER** THAT **JOGGED** ME **AWAKE.**

KEEP AMERICA WHITE

THAT PACK OF YOUNG GUYS THAT **BERNARD** INVITED ALONG—DO YOU RECALL EVER SEEIN' THEM **INSIDE** THE RHOMBUS?

UH-UH.

WHY? SOMETHIN' ABOUT 'EM **WORRY** YOU?

V**ROOOOOM.**

HOLD TIGHT.

THERE IN THE PARKIN' LOT.

HANG ON. QUICK **TURN** COMIN'...

82

BERNARD **SWORE** THERE WAS NO CALL FOR ME OR IRENE TO **HANG AROUND** WHILE HE WAITED FOR **TREATMENT.**

EMERGENCY FACILITIES WHITE ONLY

PLEASE BE QUIET

* USE MY **CAR** TO TAKE THIS SLEEPY **BOY** HOME, * IRENE.

I CAN **WALK** BACK TO MY APARTMENT ONCE I GET MY **CHEEK** LOOKED AT.

IRENE, **PLEASE** DON'T ASK ME TO DO THAT. I CAN'T **STAND** TALKING TO POLICEMEN.

YOU OUGHTA **SIC** THE **COPS** ON THOSE **FUCKERS** THAT JUMPED YOU, HON.

THEY'D JUST MAKE **FUN** OF ME LIKE THEY **ALWAYS** DO. **COPS** ARE WORSE TO QUEERS THAN THE **BASHERS** ARE.

IT'S **YOUR DECISION**. IT SURE **GRATES** ON ME, THOUGH—THINKIN' ABOUT 'EM GETTIN' **AWAY** WITH IT.

WHATEVER Y'DO, HERE'S MY **NUMBER,** BERNARD.

CALL ME IF YOU HAVE ANY MORE **PROBLEMS.**

IRENE DROVE ME HOME TO THE **WHEELERY**, THE BOTH OF US **DOG TIRED.**

PASSING THE **PHONE** IN THE HALL, I NOTICED THAT THE **RECEIVER** WAS OFF THE **HOOK.**

I DON'T **REMEMBER** HANGING IT UP, BUT I GUESS I **MUST** HAVE...

...GIVEN WHAT HAPPENED **NEXT.**

Rin-n-n·ng!

GODDAMMIT, TOLAND!—WE LEFT THAT PHONE OFF THE HOOK **ON PURPOSE!**

Rin-n·n·ng!

SOMEBODY **RECOGNIZED MAVIS** IN THE PARK TODAY AN' WE'VE BEEN GETTIN' **CRANK CALLS** EVER SINCE WE GOT **HOME.**

HELLO..?

WITH **RILEY** YELLING IN **ONE** OF MY EARS, I HAD **BERNARD** HALF-HYSTERICAL IN THE **OTHER.**

TOLAND, YOU'VE **GOT** TO COME **HELP** ME!

THAT WRETCHED **DOCTOR** ALREADY HAD A NURSE CALLING THE **POLICE** WHILE HE WAS CHANGING MY **BANDAGES**!

Shit!

BLEARY AS I **WAS,** I COULDN'T SEE ANYTHING TO **DO** BUT HEAD BACK OUT THE **DOOR** AND DRIVE DOWNTOWN TO THE **CENTRAL PRECINCT.**

I'M TOLAND POLK. I CAME DOWN TO MAKE **BAIL** FOR SOMEBODY, IF YOU'LL TELL ME HOW TO GO **ABOUT** IT.

NOW THEY'RE PUTTING ME IN **JAIL** FOR PUBLIC **DRUNKEN-NESS!**

WHAT'S HIS **NAME**?

BERNARD.

WHAT'S HIS **LAST** NAME?

UH... ACTUALLY, I DON'T **KNOW.**

I THINK HE'S IN FOR BEIN' **DRUNK.** YOU PICKED HIM UP AT **SACRED GRACE** HOSPITAL.

Chuckle! OL' **BERNARD'S** FAMILIAR ENOUGH TO THE BOYS **HERE,** MR. POLK. IT'S A SHAME HE HAD TO GET HIMSELF **HURT!**

wink!

HOW ITH IT Y'DON'T KNOW YOUR THWEETHEART'S LATHT **NAME,** GUY?

HEY, **SLOW DOWN!** BERNARD'S NO 'SWEET-HEART' OF **MINE!**

I'M NOT A **FAG!** SHIT, GUYS, I ONLY JUST **MET** THE FELLA A FEW **HOURS** AGO. HE'S A FRIEND OF A **FRIEND,** SO TO SPEAK.

AN' HERE YOU **ARE,** MAKIN' **BAIL** FOR HIM ALREADY! WHAT A **WARM-HEARTED** FELLA!

NOW FROM WHAT **I** HEAR, OL' BERNARD'S PART OF THE QUEER CROWD THAT GOES OUT TO THE **COLORED NIGHTCLUB** ON SATURDAYS.

Sniff! Sniff!

AN' FROM THE SMELL OF YOUR **BREATH,** SOMEBODY MIGHT THINK **YOU'VE** BEEN OUT THERE DOIN' A LITTLE IMBIBIN' OF YOUR **OWN!**

COULD YOU JUST **TELL** ME HOW MUCH THE **BAIL** IS?

SURE, BUT WHILE WE'RE **TALKIN'**...Y'SEE THAT **LINE** WE GOT PAINTED THERE ON THE **LINOLEUM**?

HOW 'BOUT WALKIN' **ALONG** IT FOR A FEW STEPS? JUST FOR **FUN.**

BY THE **WAY,** YOU DIDN'T HAPPEN TO DRIVE YOUR **CAR** DOWNTOWN TONIGHT, DID YOU?

TOLAND!!

NOPE. I TOOK A **TAXI.**

I WAS QUICK ENOUGH WITH THAT **LIE**...

...BUT I WASN'T TOO ADEPT AT WALKING **STRAIGHT LINES.**

TWENTY MINUTES LATER **I** WAS IN THE TANK FOR PUBLIC DRUNKENNESS **MYSELF!**

Chapter 11

THERE WAS NO HELP TO BE HAD FROM THE **WHEELERY.** A **BUSY SIGNAL** TOLD ME THAT RILEY HAD LEFT THE DAMN PHONE OFF THE **HOOK** AGAIN.

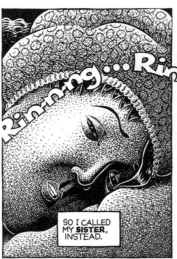

Rinnng....Rin

SO I CALLED MY **SISTER,** INSTEAD.

MEL, WHO'S CALLIN' US AT **FOUR** IN THE **MORNIN'?**

DON'T EVEN **ASK,** ORLEY!

JUST GO BACK TO **SLEEP.**

MELANIE TOLD ME LATER ABOUT THE **WAR** OF **WILLS** SHE HAD TO ENGAGE IN ONCE SHE GOT TO THE **POLICE STATION.**

YOO-HOO! WHO'S IN **CHARGE** HERE?

I WANNA BAIL MY BROTHER **TOLAND POLK** OUT OF THE **POKEY.**

HIS BUDDY **BERNARD,** TOO.

I GATHER THE TWO OF 'EM GOT OVERLY **SOUSED** TONIGHT. BUT MY BROTHER'S A **GOOD** BOY AT HEART AN' I'M SURE IF **BERNARD** HAD A SISTER HERE, **SHE'D** PUT IN A GOOD WORD FOR **HIM,** TOO.

YOU CAN REST **ASSURED** THEY'LL BOTH GET KEPT ON THE **STRAIGHT** AN' **NARROW** FROM HERE ON OUT.

AN' DON'T EVEN **THINK** ABOUT CHECKIN' **MY** BLOOD OUT FOR ALCOHOL, BY THE WAY. I'VE **HEARD** ABOUT YOUR SNEAKY **TRICKS.**

LEMME LOOK AT MY **LOG BOOK,** MA'AM.

I'M NO **HIGH-LIFE LIVER!** MY HUSBAND AN' I SPENT A NICE, SOBER EVENIN' AT **HOME** TONIGHT WATCHIN' 'GUNSMOKE.' Y'WANNA **TEST** ME ON THAT?

WAIT, MA'AM—

GO AHEAD, ASK ME WHAT CHESTER'S FUNNIEST **LINE** TONIGHT WAS.

MA'AM, Y'CAN'T GET **EITHER** O' THOSE BOYS OUT RIGHT THIS **MINUTE,** SO YOU MIGHT AS WELL CALM **DOWN.**

WHY **NOT?**

WE'VE GOT **RULES** AN' **PROCEDURES** FOR DRYIN' OUT DRUNKS.

WHAT RULES AN' PROCEDURES?

NOBODY GETS OUTA THE DRUNK TANK 'TIL THEY'VE BEEN THERE FOR **FOUR HOURS...** **BAIL** OR **NO** BAIL. IT'S DEPARTMENT **POLICY.**

FOUR HOURS?! JUST HEAR ME **OUT**, MA'AM, **BERNARD'S** BEEN DRYIN' OUT FOR **THREE** HOURS ALREADY, SO Y'CAN WALK OUTA HERE WITH **HIM** AN HOUR FROM NOW.

BUT MY LOG SAYS YOUR **BROTHER'S** DUE TO PUT IN ANOTHER **THREE** HOURS. NO GETTIN' **AROUND** IT.

SO **MY** SUGGESTION WOULD BE THAT YOU WAIT THE ONE HOUR 'TIL **BERNARD** GETS FREE, TAKE **HIM** HOME, THEN COME BACK FOR YOUR **BROTHER** LATER IN THE **MORNIN'**.

YOUR... 'SUGGESTION'... WOULD... BE... THAT...

NOW AS **'PROCEDURES'** GO, THAT'S THE **DUMBEST** I'VE HEARD OF **YET!** I'M SUPPOSED TO SPEND MY TIME SHUTTLIN' **BACK** AN' **FORTH** TO THIS POLICE STATION **TWICE**, WITH THE **MORNIN'** SUN ALREADY THINKIN' ABOUT COMIN' UP??!

FORGET **THAT!**

LOOK— TELL YOU WHAT I'LL **SETTLE** FOR... AN' DON'T MAKE ME COPE WITH ANY **HAGGLIN'** ABOUT THIS 'CAUSE IT'S THE MIDDLE OF THE **NIGHT** AN' EVERY MINUTE OF **SLEEP** I LOSE MAKES ME **CRANKIER.**

WELL, MA'AM...

DON'T **TALK**, JUST **LISTEN!**

WE'LL **SPLIT** THE **DIFFERENCE!** I'LL COOL MY HEELS HERE FOR **TWO** HOURS AN' **NOT A MINUTE MORE!** THEN I WANT 'EM BOTH **OUT!**

GOT IT? **BERNARD'LL** STAY A LITTLE **LONGER** AN' MY **BROTHER'LL** STAY A LITTLE **LESS**. **THAT** WAY, Y'BREAK **EVEN.**

IT'S **FAIR, SQUARE,** AN' I DON'T WANT TO HEAR ANY **ARGUMENTS** OUT OF YOU!

BELIEVE IT OR NOT, THE COP BOUGHT THE **DEAL.**

MELANIE WAS A FORCE TO BE **RECKONED** WITH WHEN HER **DANDER** WAS UP.

SOMETIME AFTER **SUNRISE** I DUMPED MYSELF LIKE A SACK OF **BRUISED PRODUCE** INTO MY OLD CHILDHOOD **BED** AT MELANIE'S.

SHE HAD TAKEN **BERNARD** HOME BUT SAID THAT TO DRIVE **ME** ALL THE WAY BACK TO THE WHEELERY AT THAT HOUR WOULD BE GOING **WAY** BEYOND THE CALL OF **DUTY.**

AND SHE HAD NO **INTENTION**, MELANIE SAID, OF LETTING ME GET BEHIND THE WHEEL OF MY **OWN** CAR IN MY EXHAUSTED CONDITION.

I DIDN'T **CARE**. I COULD'VE SLEPT ON A **ROLLER COASTER.**

IT WAS WELL INTO THE **AFTERNOON** WHEN I GOT JOGGED AWAKE BY WEIRD **NOISES** COMING FROM A HULKING **SHAPE** NEXT TO THE BED.

?

Choke!

Sob!

Sniff!

ORLEY??

I'M **SORRY,** TOLAND. ⁓ sniff! ⁓

I SHOULDN'T BE BEEN **IN** HERE WITH YOU **ASLEEP.**

I WAS **INTENDIN'** TO SAY A LITTLE BEDSIDE **PRAYER** ... BUT THEN I JUST STARTED **CRYIN'.**

ORLEY, WHAT'VE **YOU** GOT TO FRET ABOUT? **I'M** THE ONE WITH THE **HANGOVER!**

THAT'S RIGHT, PAL. BE **FLIP.** NEVER ACT LIKE THERE MIGHT BE ANYTHING OF **IMPORTANCE** GOIN' ON IN THE MIND OF A DUMB OL' GUY THAT **LOVES** YOU.

YOU'RE **SOMETHIN' ELSE** TO WAKE **UP** TO... THAT'S FOR **SURE!**

HEY!... **ORL!**... WHAT'S **BUGGIN'** YOU?

THE **PATH** YOU'RE SHOWIN' SIGNS OF HEADIN' DOWN.

DRINKIN' IN **BARS**... HANGIN' AROUND WITH PEOPLE THAT GET **ARRESTED**...

...IT COULD END UP WITH YOU GOIN' TO **HELL.**

OH, I KNOW YOU'RE THE **LAST** PERSON WHO'D TAKE **THAT** RISK TO HEART. YOU THINK THAT HELL'S SOME **IMAGINARY** CONCEPT!

BUT HELL IS **REAL.** IT'S AN **ACTUAL PLACE** IN THE **UNIVERSE.**

I DON'T WANT YOU TO FIND THAT OUT THE **HARD** WAY. BUT IF YOU DON'T TAKE A CAREFUL **LOOK** AT THE **LIFE** YOU'RE LEADIN'.

PLEASE, TOLAND... **THINK** ABOUT WHAT MIGHT BE IN **STORE** FOR YOU.

HORRIBLE **TORTURE** THAT'LL LAST FOR **EVER** AND **EVER.** THERE'LL BE NO **END** TO IT, TOLAND. NO **RELIEF** FROM THE **AGONY.**

SMELLY **BOILS** FESTERIN' ALL OVER YOUR **BODY.** FLAMES LICKIN' LIKE **ACETYLENE TORCHES** AT YOU WHILE **STINGIN' PUS** OOZES FROM YOUR **PORES** AN' TRICKLES LIKE A RIVER OF **ACID** DOWN EVERY INCH OF YOUR **SKIN.**

AN' THERE WON'T BE ANYTHING YOUR **SISTER** OR **I** CAN DO TO **HELP.**

WE'LL BE IN **HEAVEN,** LORD WILLIN'. BUT IT'S HARD TO SEE HOW WE CAN BE VERY **HAPPY** THERE, KNOWIN' YOU'RE IN THE PIT **SUFFERIN'.**

YOU'VE **GOT** TO BE HAPPY IN **HEAVEN,** ORLEY. HOUSE **RULES!**

FLIPPANCY!... FLIPPANCY!...

CUT RIGHT INTO MY **HEART** WITH YOUR FLIPPANCY!

NOTHIN' LEFT FOR ME TO **DO** BUT PRAY FOR YOU A HUNDRED TIMES **HARDER,** JUST TO MAKE UP FOR THE **BLINDNESS** THAT WON'T LET YOU PRAY FOR **YOUR-SELF.**

I'LL TELL MELANIE YOU'RE **AWAKE.** I'VE GOT SOME **WEEDS** TO PULL IN THE YARD.

JESUS!

WELL, LOOK WHO'S BACK IN THE **LAND** OF THE **LIVING!**

Yawn! WHAT **DAY** IS IT?

IT'S STILL **SUNDAY.** I'VE ALREADY PUT SOME HOT **COFFEE** ON THE TABLE FOR YOU.

I HOPE THE **PHONE** DIDN'T WAKE YOU UP WHEN IT RANG A WHILE AGO.

NOPE.

MAVIS CALLED, TRYIN' TO TRACK YOU **DOWN.**

SHE AN' RILEY GOT **UNEASY,** NOT KNOWIN' WHY YOU NEVER CAME BACK **HOME** LAST NIGHT.

IF THEY WOULDN'T LEAVE THEIR **PHONE** OFF THE **HOOK** ALL NIGHT, I MIGHT KEEP IN BETTER **TOUCH.**

HMM... THAT'S QUITE A **GOOSE EGG** YOU'RE SPORTIN' ON YOUR FOREHEAD.

I **TOLD** YOU I GOT IN A **FIGHT** AT **ALLEYSAX.**

WELL, IF YOU'RE PLANNIN' ON TURNIN' INTO A **BRAWLER,** BUBBA, MAYBE I SHOULDN'T BE SO **QUICK** TO SPRING YOU OUT OF **JAIL.**

Poke!

HOW MUCH DOES IT **HURT?**

DON'T COME SO **CLOSE.** I SMELL **BAD.**

WELL... I WON'T EXACTLY **CONTRADICT** YOU....

I'VE GOTTA **CLEAN UP** BEFORE I GO HOME. ORLEY WON'T MIND IF I USE HIS **SHAVIN'** GEAR, WILL HE?

NEVER **ASK** HIM AN' HE CAN'T SAY **NO.**

Y'MIGHT WANNA AVAIL YOURSELF OF A LITTLE **MOUTHWASH,** TOO, WHILE YOU'RE **AT** IT....

AN' I'M **NOT** GONNA LET YOU **LEAVE** IN THOSE FILTHY **CLOTHES,** HONEY.

LET ME **HAVE** 'EM WHILE YOU'RE IN THE **SHOWER** SO I CAN PUT 'EM IN TO **WASH.**

MAVIS SAID YOU THREE WERE IN THE **THICK** OF THAT **RUSSELL PARK FRACAS** YESTERDAY.

YEP.

SHE ALSO SAID THE **KLAN** FOLLOWED YOU OUT TO THE WHEELERY LAST WEEK.

THEY DIDN'T FOLLOW **ME**... BUT THEY **DID** PAY US A **VISIT.**

RILEY RAN 'EM **OFF.**

Sigh'!... **ORLEY'S** BEEN WORRIED THAT YOU MIGHT BE GOIN' OFF THE **DEEP END,** DEAR HEART.

WHAT A **COINCIDENCE!**...

...I'VE BEEN THINKIN' THE **EXACT SAME THING** ABOUT HIM.

I SHAVED THE **STUBBLE** OFF MY FACE AND THEN TOOK A VERY **LONG,** VERY **HOT SHOWER.**

I DIDN'T REALIZE HOW **LOST** I HAD GOTTEN IN THE SOOTHING, STEAMY SPRAY...

HI.

...UNTIL I **FINISHED** AND PULLED BACK THE **SHOWER CURTAIN.**

GINGER! WHERE DID **YOU** COME FROM?

Grope! Grope!

LOOKIN' FOR YOUR **TOWEL?**

YOU G-UESSED IT. **HEY!** STOP PLAYIN'!

RELAX, HON! IT'S **NOT** LIKE I HAVEN'T SEEN YOU NAKED **ONCE** ALREADY THIS WEEK-END!

I DIDN'T SEE **THIS,** THOUGH. HOW'D THIS **KNOT** GET RAISED ON YOUR HEAD?

IT'S A **LONG** STORY.

90

A FELLA GOT SET ON BY **BULLIES** OUT AT **ALLEYSAX** AN' SOME OTHERS OF US HAD TO STEP **IN.** IT'S NO **BIG DEAL.**

HOW **SORE** IS IT?

I WONDER HOW **BLACK** AN' **BLUE** I'M GONNA GET. GINGER, WHAT'RE YOU **DOIN'**?

JUST HELPIN' YOU **DRY OFF.**

FAIRLY **SORE.** YOU CAN STOP **PRESSIN'** ON IT NOW, THANK YOU.

UH...DO **MELANIE** AN' **ORLEY** KNOW YOU'RE **HERE?**

THEY KNOW I'M IN THE **HOUSE.** MELANIE ANSWERED THE **DOORBELL** AN' THERE I **WAS!**

SHE PROBABLY DIDN'T NOTICE ME SNEAKIN' INTO THE **BATHROOM.**

YOU'RE ACTIN' AWFULLY **FRISKY** TODAY, CONSIDERIN' THAT TWENTY-FOUR HOURS AGO YOU LOOKED DAMN NEAR **SUICIDAL.**

WELL... I CAME BY SOME **NEWS**, TOLAND...

...AN' IT FEELS LIKE A **WEIGHT'S** BEEN LIFTED OFF OF ME.

A FRIEND THAT WORKS IN THE **DEAN'S OFFICE** TIPPED ME OFF THAT **TOMORROW** I'M GONNA GET KICKED OUT OF **SCHOOL.**

??—GONNA GET—**WHAT??!**

MY **JAW** PRACTICALLY DROPPED ON THE **FLOOR** WHEN SHE SAID IT.

I **WANTED** AN EXPLANATION **THEN** AND **THERE**...

...BUT GINGER INSISTED ON **WAITING** UNTIL WE HAD MORE **PRIVACY.**

HI, ORLEY.

OOPS! **'SCUSE** ME, GINGER.

I DIDN'T KNOW THE BATHROOM WAS **OCCUPIED.**

NO **PROBLEM.**

HEY, **ORLEY**...

...I NEED TO BORROW YOUR **BATHROBE**—O.K.? MELANIE'S GOT ALL MY **CLOTHES** IN THE **WASHER.**

OH. **SURE**, TOLAND.

!

There was still the matter of retrieving my **car**, which had gotten left a block from the **police station** during the previous night's **craziness**.

You're **sure** you don't want Orley or me to drive you downtown?

There's no **need**, sis. It's an easy walk to the **bus line**.

The walk gave us **talking** time.

The stunt I pulled at the **student assembly** Friday is what **did** it.

That was serious enough to get you **booted**?

Oh, it's just an **excuse** they can use.

They **hate** havin' **integrationists** on campus. It makes the **alumni** mad an' their **wallets** tighten up.

I thought your dad had **pull** at the college.

Pull has its **limits**.

I'm **doin'** it to **myself**, Toland.

I **know** what the rules are. I break 'em **right** an' **left**.

At heart I've been **wantin'** out, probably. I don't **belong** in these parts.

I'm not sure there's anywhere I **do** belong...

...but if there **is** — this ain't **it**!

You're sure makin' me feel funny about **myself** today.

You've had an **impact** on me — y'know?

You knocked me out of a **rut**.

One place you belong is here, helpin' me see what's **what**.

Don't take too many cues from **me**, hon.

You saw me in Russell Park yesterday. **Notice** anything? I was **useless**!

I've been leadin' sing-alongs about **brotherhood** an' **nonviolence**, but yesterday all I wanted was Riley's **rifle** an' a clear shot at **sutton chopper**.

You were down there on the grass bein' a **part** of things. I just went **numb**.

It raises **questions**.

YOU DID SEEM **UPSET.** I SAW YOU LATER ON AT THE **CHURCH,** GETTIN' SOME COMFORT FROM **SHILOH.**

YOU **SAW** US? WE DIDN'T SEE **YOU.**

YOU SHOULD'VE COME **OVER.**

I DIDN'T WANNA **INTRUDE.**

ARE YOU **JEALOUS** OF SHILOH?

NO. NOT AT **ALL.**

BUT I WISH I COULD BUY A **BOTTLE** OF WHATEVER PEOPLE LIKE SHILOH HAVE.

LOOK HOW HE'S **CHEERED** YOU UP!

I'M NOT **CHEERFUL.** I'M **ADRIFT.**

THERE'S A CERTAIN **GIDDINESS** IN THAT.

WHAT'LL YOU **DO** WITH YOURSELF IF YOU DO GET KICKED OUT OF WESTHILLS?

GO BACK TO **AKRON,** I GUESS.

DO YOU **HAFTA** LEAVE TOWN...?

I'LL HAVE SOME **FENCES** TO MEND WITH MY **FOLKS.**

AT TIMES LIKE THAT, THEY TEND TO WANT ME AT **CLOSE RANGE.**

I'M **CONFUSED.** I THOUGHT THE LAST FEW MONTHS WERE WHAT YOU'D CALL **HAPPY** TIMES FOR THE TWO OF US.

BUT NOW YOU'RE ACTIN' PLEASED AS **PUNCH** AT THE THOUGHT OF LEAVIN' CLAYFIELD AN' ME BEHIND.

ANY CHANCE THE **RELIEF** YOU'RE FEELIN' COMES FROM SHEDDIN' A BOYFRIEND THAT'S GONE **QUEER** ON YOU?

GOD DAMN IT, TOLAND!

EVERYTHING THAT GOES ON INSIDE OF ME DOESN'T HAVE TO DO WITH **YOU!** QUITE A **LOT** GOES ON THAT DOESN'T HAVE **ANYTHING** TO DO WITH YOU AT **ALL!**

WELL... HERE'S THE **BUS STOP**, SHALL WE **WAIT**?

I **DUNNO**.

THERE'LL BE **MORE** OF 'EM DOWN THE **ROAD**, Y'KNOW.

THERE'S SOMETHIN' YOU SAID TO ME FRIDAY NIGHT THAT'S BEEN **BOTHERIN'** ME EVER **SINCE**, TOLAND.

YOU SAID THAT **HOMOSEXUALS** DON'T FEEL REAL **LOVE** FOR EACH OTHER.

I DON'T THINK THAT'S **TRUE**.

I woke up this mornin' rememberin' somethin' I haven't thought about in **years**. It happened when I was **six**...

...at a **party** my parents threw at our **home**.

Bein' a **kid**, I couldn't have **alcohol**, of course—but I could get **almost** drunk from soakin' up the **party noise** and **music**.

So I noticed **instantly** when somethin' made everything go **silent** out on the **patio**.

I went to see what was **up**. Everyone was watchin' two **men** who were standin' **facin'** each other. I'd seen 'em at various gatherings before...always **together**.

At first I thought it was an **argument** about to happen.

But they never **spoke**. They just looked with an awful **sadness** into each other's **eyes**.

When my aunt saw that I was about to whisper a **question**, she put a **finger** to her **lips** and looked **away**.

One of the men slid down on his **knees**...

...And pressed his **cheek** against the **leg** of the one still **standing**.

For several minutes they **stayed** that way. It was like an eerie, sad **dance** with no **movements** in it.

Finally the man on his knees wiped his **eyes**...

The one who left, I never **saw** again.

...Stood up...

...And left the **party**.

The other one came to **parties** every now and then, always by **himself**, 'til he **died** a few years later.

DID YOU EVER FIND OUT WHAT WAS GOIN' **ON**?

NOT REALLY.

MY FOLKS **BOBBED** AN' **WEAVED** 'TIL I QUIT **ASKIN'**.

I KNEW IT HAD TO DO WITH **LOVE**, THOUGH...AS YOUNG AS I **WAS**.

WE ENDED UP IGNORING BUS STOP AFTER BUS STOP AFTER BUS STOP.

ANOTHER **BUS STOP**.

ARE YOUR **LEGS** TIRED?

NOPE.

MINE EITHER.

EVENTUALLY IT HIT US THAT WE HAD WALKED ALL THE WAY **DOWN-TOWN** WITHOUT **ANY** MUNICIPAL TRANSPORT ASSISTANCE AT **ALL**.

Chapter 12

GINGER'S **SPY** IN THE **DEAN'S OFFICE** WAS RIGHT ON THE **MARK.**

ON **MONDAY** GINGER GOT CALLED IN AND OFFICIALLY **SUSPENDED** FROM **WESTHILLS.**

ON WEDNESDAY WE SAID OUR **GOODBYES** AT THE **AIRPORT...**

...PROMISING OURSELVES LOADS OF **PHONE CALLS** AND A **REUNION** WHEN PRACTICALITIES PERMITTED.

WHICH LEFT YOU FREE ON **THURSDAY** TO LAUNCH YOUR PERFORMANCE AS THE **POOR, ABANDONED SUITOR!**

I'VE NEVER SAID I DIDN'T **MILK** THE SITUATION FOR **SYMPATHY.**

I'LL ALWAYS REMEMBER SITTING AROUND THE GAS STATION WITH **STONY,** THE TWO OF US GOING **ON** AND **ON** ABOUT **LOSS** AND **LONELINESS.** I DON'T GUESS I'VE EVER FELT **STRAIGHTER.**

I KNOW HOW **ROUGH** IT IS, BUDDY. I'VE **BEEN** THERE.

I REMEMBER HOW IT **WAS** AFTER **BECKY** DROPPED ME. I WOKE UP IN THE MIDDLE OF THE NIGHT **CRYIN'** MORE THAN **ONCE,** AN' I'M NOT ASHAMED TO **ADMIT** IT.

SOMETIMES I WONDER WHAT THE FUCKIN' **POINT** IS, STONY. THE NEED TO HOLD A **GIRL** IN YOUR ARMS RUNS SO **DEEP**...BUT IS IT **WORTH** IT IF IT COMES WITH ALL THIS **PAIN?**

AND YOU CAN **BET** I LIKED THE MANLY WAY HE'D THROW HIS **ARM** AROUND MY **SHOULDER** WHILE WE TALKED.

BUT Y'GOTTA MOVE **ON.** YOU CAN'T GET STUCK IN THE **PAST.**

MY GIRL **LINDA'S** GOT A **COUSIN** NAMED **SYBIL LOUISE.** SHE'S **PRETTY** AN' SHE'S BEEN AT **LOOSE ENDS** LATELY SINCE HER BOYFRIEND JOINED THE **PEACE CORPS.**

IT'S TOO **SOON,** STONY. NOTHIN' AGAINST **SYBIL LOUISE,** BUT I NEED MORE **TIME.** Y'KNOW?

IT WASN'T JUST A **POSE.** I REALLY DID **MISS GINGER** A **LOT.**

THE FIRST FEW WEEKS OF THE SUMMER WE PHONED EACH OTHER **OFTEN** LIKE WE'D **SAID** WE WOULD.

...SO I GUESS I'LL HAVE TO TAKE THE **JOB,** BUT REALLY, TOLAND—YOU WOULDN'T **BELIEVE** THE GUY WHO **INTERVIEWED** ME!...

TELL 'ER I'M **WAVIN'** HELLO.

MM-HMM.

MAVIS SAYS TO TELL YA **HI,** BY THE WAY....

BUT THEN I FELT MYSELF GETTING MORE AND MORE **WITHDRAWN** AND CALLING HER **LESS** AND **LESS**.

IT WASN'T ONLY **GINGER** I WAS PULLING BACK FROM.

The Clayfield Banner
BIRCH SOCIETY CONDEMNS TEST-BAN TREATY TALKS

I STOPPED SHOWING UP AT **EQUALITY LEAGUE** MEETINGS OR EVEN KEEPING UP WITH HOW REV. PEPPER'S **SKIRMISHES** WITH THE **CITY** WERE FARING.

I EVEN STARTED FEELING PUT **OFF** BY SAMMY NOONE.

LOOK, TOLAND! SAMMY'S **CAST** IS **OFF**.

HEY, THAT'S **GREAT**.

LIKE OUR **LORD** ON **EASTER MORN**, MY HAND IS **RISEN** FROM THE **DEAD!**

FATHER MORRIS — BEING A GOOD **LIBERAL** WHO **APPROVED** OF PROTESTS LIKE THE ONE AT RUSSELL PARK — HAD AVERTED **ONE** POTENTIAL CRISIS BY KEEPING SAMMY ON THE CHURCH **PAYROLL** DURING THE PERIOD WHEN HE COULDN'T **PLAY**.

HOW SOON ARE YA GONNA BE READY TO **PERFORM** AGAIN?

WITH PROPER **PRACTICE** I EXPECT MY TALENTED **DIGITS** TO BE FULLY **REHABILITATED** IN **RECORD TIME!**

I'M SURE **MAVIS** WILL FREELY OFFER UP HER SEMI-VIRGINAL **BODY** FOR MY FIVE-FINGER **EXERCISES!**

NATCH! WHAT'RE FRIENDS **FOR?**

YOU'D THINK I'D HAVE SIMPLY FELT **PLEASED** FOR HIM, BUT FOR SOME REASON SAMMY'S PERPETUAL **DEVIL-MAY-CARE ATTITUDE** HAD BEGUN GETTING ON MY **NERVES**.

SOON I'LL BE TANTALIZING HER TITTIES WITH SHIMMERING TRILL-L-L-LS!...

...VISITING VENTURESOME GLISS-SANDOS ON HER QUAKING **NETHER-REGIONS!**...

AHH, MAVEEZ, ZEE **MACHO PASSION**, SHE EEZ RIZEENG...

nibble!

SAMMY, THAT TICKLES!

SPARE US YOUR **STRAIGHT** ACT, SAMMY. IT JUST AIN'T **CONVINCIN'!**

TOLAND!

BABY, WE'VE BEEN CUTTIN' LOTS OF **SLACK** FOR YOU AN' YOUR **MOODS** LATELY, BUT IF YOU'RE EVER **RUDE** LIKE THAT TO SAMMY **AGAIN**, YOU CAN START LOOKIN' FOR OTHER **QUARTERS!**

MAVIS HAD **NEVER** BLOWN HER **TOP** AT ME LIKE THAT BEFORE. MY STOMACH STILL GETS **WOBBLY** THINKING **BACK** ON IT.

MY SISTER COULD **TELL** I WAS DEPRESSED.

TOLAND, IF YOU DON'T AT LEAST MAKE A **STAB** AT SHAKIN' OFF THESE **BLUES**, YOU'RE GONNA DRIVE THE **REST** OF US OUT OF OUR **GOURDS**.

NOW, ORLEY AN' I WANT **YOU** AN' MAVIS AN' RILEY TO COME OVER SUNDAY AFTERNOON FOR A **BARBEQUE**.

AN' IF YOU DON'T BRING A BETTER **DISPOSITION** WITH YOU, IT'S GONNA BE **YOU** THAT GETS **BARBE-QUED!**

AN' FOR **GOD'S** SAKE, BRING A **DATE**.

I KNOW YOU'D RATHER **GINGER** WAS HERE, BUT YOU **CAN'T** STOP HAVIN' A SOCIAL LIFE **ENTIRELY!**

I TOOK HER **ADVICE**.

MAVIS! RILEY! IT'S REAL GOOD TO **SEE** Y'ALL AGAIN. HIYA, BUBBA.

HI, SIS.

AN' WHO'S **THIS** CUTE LI'L THING?

MELANIE, THIS IS SYBIL LOUISE BYERS.

I'M **SO** PLEASED TO **MEET** YOU, MELANIE.

SAME **HERE**. I HOPE EVERYBODY'S **HUNGRY**. ORLEY'S ALREADY IN BACK PLAYIN' WITH THE **GRILL**.

IT'S **NICE** OF YOU AND ORLEY TO HAVE ME **OVER**, MELANIE. AND YOUR **BROTHER** SEEMS REALLY NICE, **TOO**.

LET'S JUST HOPE YOU STILL **FEEL** THAT WAY WHEN YOU GET TO **KNOW** HIM BETTER, HONEY!

LEMON-ADE OR **SODA** POP?

Sizzle!

TO BE **FAIR**, TOSSING SYBIL LOUISE INTO THE SOUP WITH MY **OLD** FRIENDS AND **FAMILY** WAS PROBABLY TOO **HEAVY DUTY** FOR A **FIRST DATE**.

SHE WAS OBVIOUSLY NOT READY FOR **RILEY** WHEN HE GOT INTO ONE OF **HIS RAMBUNCTIOUS** MOODS.

WELL, WELL, WELL, WELL, **WELL!**

WELL, WELL, **WELL!** LOOK WHAT WE HAVE **HERE!**

NOW DON'T GO POINTIN' ANY FINGERS AT **ME** OVER THAT HATE SHEET, RILEY WHEELER!

IT'S **ORLEY** THAT BRINGS THOSE THINGS INTO THE **HOUSE!**

Dixie Patriot
Voice of ...thern Sanity

I SEE YOU'RE READIN' **NAZI PROPAGANDA** NOW, ORLEY. THINKIN' 'BOUT SIGNIN' UP WITH THE **BROWN-SHIRTS?**

THERE'S NOT A **THING** ABOUT ANY **GERMANS** IN THAT NEWSPAPER, RILEY.

Fizz! Crackle! Snap!

THE PEOPLE THAT PUT OUT THE DIXIE PATRIOT ARE GOOD **AMERICANS**.

SURE, ORLEY. I WAS JUST LOOKIN' AT THIS 'INTERVIEW' THEY'VE GOT WITH THE EDITOR'S **NEGRO** MAID.

Y'GOT THAT? THE 'INTERVIEWER' IS THE GUY THAT PUTS **FOOD** ON THE TABLE OF THE WOMAN GETTIN' 'INTERVIEWED.'

NOW I **ASK** YOU, MISS SYBIL LOUISE...WHAT DO YOU SUPPOSE THIS POOR WOMAN WILL CHOOSE TO **SAY** FOR PUBLICATION ABOUT ALL THESE **PROTEST MARCHES** AN' SUCH?

UH... I DON'T KN— ... I MEAN —

SHE'S **AGAINST** 'EM! **SURPRISE! SURPRISE!** SHE SAYS: 'I JES' DON'T KNOW **WHY** DOSE PEOPLES FUM DE NORTH COME DOWN HERE TO CLAYFIELD MAKIN' ALL DIS **TROUBLE!**...'

RILEY, **STOP!** IT'S PAINFUL!

'...WE DONE ALLUS GOT ALONG JES' **FINE** WID DE WHITE FOLKS. I THINKS SOME O' DESE **AGITATORS** MUS' BE **SPIES** FUM RUSSIA, FUM DE WAY DEY IS STIRRIN' THINGS **UP**...'

I DON'T SEE WHAT'S SO **FUNNY**.

NOW LISTEN TO WHAT THE INTERVIEWER-EDITOR —HER **BOSS**, MIND YA— HAS TO SAY AT THE **END**.

'IN MY OPINION THIS HUMBLE, UNEDUCATED COLORED WOMAN HAS MORE **BRAINS** IN HER HEAD THAN A **THOUSAND** OF THESE SIGN-WAVING, FOLKSONG-SINGING **HARVARD** DROPOUTS WHO KEEP SHOWING UP ON OUR DOORSTEPS TO TELL US HOW TO LEAD OUR **LIVES**.'

SHE'S GOT **BRAINS**, ALRIGHT!

BRAINS ENOUGH TO KNOW WHO'S GOT A **GRIP** ON THE **WHIP** AT THE OL' PLANTATION!

WHAT MAKES YOU SO **SURE** THE WOMAN'S NOT TELLIN' THINGS JUST THE WAY SHE **SEES** 'EM, RILEY?

AIN'T THERE SOMETHIN' A LI'L **CONDESCENDIN'** ABOUT ASSUMIN' SHE'S **NOT**?

What Jesus Said About Miscegenation

FROM WHAT **I** HEAR, A **LOT** OF NEGROES THINK THERE'S SOMETHIN' **FISHY** ABOUT ALL THESE **RADICALS** BLOWIN' INTO TOWN TRYIN' TO —

ORLEY, THAT'S **BULL-SHIT!** THE WOMAN IS **TRAPPED!**

SHE'S GOT CRACKERS ON THE **LEFT** OF HER... CRACKERS ON THE **RIGHT** OF HER... SAME AS **US!**

WE'RE **ALL** OF US STUCK IN A **GODDAM** CRACKER BOX!

CRACKERS WRITE THE **NEWS** AN' CRACKERS **READ** THE NEWS THAT THE CRACKERS **WRITE**. ALL OF **US** ARE CRACKERS, **TOO!**

WE WERE **RAISED** TO BE CRACKERS! THERE'S **NO** FUCKIN' WAY **NOT** TO BE A CRACKER AROUND HERE!

IF IT MAKES ME A '**CRACKER**' TO BE **CONCERNED** ABOUT A BUNCH OF KNOW-IT-ALL **COMMUNISTS** COMIN' DOWN TO MAKE MY WORLD OVER FOR ME, THEN I'LL BE **HAPPY** TO FLY MY CRACKER FLAG!

YOU'VE **ALWAYS** FLOWN YOUR 'CRACKER FLAG,' HON!

YOU'VE GOT ONE ON THE **CAR!** Y'KNOW THAT **REBEL-FLAG DECAL** THAT'S STUCK ON THE **WIND-SHIELD**...?

twink!

I DON'T **BELIEVE** I JUST HEARD A **SOUTHERN-BORN WOMAN** USE THE TERM '**CRACKER FLAG**' IN REFERENCE TO THE EMBLEM OF THE **CON-FEDERACY**, FOR WHICH HER **GREAT-GRANDFATHER** MAY WELL HAVE SHED HIS **BLOOD** ON THE **BATTLEFIELD!**

SYBIL LOUISE KEPT HER OPINIONS TO **HERSELF** WHILE THE REST OF US **RAVED**.

I DIDN'T REALIZE HOW **UPSET** SHE'D GOTTEN 'TIL I WAS TAKING HER **HOME** AND THE **TEARS** STARTED FLOWING:

HEY!? WHAT'S THE **MATTER**?

I DON'T THINK I CAN GO **OUT** WITH YOU **AGAIN**, TOLAND.

YOUR HOUSEMATE **RILEY** WAS BEING COMPLETELY **DISRESPECTFUL** TOWARD THE **SOUTH**, AND IT DIDN'T APPEAR TO BOTHER **YOU** IN THE **LEAST**.

AND I DIDN'T CARE AT **ALL** FOR YOUR SISTER'S **JOKE** ABOUT THE **CONFEDERATE FLAG!**

AS FOR THAT **NEWS-PAPER**... ~Sniff!~

...IT MAY BE **EXTREME** IN SOME **ASPECTS**, BUT IT **IS** TRYING TO **WARN** US ABOUT WHAT THE COMMUNISTS ARE **UP** TO.

I **DON'T** THINK I CARE TO KEEP **COMPANY** WITH PEOPLE WHO THINK THAT'S SOMETHING TO **RIDICULE.**

AND **RILEY'S LANGUAGE**, TOLAND!— **REALLY!**

THERE ARE PERFECTLY GOOD WAYS TO GET **IDEAS** ACROSS WITHOUT USING VULGAR **TERMS** OR TAKING THE LORD'S NAME IN **VAIN.**...

THE MORE SYBIL LOUISE **UNBURDENED** HERSELF, THE MORE **LOST** I GOT IN NOSTALGIC THOUGHTS ABOUT **GINGER.**

AT **WORK** THE NEXT DAY...

?

YOU CAN'T BUY GAS **HERE**, BOY. GO TO THE **COLORED** SERVICE STATION UP THE **ROAD** THREE MILES.

THAT **WON'T** BE **NECESSARY!** I ORDER ALL **MY** GAS DIRECT FROM MY **DADDY'S** COLORED **OIL FIELDS** IN **TEXAS!**

FRESH WHOLESOME ~ANDY~

ker-chunk!

THAT'S A REAL SMART **MOUTH** Y'GOT, BURRHEAD.

IT WAS ONLY A **JOKE**, MISTER!

ESMO!

YOU **KNOW** THIS **NIGRA**, TOLAND?

EVERYBODY'S BEEN **WORRIED** 'BOUT YOU, TOLE. YOU AIN'T SHOWN YOUR PRETTY FACE AT AN **EQUALITY LEAGUE** MEETIN' SINCE **GINGER** LEFT.

UH... COULD YA **BUTCH** IT UP JUST A **LITTLE**, ESMO? MY **BOSS** IS WATCHIN'.

HONEY, IF **I** EVER WENT **BUTCH**, NOBODY'D **RECOGNIZE** ME! WHAT I'M **HERE** FOR IS TO FIND OUT IF YOU WANT A **PLACE** SAVED FOR YOU ON THE **BUS**. TIME'S RUNNIN' **OUT.**

WHAT **BUS?**

THE BUS TO **WASHINGTON.**

'COURSE, THERE'LL BE A **BUNCH** OF BUSES LEAVIN' FROM CLAYFIELD, BUT **SAMMY** AN' **LES** AN' I THOUGHT YOU'D WANNA RIDE IN **OURS** SO WE CAN **AMUSE** YOU WITH OUR WITTY **REPARTEE!**

ESMO WAS TALKING ABOUT THE MAJOR **DEMONSTRATION** THAT WAS BREWING AT THE END OF AUGUST TO PUSH FOR FULL **EMPLOYMENT**, FASTER **SCHOOL INTEGRATION**, AND PASSAGE OF A **CIVIL RIGHTS ACT.**

IT WAS INTENDED TO BE **BIG**, BUT EVEN THE **ORGANIZERS** DIDN'T KNOW HOW MANY **THOUSANDS** OF PEOPLE WERE GONNA END UP POURING INTO WASHINGTON D.C. BY **PLANES**, **TRAINS** AND **BUSES** FROM ALL OVER THE **COUNTRY.**

WHAT SPRANG TO MIND INSTANTLY WAS WHAT A GOOD **BET** IT WAS THAT **GINGER** WOULD BE MAKING THE TRIP FROM **OHIO.**

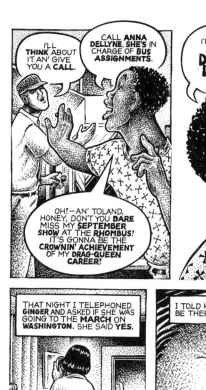

I'LL **THINK** ABOUT IT AN' GIVE YOU A **CALL**.

CALL **ANNA DELLYNE.** SHE'S IN CHARGE OF **BUS ASSIGNMENTS.**

OH! — AN' TOLAND, HONEY, DON'T YOU **DARE** MISS MY **SEPTEMBER** SHOW AT THE **RHOMBUS!** IT'S GONNA BE THE **CROWNIN'** ACHIEVEMENT OF MY **DRAG-QUEEN CAREER!**

I'M DOIN' **MISS DORIS DAY!**

NOW I **ASK** YOU — IS THAT SOME KINDA **STRETCH** OR **WHAT?!**

SORRY 'BOUT THAT **NEGRO,** GLENN. HIS **MOTHER** USED TO CLEAN OUR **HOUSE** FOR US.

HE'S KIND OF A **FAIRY,** BUT I TRY TO BE **NICE** TO HIM FOR **HER** SAKE.

THAT NIGHT I TELEPHONED **GINGER** AND ASKED IF SHE WAS GOING TO THE **MARCH** ON **WASHINGTON.** SHE SAID **YES.**

I TOLD HER I'D BE THERE, **TOO.**

♪ *It's a hammer of justice!*... ♪

♪ *It's a bell of freedom!*... ♪

OHIO WAITING STATION

THERE SHE IS!

TOLAND!

HIYA, BABE.

...AND **ESMO!** LES! SAMMY! SHILOH!

GINGER, I CAN'T **STAND** YOU HAVIN' MOVED AWAY FROM **TOWN.**

ASIDE FROM MISSIN' **CLAYFIELD'S OTHER** CULTURAL ADVANTAGES, YOU WON'T GET TO SEE MY SPECIAL **TRIBUTE** TO **DORIS DAY** AT THE **RHOMBUS** NEXT MONTH.

OH, BUT I **WILL** GET TO SEE IT, ESMO.

WE MARCH FOR EFFECTIVE CIVIL RIGHTS LAWS

VOTE DE... VOTI... RIG... NO...

101

NO MATTER HOW I HASH IT **OVER** IN MY MIND, IT KEEPS SEEMIN' LIKE **CLAYFIELD'S** THE RIGHT PLACE FOR ME TO **BE** THIS YEAR.

I **CARE** ABOUT WHAT'S **HAPPENIN'** THERE.

I THOUGHT YOU SAID YOU DIDN'T 'BELONG' THERE.

IT'S ALL **RELATIVE.** I'D FORGOTTEN HOW MUCH **LESS** I BELONG IN **AKRON.**

D'YA **KNOW** THAT FEELIN' I'M TALKIN' ABOUT, TOLAND...

iMON!

WHERE THE **QUESTIONS** YOU'VE GOT ABOUT YOURSELF STOP **MATTERIN'** NEXT TO THE SIMPLE FACT THAT YOU'RE WHERE IT'S **RIGHT** FOR YOU TO **BE**...DOIN' WHAT IT'S **RIGHT** FOR YOU TO **DO?**

YOU'VE FELT THAT WAY, HAVEN'T YOU?

HER QUESTION CAUGHT ME **SHORT** BECAUSE THE FACT WAS, I **HADN'T** FELT THAT WAY.

I'D PRETTY MUCH **ALWAYS** FELT LIKE AN INADEQUATE **BOZO** STUCK IN THE **WRONG** PLACE, DOING **WRONG** THINGS NINE-TENTHS OF THE TIME.

END SEGREGATED SCHOOLS

BUT MAYBE NOT **THIS** TIME, I THOUGHT, LOOKING AROUND ME.

THE FACT WAS, BEING THERE IN WASHINGTON THAT PARTICULAR DAY COULD **PASS** FOR THE FEELING OF RIGHTNESS THAT GINGER WAS **TALKING** TO ME ABOUT.

THERE WAS A GENERAL **HIGH** THAT PERSISTED FOR A COUPLE OF **WEEKS** AFTER WASHINGTON. **EVERYBODY** FELT IT.

♪♪ This little light of mine, Oh Lord...I'm gonna Let it shine!..♪

whew! OUT**RAGE**OUS, FOLKS!

SHILOH SAID HE COULD **SWEAR** THE KIDS IN HIS **FREEDOM CHORUS** GAINED AN **OCTAVE'S** WORTH OF RANGE **OVERNIGHT**—JUST FROM BEING PART OF THAT **THRONG.**

MELODY MOTEL

NO VACANCY

THEN CAME THE **BOMBING** AT THE **MELODY.**

NOT THE **FIRST**...BUT DEFINITELY THE **WORST.**

CAN YOU GET IN?

THERE'S SOMETHIN' **BLOCKIN'** THE DOOR.

SHILOH! CAN YOU HEAR US?

♪ Let it Shine!... Let it Shine!... ♪ Let it Shine!

SURE, PAPA.

I'M **SORRY** TO HAVE **INTERRUPTED** THINGS HERE, BUT THERE'S BEEN A TERRIBLE **TRAGEDY** THIS EVENIN'.

A **BOMB** GOT SET OFF AT THE **MELODY MOTEL.**

MOST OF THE ROOMS THAT GOT HIT WERE **EMPTY...**

...BUT THERE'S A **CONFERENCE ROOM** THEY'VE BEEN LETTIN' **SHILOH REED'S FREEDOM CHORUS** USE FOR **REHEARSALS,** AN'...

REV. PEPPER...WAS ANYBODY—?

THERE **HAVE** BEEN SOME **DEATHS,** SAMMY. I DON'T KNOW **WHO** OR HOW **MANY.**

DAMN, ESMO! I **SWEAR** I FELT THE BAR **SHAKE** EARLIER, BUT I THOUGHT IT WAS JUST MY **IMAGINATION....**

I CAN'T **STAND** ANY **MORE** OF THIS, MABEL.

THAT WAS ONE ROOMFUL OF **STUNNED QUEERS** THE PREACHER LEFT BEHIND! FOR **SURE,** NOBODY WAS OF A MIND TO HANG AROUND FOR MORE **LAUGHS!**

RILEY WAS **ADAMANT** THAT WE SHOULD **HAUL ASS** BACK TO THE **WHEELERY.**

I'M **TELLIN'** YA, THERE'S GONNA BE A LOT OF **PISSED-OFF NEGROES** RUNNIN' 'ROUND TOWN.

I **CAN'T** HEAD HOME **YET.** I WANNA FIND OUT WHAT'S HAPPENED TO **SHILOH.**

SAME **HERE.**

HERE'S MY **KEYS** TO THE **MERCURY,** RILEY. **YOU** DRIVE IT ON HOME **NOW** AN' **SAMMY** CAN BRING ME BY AFTER WE'VE **SCOUTED** THINGS **OUT.**

YOU TWO ARE **NUTS!**

YOU AN' MAVIS WON'T MIND DROPPIN' **GINGER** OFF AT THE **CAMPUS,** WILLYA?

FORGET **THAT!** I'M COMIN' WITH **YOU** AN' **SAMMY.**

WE COULDN'T GET ANYWHERE **NEAR** THE **MELODY.** STREETS WERE **BLOCKED** AND ALL YOU COULD SEE WERE **COP CARS** AND **FIRE ENGINES.**

LOOK, SAMMY— THERE'S **RAEBURN.**

ROLL DOWN THE **WINDOW.**

GOTCHA.

DON'T BOTHER WITH THE **MOTEL,** SAMMY. ANYBODY THAT'S **HURT** IS BEIN' TAKEN TO **RATTLER HILL.**

'RATTLER HILL' HAD BEEN THE DISRESPECTFUL **NICKNAME** FOR THE BLACK FOLKS' HOSPITAL FOR SO **LONG,** IT HAD ALL BUT BECOME **OFFICIAL.**

DURING THE TENSE DRIVE THROUGH **SMITH CITY** WE WERE TREATED TO **INSIGHTFUL COMMENTARY** BY OUR FAVORITE **PUBLIC SERVANT.**

Commissioner Chopper, given the motel's reputation as a focus of integrationist activity, is it true that your investigators suspect a political motive for tonight's bombing?

MORE **CLEVER SLEUTHING** BY OUR **BOYS IN BLUE!**

WHILE THE THREE OF US **LISTENED** AND **GLOWERED,** I GOT LOST IN CONTEMPLATION OF THE **MUSCLES** THAT WERE FLEXING IN SAMMY'S **JAW.**

That's right, Bill...And as shocked as we all are by this deplorable crime, I'm obliged to point out that those sweet children would be alive right now were it not for the inflammatory street demonstrations we've all been subjected to by local malcontents as well as Communistic outside agitators...

EVEN WITH HIS FACE **HIDDEN,** IT WAS CLEAR HIS **BLOOD** WAS **BOILING.**

JEROME RADLER HILL MEMORIAL HOSPITAL FOR NEGROES

AT RATTLER HILL WE HAD TO WEAVE PAST **NEWS CREWS** FROM THE LOCAL TELEVISION STATIONS.

THEY WEREN'T BEING ALLOWED **INSIDE,** BUT THAT WASN'T STOPPING THEM FROM ANGLING FOR DRAMATIC FOOTAGE IN THE **PARKING LOT.**

WE SQUEEZED INTO A LOBBY THAT WAS **PACKED** WITH **FRIENDS** AND **RELATIVES** OF THE **BOMB VICTIMS.**

HARLAND PEPPER WAS A **SIGHT** TO **BEHOLD** AS HE DASHED BACK AND FORTH TENDING TO **FIFTEEN EMOTIONAL CRISES** A MINUTE.

LES STAYED AT HIS DADDY'S **BECK** AND **CALL.** I WAS **IMPRESSED** AT HOW A **PARTYBOY** FROM THE **RHOMBUS** COULD TURN INTO A PERFECT **PREACHER'S KID** AT THE FLICK OF A **SWITCH.**

THE REST OF THE HOSPITAL WAS JUST AS **CROWDED.** FISHING AROUND FOR NEWS OF **SHILOH,** WE LEARNED HE WAS **HURT, UNCONSCIOUS** — BUT **ALIVE.**

GINGER NOTICED ANNA DELLYNE COMFORTING A **GAUNT YOUNG WOMAN** IN THE **CORNER.** WE WALKED **OVER.**

GINGER HUGGED LOTTIE AND ANNA DELLYNE AND THE THREE FEMALES WENT INTO AN INTIMATE **WHISPERING** MODE. **I** FELT **EXTRANEOUS.**

I WANDERED AROUND, WISHING I HAD SOMEBODY TO **TALK** TO.

I SAW PLENTY OF FAMILIAR **FACES** FROM THE **EQUALITY LEAGUE.** THERE WEREN'T **MANY,** HOWEVER, THAT I'D EVER BOTHERED TO STRIKE UP A REAL **FRIENDSHIP** WITH.

IT WAS SHILOH'S WIFE **LOTTIE,** WHOM I'D NEVER **MET.**

IT WAS PROBABLY COMMON **KNOWLEDGE** HOW FAR **GONE** SHE WAS FROM **CANCER,** BUT NOBODY HAD EVER BROUGHT UP THE SUBJECT TO **ME.**

SAMMY GOT **ANTSY** AND **PEELED OFF** FROM THE GROUP. AFTER EXPRESSING MY **CONCERN** TO **LOTTIE,** I DID, **TOO.**

AND **NOW** SEEMED AN AWKWARD TIME TO SET ABOUT **ICE-BREAKING!**

LES WAS OBVIOUSLY TOO BUSY FOR CONVERSATION.

I SAW **FATHER MORRIS** ACROSS THE ROOM AND THOUGHT ABOUT SAYING **HELLO**...

...BUT HE SEEMED PRETTY OCCUPIED WITH **SAMMY**, WHO WAS LOOKING SERIOUSLY **DISTRAUGHT**.

I STARTED GETTING **DEPRESSED** OVER HOW OUT OF **PLACE** I FELT.

AND WHEN I CONSIDERED HOW DAMN **TYPICAL** IT WAS OF ME TO GO INTO A FUNK OVER MY **OWN** GENERAL DISCONNECTEDNESS WHEN OTHER PEOPLE'S **CHILDREN** WERE **DEAD** OR **BLEEDING**...

...IT MADE ME EVEN **MORE** DEPRESSED!

I DIDN'T KNOW A DAMN **ONE** OF THOSE FREEDOM CHORUS KIDS THAT GOT KILLED... NOT IN A **PERSONAL** WAY.

I **DO** KNOW **SHILOH**... BUT **HE'S** NOT **DEAD**.

HOW'M I SUPPOSED TO **FEEL**? AM I SUPPOSED TO BE CRYIN'... OR **RELIEVED**... OR **WHAT**?

LES, TELL ME SOMETHIN' I CAN DO TO **HELP**.

SURE, TOLE.

PULL **MINNA BAXTER** OUT OF THE **PRAYER CIRCLE** AN' TELL HER HER **SISTER'S** ASKIN' FOR HER **INSULIN**.

·Cough!·

UH...IS **MINNA BAXTER** WITH Y'ALL?

SO AT LEAST I DID **ONE** THING THAT NIGHT THAT WAS OF SOME PRACTICAL **USE** TO SOMEBODY.

THAT'S **ME**.

TIME DRAGGED BY. IT SEEMED LIKE **HOURS**.

AT ONE POINT I SNAPPED OUT OF A **HALF-DREAM** AND REALIZED THERE WASN'T A SINGLE PERSON IN **SIGHT** THAT I **KNEW**.

A KIND OF **PANIC** GRABBED AT ME, THE WAY A **KID** CAN PANIC WHEN HE THINKS MOMMY'S **ABANDONED** HIM IN A STRANGE DEPARTMENT STORE.

THEN I SPOTTED **ESMO**.

GINGER? I **DUNNO**, HONEY. I **THINK** I SAW HER WITH **REV. PEPPER** A WHILE BACK....

ONLY **PROBLEM** IS, I DON'T SEE **HIM** ANYWHERE NOW, **EITHER**.

TALKING TO ESMO, MY **EYES** KEPT DRIFTING TO THE REMNANTS OF **DORIS DAY** IN HIS **EYEBROWS**.

I WOULDN'T SAY HE HAD **QUITE** CARRIED OFF THE DESIRED ILLUSION **VISUALLY**...

...BUT HE **HAD** CAPTURED A GOOD BIT OF HER **SPIRIT**.

THEY **KILLED** HIM, MAMA! SOME **WHITE MEN** WENT AN' **KILLED** JOAB!

DON'T **SAY** THAT, ELLIS. YOU DON'T **KNOW** THAT FOR **SURE**.

YES, I **DO**.

HARLAND, **ANNA DELLYNE** SAYS TO ASK ARE YOU READY TO TALK TO THOSE **DETECTIVES** YET.

TELL HER I'LL BE **THERE** IN JUST A FEW **MINUTES**, PAULINE.

EXIT

'SCUSE ME, REV. PEPPER.

ESMO TOLD ME **GINGER** MIGHT BE WITH YOU.

NO. IT'S JUST **ME** HERE.

OH. SORRY TO HAVE **BOTHERED** YOU.

DON'T RUN **OFF**, THOUGH, TOLAND.

THERE'S SOMETHIN' I'VE BEEN WANTIN' TO **ASK** YOU ABOUT.

DIDN'T I SEE YOU AT THE **SIT-IN** THE DAY THEY CLOSED DOWN **RUSSELL PARK?**

YES, SIR.

I **KNEW** I REMEMBERED SEEIN' YOU SITTIN' ON THE GRASS. I **APPRECIATED** YOU AN' YOUR FRIENDS **BEIN'** THERE.

AN' YOU WERE THERE AT THE **BAR** WITH **LES** TONIGHT, **WEREN'T** YOU...WHEN I CAME TO **GET** HIM?

UH... YEAH. I **WAS**.

IT WAS **DARK**, BUT I **THOUGHT** I RECOGNIZED YOU.

WANT ONE OF **THESE?**

NO, THANKS. I DON'T **SMOKE**.

YOU'RE A **SMART** YOUNG MAN.

108

I WISH **I'D** BEEN SMART ENOUGH TO STEER **CLEAR** OF THESE THINGS BEFORE THEY GOT THEIR **HOOKS** INTO ME.

THEY CALL 'EM **'COFFIN NAILS,'** Y'KNOW. IT DON'T TAKE A **GENIUS** TO SEE **WHY!**

ANNA DELLYNE'S **ALWAYS** AFTER ME TO **QUIT.** I DO TRY AT LEAST TO STAY OUT OF **VIEW** WHEN I'M PUFFIN'.

THERE'S SEVERAL IN THE **CONGREGATION** THAT JUST WON'T LET **UP** ON ME ABOUT IT.

PEOPLE LIKE THAT ARE APT TO MAKE YA DO STUFF **MORE** JUST TO BE **CONTRARY.**

WELL...THEY'RE **RIGHT** IN WHAT **THEY SAY.** THAT'S THE INESCAPABLE **TRUTH** OF IT.

AN' I **DO** QUIT.

ALMOST.

FOR **GOOD** PERIODS OF TIME.

BUT THEN SOMETHIN' **HORRENDOUS** HAPPENS LIKE IT DID **TONIGHT** AN' I'M **OFF** TO THE **RACES** AGAIN!

I SHOULD BE **IN** THERE RIGHT NOW WITH ALL THE **FAMILIES** WHO'RE GRIEVIN'.

IT'S SUCH A **TERRIBLE** THING THAT'S HAPPENED.

BUT I'VE BEEN RUN **RAGGED** THESE LAST FEW HOURS. I **HAD** TO HAVE ME A **BREAK!**

Y'WON'T HEAR **ME** CRITICIZIN' YOU!

BUT TO GET TO WHAT WAS ON MY **MIND**...

...I'VE HAD SOME PEOPLE COMIN' TO ME LATELY SAYIN' THAT **MABEL LAKE** SHOULDN'T PARTICIPATE IN OUR **MARCHES** OR **DEMONSTRATIONS** ANYMORE.

HUH?

DON'T GET ME **WRONG,** NOW. EVERYBODY **LOVES** MABEL TO **DEATH,** JUST LIKE I DO.

SHE'S PLAYED PIANO AT OUR **CHURCH SERVICES** FOR **YEARS.** I WOULDN'T GIVE UP HEARIN' HER MUSIC FOR **ANYTHING!**

NOBODY WOULD **EVER** WANT TO **SIDELINE** A FINE WOMAN LIKE **MABEL.**

BUT THERE ARE **OTHER** PARTS TO OUR EFFORT BEYOND THE ACTUAL **DEMONSTRATIONS.**

I DON'T UNDER-STAND.

PEOPLE **HAVE** TO BE CONCERNED ABOUT **DISCIPLINE** IN A MOVE-MENT.

OUTSIDE OF A **MOVEMENT CONTEXT**, I SUSPECT A MAJORITY WOULD **SIDE** WITH YOU ON THAT.

NOW, **SOME** INDIVIDUALS MIGHT ASK WHETHER IT'S FAIR TO **PUNISH** A DUMB **ANIMAL** FOR DOIN' WHAT ITS **TRAINERS** HAVE **TAUGHT** IT WAS THE **RIGHT** THING TO **DO**.

GIVEN THE **IMPERFECTIONS** OF ALL THE **HUMANS** INVOLVED, I'LL BET THOSE **DOGS** WERE THE **LEAST BIGOTED** CREATURES IN THE **PARK**.

DON'T I REMEMBER THAT **SAMSON** KILLED A **LION**?

CHANCES ARE THAT **LION** WASN'T A JEW-HATER, BUT—

WELL, **MY GOODNESS GRACIOUS!**

NOW YOU'RE THROWIN' **BIBLE STORIES** AT A **PREACHER**! AREN'T **YOU** THE **DAREDEVIL** OF THE DAY!

I **HOPE** YOU DON'T THINK THAT ANALOGY WOULD STAND UP UNDER ONE **SECOND** OF SERIOUS **SCRUTINY!**

IT WAS JUST A **PASSIN' THOUGHT**.

OH, I COULD THROW BIBLE STORIES **BACK** AT YOU AN' TALK ABOUT THINGS **JESUS** SAID, BUT I TRY AN' SAVE MY **SERIOUS** PREACHIN' FOR THE **SUNDAY** SERVICES.

I COULD EVEN TELL A FEW TALES ABOUT MISTER **GANDHI**—BUT THERE'S NO NEED TO GET SO **HISTORICAL**.

LET'S JUST TALK ABOUT THE PETTY LITTLE **SUTTON CHOPPERS** OF THE WORLD.

THEY **BARK** AN' **SNARL**, BUT THESE PEOPLE ARE TOTALLY AT **SEA** WHEN YOU REFUSE TO TAKE THEIR **BAIT**.

IT BORDERS ON THE **COMICAL** HOW AT SEA THEY ARE!

OR IT **WOULD**, IF THE **CIRCUMSTANCES** WEREN'T SO **GRAVE**.

IT'S IMPORTANT TO **RECOGNIZE** THAT STRATEGIC **ADVANTAGE** AN' BE **RESOLUTE**.

I DO RECALL A FLEETING **WISH** I HAD THAT MY **DADDY** COULD'VE BEEN MORE LIKE HARLAND PEPPER.

THAT MADE ME FEEL **GUILTY**, SINCE THERE'D BEEN NOTHING REALLY **WRONG** WITH MY DADDY AS HE **WAS**.

WE KEPT ON TALKING FOR SEVERAL MORE MINUTES. I CAN'T REMEMBER ALL THE **DETAILS**, JUST THE OVERALL **FEELING** OF IT.

OUT OF THE **BLUE**, I THOUGHT ABOUT ASKING THE REVEREND IF HE HAD EVER READ *SEEING THROUGH THE LORD*...

...BUT THEN WE GOT **INTERRUPTED** BY A **CLAMOR** IN THE **HALL**.

TOLAND! WHERE'VE YOU BEEN?

CONFERRIN' WITH THE REVEREND. WHAT'S ALL THE NOISE?

SAMMY NOONE'S DOWN IN THE PARKIN' LOT THROWIN' A FIT FOR THOSE TV PEOPLE.

HOLY SHIT, ESMO!

GRAB YOUR NOTEBOOK IF YOU'RE WATCHIN' THIS, COMMISSIONER CHOPPER! I'LL TELL YOU WHO SET OFF THAT BOMB TONIGHT!

IT'S YOU, CHOPPER!

YOUR FINGER-PRINTS ARE ALL OVER THAT STINKIN' FUSE!

IT'S YOU AN' EVERY WHITE BIGOT IN THIS TOWN THAT EVER USED THE WORD 'NIGGER'!

Y'DON'T EVEN HAVE TO STRIKE A MATCH, YOU BASTARD!...

whew! HEAR HER RAVE!

I HOPE SAMMY KNOWS WHAT HE'S DOIN' —TALKIN' WILD LIKE THAT WITH A CAMERA RUNNIN'!

LOOK! THERE COMES LES OUT THE DOOR TO DAMP HIM DOWN....

...YOU DO IT WITH WORDS!

HEY! SAMMY!

DRIVING US HOME LATER ON THROUGH THE DARK CITY STREETS, SAMMY CONTINUED MUTTERING ANGRILY AT SOME INVISIBLE TELEVISION NEWS CREW IN HIS HEAD.

...IGNORANT SONS-O'-BITCHES... ...RACIST... ...MURDERIN'...

THE LAST REPORT WE'D GOTTEN BEFORE LEAVING THE HOSPITAL WAS THAT SHILOH WAS STILL HANGING ON. IT WAS STILL TOO SOON TO KNOW HOW MUCH HIS BRAIN WOULD STAY DAMAGED, EVEN IF HE PULLED THROUGH.

OF THE KIDS IN THE FREEDOM CHORUS, THREE WERE DEAD. FOUR OTHERS WERE BAD OFF.

...FUCKHEADS... ...OUGHTA BURN IN HELL...

I'VE GOTTA REMEMBER TO PHONE **ODETTA BEEMON** TOMORROW AND SEE IF SHE NEEDS ME TO SCARE UP A **BABYSITTER** FOR **REBECCA** UNTIL... UH...

GINGER ALTERNATED BETWEEN LONG, GRIM **SILENCES** AND SUDDEN BURSTS OF **TALK** ABOUT **PRACTICAL** MATTERS.

AS FOR **ME**, I LET MY MIND DRIFT BACK OVER THE THINGS REV. PEPPER HAD **SAID** DURING OUR **CONVERSATION** IN THE **STAIRWELL**.

HITTIN' **DOGS** OR HITTIN' **PEOPLE**— IT'S THE **WRONG** WAY TO **GO**, TOLAND. REALLY, IT **IS!**

STRATEGICALLY...MORALLY... FROM ANY **NUMBER** OF STANDPOINTS!

klunk!

STILL, I'LL TELL YOU A **SECRET**, SON. DON'T YOU TELL **ANYBODY** I **SAID** THIS, THOUGH.

Y'SEE, **I'M** A HUMAN BEING WITH **FAULTS** AN' **WEAKNESSES** LIKE ANYBODY **ELSE**, AN'... WELL...

...WHAT I'M **ADMITTIN'** IS: AS LONG AS MABEL'S **PURSE** WAS FLYIN' **ANYWAY**, I WISH I COULD'VE **BEEN** THERE TO **SEE** IT!...

Chuckle! A DOG THAT GETS HIT WITH A **BRICK**, HE MIGHT THINK **TWICE** ABOUT BITIN' HIS NEXT **NEGRO!**

CRACK!

SHIT!

WHAT WAS **THAT?**

SOMEBODY THREW A **ROCK** AT US.

MAYBE I'LL RIDE THE **GAS PEDAL** A LITTLE **HARDER** FOR A MILE OR TWO....

JESUS! MY SKIN'S **NEVER** FELT SO **WHITE!**

I'M SURPRISED THEY **RAN** IT. I GUESS THEY THOUGHT SAMMY WAS **COLORFUL**!

GONNA CATCH UP ON YOUR **READIN'** DURIN' THE FUNERAL?

VERY **FUNNY**!

I WAS SO **DISTRACTED** WALKIN' OUT OF THE DORM, I FORGOT THIS WAS IN MY **HAND**.

WOULD YOU BELIEVE I'VE GOTTA TAKE A **TEST** ON **NATHANIEL HAWTHORNE** THIS AFTERNOON AT **FIVE**?

I'LL GO YA ONE **BETTER**.

WOULD YOU BELIEVE I GOT MYSELF **FIRED** THIS MORNIN'...?

IF GINGER AND I WERE ENTERTAINING ANY **ILLUSIONS** WHILE DRIVING TO THE CHURCH THAT WE WERE GONNA GET TO **SIT DOWN** DURING THE FUNERAL, WE GOT OVER 'EM **FAST** ONCE WE GOT A LOOK AT THE HUGE **CROWD** THAT WAS GATHERING.

IT WAS OBVIOUS THE **SANCTUARY** WAS ALREADY **FULL** AND THAT YOU COULD'VE FILLED **RUSSELL PARK TWICE** WITH THE **OVERFLOW**.

OF COURSE, SINCE THE **PARK** WAS STILL **FENCED OFF** AND **UNAVAILABLE**, IT WAS THE ADJACENT **STREETS** THAT WERE GETTING SWAMPED WITH **MOURNERS**...

...WHILE AN ARMY OF **COPS** KEPT WATCH, CHARGED WITH MAKING SURE THAT THE **EMOTIONS** OF THE MOMENT DIDN'T START THREATENING **PUBLIC ORDER**.

IN THE COURSE OF THE **SERVICE** WE CAUGHT QUICK GLIMPSES OF **SAMMY** AND A FEW OTHER FRIENDS...

...BUT MOSTLY ALL WE COULD SEE WERE THE **HATS** AND **HEADS** OF THE **STRANGERS** AGAINST WHOM WE WERE BEING PRESSED LIKE **SARDINES**.

FROM ATOP VARIOUS PERCHES **TV NEWS CREWS** SQUINTED INTO THEIR **VIEWFINDERS** AND PLAYED WITH THEIR **ZOOMS**.

THEY KNEW THE DRAMATIC **FOOTAGE** THEY WERE GETTING WOULD PLAY ON THE TUBE LIKE **GANGBUSTERS**. ESPECIALLY UP **NORTH**.

EVERYONE LISTENED SORROWFULLY TO **HARLAND PEPPER'S EULOGY**...

...WHICH WAS **MOVING** DESPITE THE **CRACKLE** MIXED INTO IT BY THE CHURCH'S **PUBLIC ADDRESS SYSTEM**.

I WAS SURPRISED BY HOW **PERSONALLY** IT WAS HITTING ME, CONSIDERING HOW I'D SCARCELY KNOWN A **ONE** OF THE MURDERED KIDS TO **SPEAK** TO.

♪ ...Deep in my heart, ♪ I do believe... ♪ ♪

AS THE **CASKETS** WERE BROUGHT DOWN THE STEEP STONE STEPS, **FAMILIES** FOLLOWED AND THE **SCREAMS** AND **CRYING** GOT **LOUD**.

THEN, ONCE THE **DOORS** ON THE **HEARSES** HAD CLICKED SHUT...

...THE MOURNERS SWAYED AND SANG '**WE SHALL OVERCOME**.'

BUT NOT **ME**. I COULDN'T GET THE **WORDS** TO **COME**.

WE HAD TO **FOREGO** FOLLOWING THE HEARSES OUT TO THE **CEMETERY** BECAUSE OF THE **TEST** GINGER WAS SUPPOSED TO TAKE AT THE **COLLEGE**.

WELL... BE **SMART**!

THANKS.

IT MUST'VE BEEN A HELLUVA **FUNERAL PROCESSION**, THOUGH.

AFTER DROPPING GINGER OFF I DROVE BACK TO **GLENN'S GULF & TUNE-UP**.

ARE YA **SURE** YA WANNA SHOW YER FACE IN THERE AGAIN, SLICK?

I THOUGHT THAT GLENN MIGHT HAVE **RECONSIDERED** SINCE OUR **ARGUMENT**.

GLENN—

BE ON YOUR **WAY**, SON. I'M **NOT** LETTIN' **MY BUSINESS** GET BURNED DOWN ON ACCOUNT OF **YOUR POLITICS**.

NO SUCH **LUCK**.

I SAT ON THE BANK OF A NEARBY **CREEK** FOR A WHILE AND TRIED TO **SORT** THINGS OUT.

THEN I REALIZED WHERE I NEEDED TO **BE**.

GINGER, MEANWHILE, WASN'T IN THE BEST FRAME OF **MIND** TO BE QUIZZED ABOUT **NATHANIEL HAWTHORNE**.

FINISHED **ALREADY**, MISS RAINES...?

PLOP!

SHE WALKED TO THE CAMPUS **CAFETERIA**.

IT WAS WHERE YOU REFLEXIVELY **WENT** AT THAT TIME OF DAY.

WHO AM **I** TO SING THAT SONG? WHAT **DUES** HAVE I PAID?

I HAVEN'T HELPED ANY-BODY 'OVERCOME' A FUCKIN' **THING!**

YOU'VE BEEN DOIN' O.K.

MAYBE I'M MORE **WAKED UP** TO SOME STUFF THAN I WAS, THANKS TOTALLY TO **YOU.**

THE **QUESTION** IS: DOES A **WAKED-UP TOLAND POLK** DO ANYBODY ON THE PLANET ANY **GOOD?**

YOU'VE DONE **ME** GOOD.

YOU'VE PULLED ME DOWN TO **EARTH** A LITTLE.

DON'T LET ME DO THAT TOO **MUCH.** I LIKE THE **LOOK** OF YOU FLYIN' UP THERE.

I THINK I'VE BEEN LETTIN' MYSELF BELIEVE THAT **EVENTUALLY** SOMEBODY'D PUT A **HELP-WANTED AD** IN THE PAPER FOR AN EXTRA **JOAN BAEZ** OR TWO AN' I COULD APPLY FOR THE **POSITION.**

BUT ALL THE **SINGIN'** THAT JOAN BAEZ AN' THE OTHERS DO ISN'T MAKIN' THAT MUCH OF A **DENT** IN THINGS, IT SEEMS LIKE.

I **LOVE** YOU, GINGER.

I **ADMIRE** YOU AN' **LOVE** YOU AN' WISH TO HELL I WAS MORE **LIKE** YOU.

I LOVE YOU, **TOO,** TOLAND.

WHEN I WAS **GROWIN' UP,** THEY ALWAYS TOLD ME I'D FALL IN LOVE WITH A **GIRL** SOMEDAY AN' GET **MARRIED.**

AN' NOW I'M IN LOVE WITH **YOU** AN'... WELL....

IT'S **COMPLI-CATED.**

I WISH YOU COULD **FORGET** WHAT I **TOLD** YOU ABOUT ME.

THERE'S NO **FORGETTIN'** SOMETHIN' LIKE THAT.

I CAME ACROSS A **BOOK** THAT SAYS **LOTS** OF GUYS GO THROUGH HOMO PERIODS ...BUT THEN IT **PASSES** AN' THEY'RE **NORMAL.**

—AN' THERE'S NO WISHIN' IT **AWAY.**

121

FIREMEN GOT THE **FLAMING UPHOLSTERY** IN SAMMY'S CAR **DOUSED** WITHOUT THE **GAS TANK** BLOWING, BUT IT WAS STILL AN UNDRIVABLE MESS OF **BLACKENED SPRINGS** AND **ASHES** BY THE TIME THE **SMOKE** CLEARED.

FELTON, SHOW FATHER MORRIS THAT **NEWSPAPER** I GAVE YOU.

OH, YEAH. I ALMOST **FORGOT.**

THIS CAME OUT YESTERDAY **EVENIN'.**

WE THOUGHT IT MIGHT HAVE SOMETHIN' TO DO WITH WHAT **HAPPENED** TONIGHT.

OH, GOOD HEAVENS!

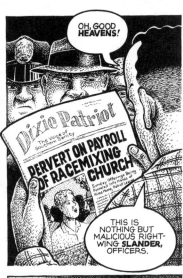

Dixie Patriot
The Voice of Southern Sanity

PERVERT ON PAYROLL OF RACEMIXING CHURCH

Sunday Offerings Being Funneled Into Hustler Hideaway, Patriot Learns

THIS IS NOTHING BUT MALICIOUS RIGHT-WING **SLANDER,** OFFICERS.

THERE'S CERTAINLY NO **BASIS** FOR THIS IN **FACT!**

IS THERE, SAMMY?

HOLY **MOSES,** EDGAR— HOW COULD YOU EVEN **ASK?!**

cough! THE EXTREMISTS WHO WILL STOOP TO **ANYTHING** TO DISCREDIT MY CHURCH'S STAND ON **RACIAL** ISSUES. IT'S AN EXAMPLE OF ~~~ ~~~ . . .

FATHER MORRIS REACTED WITH A FIRM **DEFENSE** OF SAMMY WHILE THE **POLICE** WERE THERE.

SAMMY **HIMSELF** SCARCELY HAD TO SAY A **WORD,** HE TOLD US LATER.

STILL, IT DIDN'T HAVE THE **FEEL** OF SOMETHING LIKELY TO **BLOW OVER.**

THE FIREMEN, POLICE AND REPORTERS **LEFT** EVENTUALLY AND THINGS QUIETED DOWN...

...BUT SAMMY NEVER **SLEPT** A WINK.

NEITHER DID **FATHER MORRIS,** APPARENTLY.

AROUND **DAWN** HE SHOWED BACK UP AT SAMMY'S **DOOR.**

SAMMY! WAKE **UP!** LET ME **IN!**

Knock, Knock!

FATHER MORRIS CAME **IN,** TOOK A DEEP **BREATH...** ...AND **LOWERED** THE **BOOM.**

WHO'S **SLEEPIN'?**

YOU'RE GOING TO HAVE TO **GO,** SAMMY. YOU CAN'T **LIVE** OR **WORK** HERE AT THE **CHURCH** ANYMORE.

WHEN MY **PHONE** STARTS RINGING THIS MORNING, I NEED TO BE ABLE TO SAY YOU'RE ALREADY **PACKING.**

TODAY? YOU WANT ME OUT **TODAY**?

IT'S A **DELICATE POLITICAL SITUATION**. PLEASE UNDERSTAND.

I'LL PAY FOR A **MOTEL ROOM** FOR YOU OUT OF MY OWN **POCKET** UNTIL YOU DECIDE WHERE YOU'D LIKE TO **SETTLE**.

A CHANGE OF **CITIES** MIGHT BE SOMETHING TO **THINK** ABOUT.

BUT YOU MUSTN'T **TELL** ANYONE THAT I'M **HELPING** YOU.

THERE ARE GOING TO BE ENOUGH **AWKWARD QUESTIONS** TO FIELD WITHOUT ME LOOKING **INDECISIVE** IN A **CRISIS**—

HEY, **EDGAR**— SAVE YOUR **MONEY**!

I'VE GOT **FRIENDS** WHO'LL HELP ME OUT!

DON'T **CALL** ME '**EDGAR**'!

I'VE **ASKED** YOU NOT TO CALL ME '**EDGAR**' IN **PUBLIC**, BUT YOU **DID** IT TONIGHT IN FRONT OF THE **POLICE** AND **REPORTERS**.

I **BEG** YOUR **PARDON**, FATHER...

...I'D **NEVER** WANT TO SHOW **DISRESPECT** FOR THE **CLOTH**!

SAMMY, I'VE GOT TO BE **FIRM** ABOUT THIS. THERE ARE **IMPORTANT THINGS** AT STAKE AND YOU **KNOW** IT.

TRINITY EPISCOPAL IS ALREADY A **TARGET** BECAUSE OF THE POSITION I'VE TAKEN ON **INTEGRATION**.

THE **RACE-BAITERS** WILL MAKE **HASH** OF ME IF I'M SEEN AS CONDONING **HOMOSEXUALITY**.

I **KNOW** THAT YOU **CARE** ABOUT RACE RELATIONS IN **CLAYFIELD**. YOU EVEN PUT YOURSELF AT **RISK** BY DEMONSTRATING IN **RUSSELL PARK**.

I **SUPPORTED** AND **APPLAUDED** YOU FOR THAT.

BUT NOW THERE'S **THIS** TO DEAL WITH... AND THERE'S NO **GENEROUS** WAY TO **HANDLE** IT.

YOU'RE REALLY BEING A **CHICKENSHIT**, EDGAR.

DON'T **CALL** ME '**EDGAR**'.

WE **LEARNED** ABOUT ALL OF THIS LATER IN THE **DAY**, AFTER SAMMY CALLED **MAVIS** AT THE **DRUG STORE** TO ASK IF SHE AND RILEY AND I COULD TAKE TIME OUT TO COME HELP HIM **MOVE**.

SAMMY! HOW **ARE** YA, HON?

NO **JOB**. NO **HOME**. NO **WHEELS**. HOW 'BOUT **YOU**?

MAVIS AND RILEY **INSISTED** THAT SAMMY MOVE INTO THE **WHEELERY** WITH US, AT LEAST FOR THE **TIME BEING.**

IT'LL BE KINDA **PRIMITIVE,** SAMMY, BUT YOU CAN STOW YER **STUFF** IN THE **CORNER** AN' CAMP OUT ON OUR **ROLL-AWAY BED.**

OH, BUT I **ADORE** 'PRIMITIVE,' RILEY! IT'LL BE LIKE AN INDOOR **BOY SCOUT JAMBOREE!**

LET'S SET **FIRE** TO YOUR **ARMCHAIR** RIGHT NOW AN' ROAST **MARSH-MALLOWS!**

SAVE YER MARSHMALLOWS FOR THE **CROSSES** WE MIGHT FIND BURNIN' IN THE FRONT YARD BEFORE THIS SHIT'S OVER!

AN' DON'T WORRY ABOUT PAYIN' ANY **RENT** 'TIL YOUR **GUITAR STUDENTS** START FINDIN' THEIR WAY OVER HERE, **BABY.**

I'M **BETTIN'** MOST OF 'EM WILL **STICK** WITH YOU.

MAYBE.

IT DIDN'T TAKE **LONG** FOR SAMMY TO GET **SETTLED** IN — IF YOU CAN CALL DUMPING A **GUITAR** AND A COUPLE OF **DUFFEL BAGS** IN THE CORNER **'SETTLING IN'!**

WE SAT AROUND AND CHEWED OVER THE DAY'S **EVENTS** UNTIL OUR **EYES** GOT **HEAVY.**

THEN RILEY UNFOLDED THE **COT** FOR SAMMY AND WE ALL GOT READY FOR **BED.**

FOR A WHILE, ONCE THE **WHEELERY** WAS **DARK,** NOTHING **STIRRED.** THEN...

TOLAND...?

TOLAND? ARE YOU **AWAKE...?**

NO.

LOCO KEEPS PUTTIN' HIS **NOSE** ON MY **PILLOW** AN' **PANTIN'** IN MY **EAR.**

ALSO— I CAN'T **SLEEP** FOR **THINKIN'.**

WHAT **ABOUT?**

ABOUT HOW I SHOULD MAYBE DRIVE UP TO **RIDGELINE** AN' VISIT MY **FATHER.**

SOUNDS GOOD TO **ME.** PEOPLE **SHOULD** VISIT THEIR PARENTS.

CLICK!

YOU DON'T **UNDER-STAND.**

IT'S NO SIMPLE **MATTER,** ME WALKIN' IN AN' LOOKIN' THAT LOATHSOME **THROWBACK** IN THE EYE. THERE'S A LOT OF **BAD BLOOD** BETWEEN ME AN' HIM.

AN' MY **STEPMOTHER RACHEL'S** NO **HELP!**

SO DON'T **GO.**

BUT I **NEED** HIM.

DADDY'S **RICH** AS **SIN** AN' I'M NEARLY **BROKE.**

HE'S GOT **HOUSES** AN' **CARS** RUNNIN' OUT OF HIS **EARS**...**ACRES** OF **LAND**...HE USED TO RUN OFF TO **EUROPE** WITH RACHEL **ALL** THE TIME...

...'TIL HIS **HEALTH** WENT BAD.

NOW HE'S SO BAD OFF HE CAN'T **ARCH** HIS **EYEBROW** WITHOUT A **FORKLIFT!**

REALLY?

I'M TALKIN' ABOUT **MAJOR PARALYSIS.**

THAT'S **SAD.**

YEAH. **SEE** SAMMY CRY.

SO GO **SEE** HIM.

SO WHAT **GOOD'S** ALL THAT MONEY TO DADDY' **NOW?** THERE'S NOTHIN' LEFT HE CAN **DO** WITH IT BUT **PISS** ON IT JUST TO WATCH IT **DRY!**

MEANWHILE **I'M** GETTIN' VERY **POOR** VERY **QUICK!**

BUT HE **HATES** ME.

HE **HATES** THE FACT THAT ONCE UPON SOME ENCHANTED EVENING HE WAS SCREWING MY LOVELY **MOM** AN' A SILLY LITTLE **FAIRY SPERM** CAME WIGGLING OUT OF HIS BIG, BUTCH **DICK.**

BUT I'M NOT EXACTLY **OVERLOADED** WITH **OPTIONS.** COULD BE I SHOULD TAKE THE **BULL** BY THE **HORNS** AN'—

YA **MIGHT** BE SELLIN' THE OL' GUY **SHORT,** Y'KNOW. PEOPLE DO **CHANGE**...'SPECIALLY IN TIMES OF **ADVERSITY.**

WILL YOU DRIVE ME UP TO **RIDGELINE,** TOLAND? IN **YOUR** CAR?

YOU WANT **ME** TO GO **WITH** YOU?

I'M **NERVOUS** ABOUT GOIN' **ALONE.**

AN' I DON'T THINK **MY** CAR'S SO **ROADWORTHY** SINCE THOSE FELLAS MISTOOK IT FOR A **POTATO** LAST NIGHT AN' TRIED TO **BAKE** IT!

WHEN WOULD YA WANNA **GO?**

I'M NOT **SURE.** IT'LL TAKE ME A **LITTLE** WHILE TO BUILD UP MY **NERVE.**

BUT WE'LL MAKE IT A **WEEK-END,** FOR **SURE,** SO IT WON'T INTERFERE WITH YOUR **JOB.**

WHAT **JOB?**

OOPS! I KEEP **FORGETTIN'** YOU'VE SEVERED YOUR TIES WITH THE **PETROLEUM INDUSTRY!**

HEY, WE'RE **BOTH** OUT OF WORK AT THE **SAME** TIME. LET'S START A **CLUB!**

SERIOUSLY, KID...HOW MUCH OF A **BIND** DOES IT PUT YOU IN?

OH, I'M **O.K.** FOR A **WHILE....**

I'VE STILL GOT SOME SAVINGS FROM MY FOLKS' **INSURANCE** AN' FROM SELLIN' MELANIE AN' ORLEY MY SHARE OF THE **HOUSE.**

BUT IF YOU **POSTPONE** YOUR LI'L FAMILY REUNION TOO **LONG,** I MIGHT HAFTA TAKE SOME JOB THAT'D **KEEP** ME FROM—

IT'LL BE **SOON.** I'VE JUST GOTTA WORK ON WHAT TO **SAY.**

I'M **SCARED**, TOLAND. I DON'T KNOW WHAT'S GONNA **HAPPEN** TO ME.

I'VE ALWAYS TAKEN **PRIDE** IN MY **CHECKERED HISTORY**, BUT I'VE NEVER GOTTEN MYSELF BRANDED A **PERVERT** ON THE FRONT PAGE OF A **NEWSPAPER** BEFORE!

WHERE'D THAT PHOTO OF YOU **COME** FROM, ANYWAY?

THE **RUSSELL PARK SIT-IN**, AS FAR AS I CAN TELL.

MAVIS SAYS I SHOULD POP INTO THE DIXIE PATRIOT **OFFICE** AN' ASK IF THEY'LL SELL ME SOME **EXTRA PRINTS** OF THE PHOTO FOR MY **RELATIVES!**

THE **CLAYFIELD BANNER** IS **ALWAYS** WILLIN' TO DO THAT, Y'KNOW...

...IF THEY PRINT YOUR **PICTURE**, YOU CAN ORDER A **COPY**.

IT'S A REGULAR **SERVICE**.

Chuckle!
THAT'D BE A SIGHT TO SEE!

I CAN JUST **IMAGINE** THOSE DIXIE PATRIOT WEASELS **QUAKIN'** IN THEIR **BOOTS**, WATCHIN' ONE OF THE LOCAL **UNDESIRABLES** THEY'VE FINGERED COME SAUNTERIN' UP THE **DRIVEWAY!**

LOOK, PAL, I'LL DRIVE YOU TO RIDGELINE IF YOU **NEED** ME TO. IT WON'T BE MUCH TROUBLE.

THANKS, TOLAND. YOU'RE A REAL **FRIEND**.

CAN I LIE DOWN **NEXT** TO YOU AN' HOLD **ON** TO YOU FOR JUST A **MINUTE?**

SAMMY... I WISH YOU WOULDN'T **ASK** THAT.

I'M NOT TALKIN' ABOUT **SEX**.

I JUST WANNA **HOLD ON** TO SOMEBODY FOR **FIVE MINUTES**. I'LL GO AWAY THEN.

THAT'S O.K.— **FORGET** IT.

I JUST **REMEMBERED:** **LOCO** MIGHT HEAR THE **BEDSPRINGS** CREAKIN' AN' THINK I'M BEIN' **UNFAITHFUL!**

NEVER **TRIFLE** WITH THE AFFECTIONS OF A **CARNIVORE**, IS MY MOTTO!

G'NIGHT.

Chapter 15

SOME DAYS YOU REMEMBER FOR THE **SOUR** NOTES.

Sproin-n-ng!

THERE WAS NO SHORTAGE OF **THOSE** THE DAY GINGER PHONED TO TELL ME SHE WAS **PREGNANT**.

WE AGREED WE'D MEET TO TALK THINGS **OVER** IN ONE OF THE LITTLE **PRACTICE ROOMS** AT THE COLLEGE **MUSIC BUILDING**.

PRACTICE ROOMS

I WAS SO **AGITATED**, I GOT **LOST** AND WANDERED DOWN EVERY CORRIDOR BUT THE **RIGHT** ONE.

THE PRACTICE ROOM **DOORS** HAD TINY **WINDOWS** IN THEM.

I PEERED INTO **EACH** ONE AS I PASSED **BY**.

IT SEEMED LIKE **EVERYBODY** IN THE **BUILDING** WAS A FUCKING WHIZ AT DOING **SOMETHING**!

ANY **SECOND** I EXPECTED TO GET ASKED WHAT THE HELL **I** WAS DOING IN A BUILDING LIKE **THAT**!

PRACTICE ROOMS

PRACTICE ROOMS

HEY, **THERE** YOU ARE!

FINALLY I FOUND GINGER.

I ALMOST COULDN'T **SEE** YA, Y'KNOW... ...WITH YOU DOWN ON THE **FLOOR** LIKE THAT.

SO... Y'WANNA GET **MARRIED**?

MARRIED?

ISN'T THAT WHAT PEOPLE **DO**?

YOU DON'T HAVE A **JOB**.

I'M GONNA **GET** A JOB. I'VE GOT **APPLICA-TIONS** IN.

IT'S **NOT** LIKE I'M **UNEMPLOYABLE**! I'M **NOT** GONNA LIVE OUT MY LIFE ON **RELIEF**!

THIS'LL HELP ME GET **SERIOUS**.

WHILE WE **TALKED**, GINGER KEPT IDLY NOODLING OUT LANGUID **TUNES** ON HER **GUITAR**.	EVERY NOW AND AGAIN SHE'D HIT A JARRING **SOUR NOTE**.	STRANGELY, SHE NEVER **PAUSED** OR MADE A MOVE TO **TUNE UP**.	FROM HER **EXPRESSION**, YOU WOULDN'T EVEN THINK SHE **KNEW**.	SHE WAS **WAY** TOO GOOD A **GUITARIST**, THOUGH, NOT TO **KNOW**.

TOLAND, YOU **KNOW** I'VE ALWAYS PLANNED ON TRYIN' TO BE A PROFESSIONAL **SINGER** ONCE I GRADUATE.

I MIGHT NEED TO GO LIVE IN **NEW YORK**...AN' TAKE **LESSONS** AN' BE **POOR** AN' SPEND TIME SCOUTIN' AROUND FOR—

I CAN GO TO NEW YORK **WITH** YOU AN' HELP TAKE **CARE** OF—

I MIGHT LIKE TO BE **ALONE** IN NEW YORK.

Sproing

THOSE SOUR NOTES MADE ME **EDGY** AND **DOLEFUL**.

ANNA DELLYNE TALKS ABOUT HOW MUCH IT **MEANT** TO HER TO BE ON HER **OWN** IN NEW YORK WHEN SHE WAS STARTIN' HER CAREER.

SHE WAS '**ALONE**' WITH HER **DEMONS**, SHE SAYS.

SHE SAYS THAT'S WHAT SHE **NEEDED**.

MY **IMPRESSION** WAS YOU'D GOTTEN HOOKED ON WORKIN' WITH THE **MOVEMENT** HERE IN **CLAYFIELD**.

THAT'S THE WAY I WAS LOOKIN' AT THINGS WHEN WE WERE IN **WASHINGTON**.

BUT I'M FEELIN' **SHAKY** ABOUT THAT. I'M NOT SURE I'VE GOT ENOUGH **MORAL SPINE** FOR THIS MOVEMENT.

I **HATE** TOO MANY PEOPLE.

I WAS **TRYING** TO LISTEN...

...BUT AT THE SAME TIME A **JUMBLE** OF ALL THE THINGS SHE'D **SAID** TO ME OUT AT **BLUERABBIT LAKE** WERE BUSY **BARRELING AROUND** IN MY **HEAD**.

A FEW HAD BEGUN TO RING **HOLLOW**.

WHAT'S **REALLY** GOIN' ON IS, YOU'VE DECIDED YOU DON'T WANNA BE MARRIED TO A **HOMOSEXUAL**.

TOLAND...

...DO YOU FIND THAT SO **STRANGE**??

SO...LIKE, WHAT AM I SUPPOSED TO **DO**?

WHAT ARE THE **RULES**?

DO I PAY FOR AN **ABORTION**? IS **THAT** WHAT HAPPENS?

ANNA DELLYNE SAYS SHE KNOWS SOMEONE I CAN **TALK** TO... ABOUT THAT.

THAT'S WHEN A WHITE **RAGE** SWELLED UP INSIDE OF ME.

SHE'D TALKED IT ALL OVER WITH **ANNA DELLYNE**... ...EVEN **BEFORE** SHE'D SAID ANYTHING TO **ME**!

DO YOU REALLY **WANT** AN ABORTION?

NO.

BUT I WANT MY **LIFE**.

I DON'T WANNA ABORT MY **OWN LIFE**, EITHER.

I DON'T WANNA GET **STUCK**—ALONE OR WITH **YOU**—JUST BARELY SCRAPIN' **BY**... GIVIN' UP ON BEIN' WHO I **WANT** TO BE.

I GOTTA GO **THINK**.

MAYBE IF **YOU** HAD SOMEBODY **YOU** REALLY WANTED TO BE, YOU'D UNDER-STAND.

REV. PEPPER!

DRIVING BACK FROM THE WESTHILLS CAMPUS, MY **THOUGHTS** WERE RACING IN EVERY **DIRECTION** AT **ONCE.**

THEN, AS I WAS PASSING **RUSSELL PARK,** I NOTICED **HARLAND PEPPER** STOMPING UP THE STREET TOWARD HIS **CHURCH.**

DON'T TRY TO **TALK** TO ME **NOW,** TOLAND. I'M **NAIL-SPITTIN'** MAD!

WHAT'S THE **MATTER?**

WE WON!

Y'SEE THE CHOPPER'S PRETTY **FENCE** HERE?

ITS DAYS ARE **NUMBERED.**

SO SAID THE **LAW**...AS OF **YESTER-DAY!**

THEN WHY ARE YOU —??...I MEAN, THAT'S **GOOD,** ISN'T IT?

SON, **YOU** KNOW HOW MANY **MONTHS** WE'VE HAD OUR LAWYERS TROOPIN' THROUGH EVERY ROOM OF THE **COURTHOUSE** SUIN' TO GET THIS FARCICAL **'PARK RENOVATION'** BROUGHT TO AN END.

I'VE LISTENED TO SO MUCH TALK ABOUT **LANDSCAPIN',** I'VE STARTED HAVIN' **DREAMS** ABOUT **BULLDOZERS** AN' **BACKHOES!**

SO WE GO THROUGH **FIFTEEN HEARINGS** AN' DO A DANCE WITH **TWO HUNDRED CITY LAWYERS...**

...'TIL WE **FINALLY** GET THE JUDGE TO SAY: NO QUESTION **ABOUT** IT, THE FENCE HAS GOTTA **GO!**

NOW I **ASK** YOU: DO YOU SEE ANY **FENCE** COMIN' DOWN? I **DON'T!** NOR DO I SEE THE FIRST **SIGN** OF ANY **RENOVATION** UNDER WAY.

THE ONLY THING **UNDER** WAY AS WE SPEAK IS MORE **FANCY FOOTWORK** AT CITY HALL! THEY JUST WAVED A **STAY** OF **ENFORCEMENT** AT ME THAT'LL MAKE **SURE** WE DIDDLE AWAY ANOTHER **SIX MONTHS** OR SO PLAYIN' **PING-PONG** WITH **APPEALS!**

I'M TRYIN' TO DO SOMETHIN' ABOUT **RACISM** AN' THEY'VE GOT ME BALLED UP IN GLORIFIED **CHICKEN WIRE!**

IT NEVER **STOPS!** THEY JUST **WEAR** YOU **DOWN!**

BUT...IT'S ALL **ABSURD!** THEY'RE **STALLIN'!** YOU'LL GET YOUR PARK BACK IN THE **END.**

OH... I **KNOW** WE WILL. I JUST GET SO **FED UP** WITH HAVIN' TO SPEND MY **ENERGY** EVERY DAY THINKIN' ABOUT ALL THIS **CRAP!**

WHEN THE PREACHER HAD GOTTEN ENOUGH OF HIS **FUMING** DONE FOR ME TO DARE CHANGE THE **SUBJECT,** I ASKED HIM IF **ANNA DELLYNE** WAS ANYWHERE AROUND THE CHURCH THAT AFTERNOON.

NO, SHE WAS OUT VISITING **SHILOH** AT **RATTLER HILL,** REV. PEPPER TOLD ME.

JEROME RADLER HILL MEMORIAL HOSPITAL FOR NEGROES

SEEING **HARLAND** HAD MADE SOMETHING **CLICK** IN MY **MIND;** THERE WERE SOME **WORDS** THAT HIS WIFE AND I NEEDED TO HAVE. I DROVE TO THE **HOSPITAL.**

WHEN I GOT OFF THE **ELEVATOR** I NOTICED THAT A WHOLE BUNCH OF **NURSES** WERE HOVERING EXCITEDLY AROUND THE DOOR TO **SHILOH'S ROOM.**

THEY **SHUSHED** ME AS I WALKED **OVER** TO THEM.

THEN I SAW **WHY.**

ANNA DELLYNE WAS SITTING ON THE EDGE OF SHILOH'S **BED,** LOVINGLY SINGING ONE OF HER OLD-TIME **SONGS** FOR HIM.

♪ *You may try forgetting me, but you will not succeed... Your soul is under lock and key...* ♪

HIS **EYES** WERE **CLOSED.** WHO COULD TELL IF HE WAS EVEN **HEARING** HER?

THE AUDIENCE IN THE **DOORWAY,** THOUGH, WAS TOTALLY **RAPT.**

♪ *...And it will not be freed... You'll always be a part of me...* ♪

HER VOICE WAS **SOFT.** IT WASN'T LIKE SHE WAS ON A **STAGE...**

...BUT MY **IMAGINATION** GAVE HER A **MICROPHONE** TO SING INTO, AND SHILOH'S **ROOM** TURNED INTO A SMOKY HARLEM **NIGHTSPOT** FROM **DECADES BEFORE.**

WHAT KIND OF A DIFFERENT **LIFE** WOULD I HAVE BEEN LIVING, I WONDERED, IF I COULD'VE **BEEN** THERE, BACK THEN, TO **HEAR** HER?

♪ *...Forever in the heart of me... You may have left me before...* ♪

♪ *...But you can't leave me behind!* ♪

I **SAW** YOU PEEKIN' IN AT MY 'PERFORMANCE'!

I SHOULD GET MYSELF LAID UP IN HERE SOMETIME. MAYBE YOU'LL COME AND SING THOSE OLD SONGS FOR **ME!**

DO ME A **FAVOR** AN' DON'T GET YOUR **HEAD** BASHED IN WITH A **MOTEL WALL** JUST FOR THE PLEASURE OF HEARIN' ME **WAIL!**

JUST CATCH ME WHEN I'M CHOPPIN' GREENS FOR A **SALAD** OR WEEDIN' MY **GARDEN.** I'LL WARM UP YOUR **EARS** SOME!

YOU'RE A HARD LADY TO BE **MAD** AT.

YOU'VE GOT SOME CALL TO BE **MAD** AT ME?

GINGER SAYS YOU'RE GONNA HELP HER GET AN **ABORTION.**

WHOA, BETSY! THAT'S PUTTIN' THE WRONG **SLANT** ON IT!

I SAID **IF** SHE CHOOSES THAT ROUTE, I'LL STEER HER TOWARD SOMEBODY WHO WON'T BE GOIN' AT HER WITH **HEDGE CLIPPERS** AN' A **HOOVER!**

ANNA DELLYNE, IT'S **IMPORTANT** TO ME THAT YOU **UNDERSTAND** SOMETHING. I'VE **OFFERED** TO DO THE RIGHT THING AN' **MARRY** GINGER.

WELL, MORE **POWER** TO YOU! YOUR **FOLKS** RAISED YOU **WELL.**

I CAN'T HELP **WONDERIN',** THOUGH, IF YOU'RE LOOKIN' IN A **CLEAR-EYED** WAY AT WHAT THE **MARRIED** LIFE YOU'RE PROPOSIN' MIGHT TURN OUT TO BE **LIKE.**

SOMETHIN' ABOUT THIS IS **REMINDIN'** ME OF THE FIX MY OL' FRIEND **SHELBY** GOT IN.

He was in a **band** I was with, back when I was a **singer** up **north.** He was a **good musician,** now!...

...An' **Shelby,** bless his heart, was as **gay** as a **peacock!**

I FELT MY **CHEEKS** FLUSHING AS SOON AS I SAW WHERE WE WERE **HEADING.**

We all **knew** Shelby was that **way.** You couldn't **not** know!

There were **jokes** made at his expense when he first signed **on,** but he'd be so **funny** about everything **himself** that he got to be as **popular** as anybody in the **band.**

But then **somethin'** made Shelby decide he just **had** to go **straight.**

He got **married,** had **children,** an' memorized more **Bible** verses than the Lord **Himself** ever knew!

He built up a whole **make-believe world** for himself.

He **walked** different, **talked** different, an' tried to **be** somebody **altogether** different from the Shelby we'd known **before.**

BUT HE COULDN'T **KEEP UP** THE MAKE-BELIEVE, TOLAND. IN **TIME,** THE WHOLE HOUSE OF CARDS **FELL DOWN** AROUND HIM.

HE WOUND UP WITH AN **EX-WIFE** AN' THREE **KIDS** WHO'D LOST ALL **RESPECT** FOR HIM BECAUSE OF HIS **LIES.**

An' the **crazy** thing was, everybody **respected** Shelby when he was **gay**, but I can't think of a **soul** who liked him much when he was **straight**!

HE WASN'T **GEARED** TOWARD BEIN' STRAIGHT.

TO PUT IT **BLUNTLY**, **SHELBY** BEIN' **STRAIGHT** BORDERED ON THE **LUDICROUS**!

BEIN' **GAY**, ON THE OTHER HAND, HAD ALWAYS COME **NATURAL** TO HIM.

Tsk, tsk, tsk!..I DO **MISS** OL' **SHELBY**!

OH' - NOT THAT **YOU'D** BE LUDICROUS PLAYIN' STRAIGHT, SUGAR!

THERE'S NOT A **DOUBT** IN MY **MIND** YOU'D PULL IT OFF BETTER THAN **SHELBY** DID!

STILL, I'D **THINK** A LITTLE MORE ABOUT IT IF I WAS YOU... ABOUT TRYIN' TO BE WHAT YOU'RE **NOT**.

IT THREW ME OFF **BALANCE** TO LEARN HOW GINGER HAD SPILLED THE **BEANS** ABOUT ME, BUT I KEPT MY **COOL**.

OH, LOOK — **LES** IS BACK. I SAW HIM DUCK INTO **SHILOH'S** ROOM.

LET'S GO SAY **HELLO**.

HAS SHILOH **WAKED UP** AT ALL?

WELL, Y'KNOW, TOLAND, HE'S HAD HIS **EYES** OPEN...AN' HE'S EVEN **SMILED** A TIME OR TWO.

BUT IT'S BEEN HARD TO TELL HOW MUCH HE'S REALLY **WITH** US.

ANNA DELLYNE...UH... THIS IS KINDA OUT OF **LEFT FIELD**, BUT... UH...

IF Y'GOT SOMETHIN' ELSE ON YOUR **MIND**, TOLAND, SPIT IT **OUT**.

HAS IT EVER **BOTHERED** YOU THAT YOU GAVE UP BEIN' A **PROFESSIONAL SINGER**?

DOES THAT BOTHER **YOU** ABOUT ME?

IT'S NONE OF MY **BUSINESS**, BUT SOMEHOW IT **NAGS** AT ME.

I MEAN, IT MUSTA BEEN **EXCITING** BACK THEN! AN' YOU WERE DOIN' **GOOD**! YOU MADE SOME **RECORDS**! PEOPLE WERE PACKIN' THE **CLUBS** TO HEAR YOU **SING**!

OH, I DON'T KNOW HOW MANY CLUBS I '**PACKED**'!

BUT IT WAS **WORKIN'** FOR YOU! DON'T YOU EVER **RESENT** THAT YOU GAVE THAT **UP**?

133

'CAUSE YOU'RE ENCOURAGIN' **GINGER** TO GO TO NEW YORK BY HERSELF LIKE **YOU** DID.

BUT WHEN ALL WAS SAID AN' DONE, **YOU** CAME BACK **HOME**.

WHAT IF NEW YORK DOESN'T WORK FOR **HER**...AN' **SHE** COMES BACK?

THEN **SHE** WON'T HAVE WHAT **SHE** WENT UP THERE LOOKIN' FOR...

...AN' MEAN-WHILE, THE ONLY **CHILD** I'M EVER LIKELY TO **HAVE** WILL BE **GONE FOREVER!**

I CAN'T CUT A PATH THROUGH **THAT** THICKET FOR YOU.

YOU AN' GINGER HAFTA FIND YOUR **OWN** RIGHT WAY TO GO.

ARE YOU **FREE** NOW?

HUH?

ARE YOU **FREE** NOW?

OH. YEAH.

Y'GOT YOUR OWN **WHEELS** HERE?

YEAH.

MAMA, THE CAR'S **YOURS** TONIGHT. ME AN' TOLAND ARE GONNA GO CATCH A **BITE**.

C'MON. LET'S GET THE HELL **OUTA** HERE.

WELL, THE PREACHER SAID YOU WERE **O.K.** IN **HIS** BOOK.

HE SAID YOU AN' HIM TALKED **PHILOSOPHY.**

⸮Snort!⸮ I'D LIKE TO OF SEEN **THAT!**

I'LL BET THAT WAS A REAL **TWO-WAY CONVERSATION,** WASN'T IT, TOLE!

CORRECT ME IF I'M **WRONG,** BUT 'TALKING PHILOSOPHY' WITH MY PAPA **USUALLY** MEANS DOIN' LOTSA **SMILIN'** AN' **NODDIN'** WHILE HE PREACHES A **SERMON** AT YOU.

I GOT SOME WORDS IN.

Y'KNOW, LES, THIS PLACE IS **DIFFERENT** WHEN IT'S **QUIET.** THERE'S ALWAYS BEEN A **BAND** PLAYIN' WHEN I'VE BEEN HERE BEFORE.

Y'GOTTA BE HERE **LATE** AT **NIGHT** TO GET **LIVE** MUSIC.

THERE'S SOME NICE COZY TUNES ON THE **JUKEBOX,** THOUGH.

WHY DON'T I GO PUT ONE OF 'EM **ON** SO YOU AN' ME CAN **DANCE?**

BUT DONCHA THINK I CAN **SEE** WHICH WAY YOUR **EYEBALLS** DRIFT EVERY TIME A HANDSOME **MAN** PASSES BY?

LES...

C'MON. GIVE **IN** A LITTLE. **I** CAN READ YOUR **BEADS.**

DID YOUR **MOTHER** TALK TO YOU ABOUT ME?

MY MOTHER AIN'T SAID A FUCKIN' **WORD** ABOUT YOU.

C'MON, BABY. LET'S DO THE **SCARY** THING.

I'M GONNA GO PUT MY **MONEY** IN THE SLOT. THEN I WANT YOU TO COME **OVER** TO ME.

♪ Give me ♪ just one minute... ♪ ♪

...of the Love of a Lifetime... ♪ ♪

Put your whole heart in it. ♪

♪ I won't keep it... ♪

♪ ...for long. ♪

♪ It's worth a fortune in gold, dear... ♪

♪ ...To have the Love of a Lifetime. ♪

ALLEY SAX

♪ Before I'm too old, dear... ♪

♪ won't you help me... ♪

♪ ...feel young? ♪

O.K... IT WAS A BAD **CALL** I MADE.

IN **PUBLIC'S** TOO **FAST** FOR YOU NOW.

FROM THE WAY THE MELODY'S **SECURITY GUARDS** AND **DESK CLERKS** ACTED, I GATHERED IT WASN'T THAT **UNUSUAL** FOR LES TO WHEEL INTO THE MOTEL AT ODD HOURS WITH A **MALE COMPANION** IN TOW.

MELODY MOTEL

NO VACANCY

IN FACT, THEY LOBBED A **KEY** AT US WITHOUT EVEN ASKING FOR **PAPERWORK**, WHICH I THOUGHT WAS **GRACIOUS** OF 'EM. WE PASSED **BOMB DEBRIS** ON THE WAY TO OUR ROOM, BUT I DIDN'T **DWELL** ON IT.

137

WELL... HERE WE **ARE.**

CLICK!

I NEED TO MAKE A **PHONE CALL.**

I PHONED **RILEY** AND TOLD HIM A **LIE** ABOUT WHERE I **WAS** SO HE AND MAVIS WOULDN'T GET **WORRIED** IF I DIDN'T COME **HOME** ALL NIGHT.

HIYA, RILEY.

LISTEN, **GINGER** GOT IT INTO HER HEAD THAT WE SHOULD DRIVE UP TO THE **FAIR** AT **PINERISE** TONIGHT. CHANCES ARE WE'LL **STAY OVERNIGHT** SOMEWHERE ON THE **ROAD.**

...IT DIDN'T EVEN **REGISTER** ON ME WHEN LES LEFT THE BED TO GO TAKE A **SHOWER.**

Y'KNOW ONE OF THE **GOOD** THINGS ABOUT **QUEER SEX**, LES...?

NOBODY GETS **PREGNANT.**

LISTENING TO THE **WATER** SPRAYING IN THE BATH-ROOM, I THOUGHT ABOUT **ANOTHER** BLACK PLAYMATE I'D ONCE HAD...AND ABOUT ANOTHER **BATH.**

IT WAS BACK WHEN I WAS A **KID** AND USED TO PLAY IN THE **YARD** WITH STETSON'S SON, **BEN.**

OUT OF **BOREDOM** ON ONE PARTICULAR DAY, BEN AND I CAME UP WITH A SILLY **PRANK** TO PLAY ON HIS **PA.**

LET'S SWAP OUR **CLOTHES.**

SWAP OUR CLOTHES?

AN' WALK AROUND THE **YARD.** WE'LL SEE HOW LONG IT TAKES YOUR **PA** TO **CATCH ON!**

Giggle!

AS A RULE, MAMA **DISCOURAGED** ME FROM BRINGING BEN **INSIDE** THE **HOUSE...**

WHERE'S YOUR PA **NOW?**

HE'S BACK O' THAT WOOD **GATE.**

...SO WE SNUCK INTO THE **WORKSHOP** IN BACK OF OUR **CARPORT** TO DO THE SWAP.

Hee hee!

Snicker!

THE TWO OF US FELT FREE TO BE **DEVILISH** THAT AFTERNOON...

...SINCE MY **MAMA** AND **SISTER** WERE OFF SOME-WHERE **SHOPPING** AND MY **DADDY** WAS AT **WORK.**

OUR **TIMING** WAS OFF, THOUGH. BEFORE BEN OR I HAD GOTTEN A CHANCE TO PARADE PAST **STETSON...**

Slam!

...MELANIE AND MAMA CAME **HOME.**

Slam!

BEN?

BEN?

MAMA CAUGHT SIGHT OF **BEN** BEFORE SHE SAW **ME**...

...AND REALIZED IN A **FLASH** WHOSE **CLOTHES** HE HAD ON.

WHAT ARE YOU **DOING** IN THOSE CLOTHES?

ARE YOU TRYING TO **STEAL** TOLAND'S **THINGS**?

NO, MIZ POLK!

STETSON!

MAMA! WAIT!

STETSON! I WANT YOU TO **SEE** THIS!

MAMA, IT'S JUST A **GAME**.

OH, **NO**, TOLAND! **LOOK** AT YOU!

TOLAND'S WEARIN' NIGGER CLOTHES!

SMACK

OW!

I'VE **TOLD** YOU **NEVER** TO USE THAT **WORD**!

WHAT'S **WRONG**, MIZ POLK?

STETSON, AREN'T YOU **ABLE** TO KEEP **TRACK** OF THESE BOYS ANY BETTER THAN **THIS**?

~Sob!~

WHU'D THEY **DO**, MA'AM?

SEE FOR **YOURSELF**! **BOTH** HAVE GOT ON WHAT THE **OTHER** SHOULD BE WEARING!

MY, **MY**! JUS' **LOOK** AT **THAT**! I **SURE** SHOULDA BEEN **WATCHIN'** 'EM CLOSER, MA'AM.

BEN, **YOU** KNOW BETTER THAN TO GET INTO SUCH **MISCHIEF**.

YOU BOYS GO SWITCH BACK INTO YOUR **RIGHT** THINGS NOW —Y'HEAR?

TOLAND'S **MY** SON, STETSON. **I'LL** TELL HIM WHAT TO DO.

TOLAND, YOU GO INSIDE AND TAKE A **BATH** RIGHT **NOW**!

A BATH?!

AND CHANGE INTO **FRESH CLOTHES** WHEN YOU'RE DONE.

A **BATH**, MAMA?? **NOW**??

MAKE **QUICK** BUSINESS OF IT AND IT WON'T TAKE **LONG**.

BEN, AS SOON AS TOLAND IS OUT OF YOUR **CLOTHES**, I'LL **BRING** THEM TO YOU.

YES'M.

YOU CAN CHANGE IN THE **CARPORT**.

BUT THERE'S LOTS MORE **PLAYIN' TIME** LEFT THIS AFTERNOON, MAMA—

TOLAND POLK, ARE YOU **ARGUING** WITH ME...?

NO, MA'AM.

GOOD.

SCRUB YOURSELF **GOOD. THEN** YOU CAN PLAY WITH BEN SOME MORE.

IT WAS **CONFUSING.**

I COULDN'T SEE WHERE ALL THE **URGENCY** WAS COMING FROM.

WHY DID I HAVE TO TAKE A BATH **THAT** VERY **MINUTE?**

WHY WAS IT SO **IMPORTANT?**

MAMA....

WELL... LOOK WHO'S **HERE.**

LET'S RUB A LITTLE **SOAP** ON THIS WHITE BOY'S SKIN.

141

Chapter 17

I THOUGHT IT WAS A **DREAM** AT FIRST: SOME **STRANGER** STANDING AT THE DOOR ONLY A FEW FEET **AWAY** FROM ME, EXCHANGING **WHISPERS** WITH LES.

THEN THE SOLID SOUND OF THE DOOR **CLOSING** TOLD ME: NO, IT **HADN'T** BEEN A DREAM.

I WAS **EMBARRASSED**, REALIZING I'D BEEN RIGHT THERE IN FULL **VIEW** THE WHOLE **TIME**, NAKED ON A CLUMP OF TANGLED **BEDSHEETS**.

BUT IT DIDN'T SEEM TO HAVE BOTHERED **LES**, SO I FIGURED, WHAT THE **HELL!**

MORNING **LIGHT** WAS WARMING MY **EYELIDS**, BUT I KEPT THEM SHUT AND TRIED TO GO BACK TO **SLEEP**. I WANTED MORE OF THE DREAMS I'D BEEN HAVING **EARLIER**.

I **DRIFTED** UNTIL I FELT SOMETHING **BLOCKING** THE LIGHT. IT WAS **LES** BENDING **OVER** ME.

HEY. TIME TO WAKE UP.

Whoops!

C'MERE. BACK TO **BED**.

MAN! LOOK AT SLEEPIN' BEAUTY GET WIDE AWAKE **FAST!**

NO MORE **TOMFOOLERY**, NOW. IT'S TIME TO HAUL OUR DECADENT ASSES OUT INTO THE **COLD, CRUEL WORLD!**

LIKE, I NEED YOU TO DRIVE ME TO **WORK!**

HEY, **THAT'S** NOT THE **SHIRT** YOU HAD ON LAST NIGHT.

WHERE'D YOU GET A CHANGE OF **CLOTHES?**

MY FRIEND **RUPE** WAS JUST HERE.

HE LOOKS **OUT** FOR ME WHEN THESE '**SPECIAL OCCASIONS**' ARISE.

RUPE WORKS FOR THE **MOTEL**.

HE LETS ME STOW FRESH **CLOTHES** AN' OTHER EMERGENCY PROVISIONS IN THE **OFFICE SAFE**.

IT WOULDN'T BE **COOL**, SHOWIN' UP FOR WORK ALL **RUMPLED** AN' **UNPRESENTABLE**.

WHICH **REMINDS** ME: I'VE STILL GOTTA **SHAVE**.

YOU'VE GOT A **RAZOR**?

LIKE I **SAY**, RUPE TAKES **CARE** OF ME. **YOU** CAN USE IT **AFTER** ME, IF YOU **WANT**.

NAH. I'LL SHAVE **LATER**, AT **HOME**.

Bzzzzzzzzzzz

TOO BAD IT'S STILL **RAININ'**, OTHERWISE THE **CONSTRUCTION CATS'D** BE IN VIEW ACROSS THE COURTYARD THERE, WORKIN' ON **BOMB** REPAIRS.

I INVITED ONE OF 'EM INTO A **ROOM** LAST WEEK, AN' **GUESS WHAT**?

HE PULLED A **REEFER** OUT OF HIS POCKET AN' WE SPENT **TEN MINUTES** HAVIN' THE **SEXIEST** TIME TWO MEN EVER HAD WITH THEIR **PANTS** ON.

LES... I'VE GOTTA **SAY** SOMETHING.

WHAT'S **THAT**?

I **LOVE** YOU.

NO, YOU DON'T.

BUT DON'T FEEL STUPID FOR **THINKIN'** YOU DO, **TEMPORARILY**. BELIEVE ME, I'VE **BEEN** THERE!

IT THROWS YOU **OFF**, DOIN' IT FOR THE FIRST TIME.

MY FIRST TIME, I WAS LIKE A **BABY GOOSE** RIGHT OUT OF THE **EGG**, READY TO WADDLE AFTER THE FIRST WARM **BODY** THAT COULD **PASS** FOR A **MAMA!**

DON'T **WORRY**...YOU'LL GET YOUR **SEA LEGS**.

I TELL YOU, THOUGH, TOLE— I HAD A **FINE TIME** WITH YOU LAST NIGHT. I SEE A GREAT **FUTURE** FOR YOU IN THE **LAND O' LOVESVILLE!**

DON'T FORGET YOUR **JACKET.**

NOW IF I WAS **SMART**, I'D OF HAD A COUPLE OF **UMBRELLAS** SQUIRRELED AWAY IN RUPE'S SAFE.

BUT **NOT BEIN'** SMART, I **DON'T!** I'VE **LUCKED OUT** ON WEATHER SO MUCH UP TO NOW, I GOT **COMPLACENT!**

YOU THINK YOU'VE PLANNED FOR **EVERY CONTINGENCY**, BUT YOU ALWAYS FORGET **SOMETHIN'!**

SPEAKING OF **PLANS**...

...MY PLAN WAS TO DROP **LES** OFF AT WORK AND THEN GO FIND **GINGER** AT **WESTHILLS.**

G'BYE. DON'T GET **WET.**

VERY **FUNNY.**

THE **CONTINGENCY** I WAS FORGETTING WAS THAT SHE HAD **THREE CLASSES** IN A **ROW** THURSDAY MORNINGS, STARTING AT **EIGHT.**

DAMN!...

THAT WAS TOO LONG TO **WAIT.** I WAS ALL **CHARGED UP** AND IN NEED OF A **FRIEND** TO TALK TO **NOW!**

SO I CALLED UP MY **SISTER** AND ASKED HER OUT.

HEY, MELANIE— WANNA GO TO THE **PANCAKE HOUSE?**

ON MY WAY TO THE PANCAKE HOUSE I MUST'VE MADE A **DECISION** WITHOUT EVEN NOTICING I WAS **DOING** IT...

...BECAUSE THE **FIRST** THING I DID ONCE **COFFEE** WAS POURED WAS TELL MELANIE THAT I HAD GOTTEN GINGER **PREGNANT.**

AND **THEN** I TOLD HER ABOUT THE NIGHT I'D JUST SPENT WITH **LES.**

I COULDN'T QUITE **BELIEVE** THAT MUCH **TRUTHFULNESS** COMING OUT OF MY MOUTH IN ONE **SITTING!**

IF I EXPECTED **HYSTERICS** FROM HER OVER HAVING A **PERVERT** FOR A **BROTHER,** SHE **SURPRISED** ME. WHO KNOWS? — MAYBE SHE'D BEEN NURSING SOME UNFORMED **SUSPICION** ABOUT ME **ALREADY.**

OR MAYBE THE PARADOXICAL **OTHER** NEWS ABOUT MY HAVING KNOCKED UP **GINGER** WAS JAMMING HER **CIRCUITS** A BIT.

WHATEVER WAS COOKING INSIDE OF HER, HER FIRST REACTION WASN'T TO EMBED A **SYRUP PITCHER** IN MY **CRANIUM,** WHICH HAD BEEN MY **WORST-CASE SCENARIO** GOING **IN.**

IN FACT, FOR A **MINUTE** OR SO SHE ACTED SO **CALM,** I BEGAN TO WONDER IF SHE'D COME DOWN WITH SOME **HEARING** PROBLEM I WASN'T AWARE OF.

THEN SHE STARTED **TREMBLING.**

SHE **WAS** MAD AFTER **ALL** — BUT AT **FATE** MORE THAN **ME.**

IT'S NOT FAIR!

ORLEY AN' I GET **MARRIED** AN' DO ALL THE THINGS WE'RE **SUPPOSED** TO DO — BUT **WE** CAN'T GET A BABY GOIN' TO SAVE OUR **LIVES!**

CLANK!

MEAN- WHILE, MY SWEET BABY **BROTHER...**

...(WHOM I DEARLY **LOVE** AN' WANT TO **KILL** RIGHT NOW)...

...IS **SINGLE** AN' A **HOMOSEXUAL** AN' NOT EVEN SUPPOSED TO **LIKE** WOMEN...

AN' **HE** GETS A BABY WITHOUT EVEN **TRYIN'** TO!

BEAR IN **MIND,** SIS...

...THAT I'M NOT ABSOLUTELY **SURE** THAT I'M REALLY A **HOMO.** THINGS AREN'T ALWAYS WHAT THEY **SEEM,** Y'KNOW, AN'—

OH, TOLAND, I HATE TO **UNDERMINE** YOUR ASPIRATIONS IN ANY **WAY,** BUT YOU REALLY DO **SOUND** GAY TO ME.

WHAT YOU AN' LES **DID** — THAT'S WHAT **GAY** PEOPLE DO.

I THOUGHT EMOTIONS WERE RUNNING HIGH AT **THAT** POINT...

squeeze!

...BUT YOU SHOULD'VE **SEEN** MELANIE **FREAK** OUT THE FIRST TIME THE WORD **ABORTION** CROSSED MY LIPS!

TOLAND POLK — I WON'T **HEAR** OF YOU **KILLIN'** THAT **BABY!**

C'MON, IT'S **NOT** A BABY YET! IT'S JUST A LITTLE GLOB OF **CELLS!**

YOU WASH MORE STRAY CELLS THAN **THAT** DOWN THE **BATHTUB DRAIN** EVERY DAY!

HONESTLY, TOLAND! IT'S JUST **LIKE** YOU TO LOOK AT THINGS IN A **NUMBSKULL WAY** LIKE **THAT!**

THAT '**GLOB** OF **CELLS**' YOU'RE PLANNIN' ON WASHIN' DOWN THE DRAIN HAS A LITTLE BIT OF **YOU** AN' A LITTLE BIT OF **GINGER** IN IT—AN' IT'S **ALIVE!** THINK ABOUT IT!

JESUS, MELANIE! DON'T GET SO **OVER-WROUGHT!**

YOU'RE GONNA FIND OUT WHAT '**OVERWROUGHT**' **IS** IF I HAVE TO LISTEN TO MORE **DOUBLETALK** FROM YOU ABOUT '**CELL GLOBS?**'

GINGER'S SO **SMART** AN' **TALENTED.** I'VE **ENVIED** HER RIGHT FROM THE **BEGINNING.**

AN' EVEN **YOU** HAVE BEEN KNOWN TO EXHIBIT A **TRAIT** OR TWO WORTH **PASSIN'** ON.

A **BABY** MADE OUT OF THE **TWO** OF YOU COULD GROW UP TO BE SOMEBODY REALLY **SPECIAL.** OR **INTERESTING,** AT **LEAST!**

NOW I WANT YOU TO LOOK ME **DIRECTLY** IN THE **EYE,** DEAR HEART, AND **TELL** ME THAT NONE OF THAT **MATTERS** TO YOU AT **ALL.**

I **SIDESTEPPED** HER CHALLENGE WHILE WE WERE THERE AT THE **PANCAKE HOUSE...**

...BUT IT HAD **CLAMPED** ITSELF ONTO MY **MIND** THE WAY A **DOG** CLAMPS ONTO **PANTS CUFFS.**

THE **RAIN** HAD STOPPED BY THE TIME MY SISTER AND I PARTED COMPANY. THERE WERE **PUDDLES** EVERYWHERE AND A GRAY OCTOBER **CHILL** HAD SETTLED IN.

NOT THE MOST **INVITING** CONDITIONS FOR A TRIP OUT TO BLUERABBIT LAKE—BUT **THAT'S** WHERE I FELT LIKE **GOING.**

IT BEING TOO **MUDDY** FOR ME TO SPRAWL ON THE **BANK** IN MY **USUAL** FASHION, I FOUND A DAMP **TREE STUMP** TO SIT ON.

PART OF ME STAYED AWARE OF THE STUMP'S **WETNESS,** WHICH CREPT THROUGH MY **JEANS** UNTIL MY **HINDSIDE** WAS **NUMB** AND **CLAMMY.**

ANOTHER PART WATCHED THE IMAGINARY **CHILDREN** WHO WERE SCAMPERING OVER THE WATER'S RIPPLING **SURFACE.**

IMAGINARY **DADS** AND **MOMMIES** SOON ARRIVED ON THE SCENE.

I'D BEEN RAISED TO EXPECT I'D BE ONE OF THEIR **NUMBER** SOMEDAY.

FUNNY HOW EXPECTATIONS CAN **EVAPORATE!**

THEY LEAVE A **MARK**, THOUGH.

MELANIE WAS **RIGHT.** I COULD **NEVER** CLAIM IT DIDN'T **MATTER.**

IT MATTERS TO **ME, TOO,** TOLAND.

BUT KNOWIN' THAT SOMETHIN' **MATTERS** DOESN'T MEAN YOU KNOW WHAT TO **DO** ABOUT IT.

Y'KNOW, MAYBE WE'RE NOT APPROACHIN' THIS SITUATION IN AS **EXPERIMENTAL** A SPIRIT AS WE SHOULD.

YOU SOUND LIKE YOU'RE STILL ANGLIN' FOR US TO GET **MARRIED.**

Sigh!...I KEEP TRYIN' THE IDEA ON FOR **SIZE....**

EVEN THOUGH YOU'RE **GAY?**

IT'S **NOT** LIKE I'M **ALL-THE-WAY** GAY!

MAKIN' A **BABY'S** GOTTA COUNT FOR **SOME- THING!**

BUT YOU'D WANNA BE ABLE TO SLEEP WITH **MEN** ONCE IN A WHILE...?

WELL... THAT'S WHERE BEIN' **EXPERI- MENTAL** COMES IN.

I'D NEED TO DO **SOMETHIN'** WITH THE GAY PART OF MYSELF! BUT I'D STILL BE A GOOD **HUSBAND** AN' **FATHER.** I **SWEAR** I WOULD.

AN' IF **I** WANNA SLEEP WITH SOMEBODY ELSE, **TOO**— THAT'LL BE FINE WITH **YOU...?**

UH...

WHY WOULD YOU WANNA DO **THAT?** YOU'RE NOT GAY.

HMM. HELP ME GET A CLEARER **IDEA** OF HOW YOU'RE **PICTURIN'** THIS MARRIAGE WE'RE EXPERIMENTIN' WITH – O.K?

BOTH OF US ARE GONNA MOVE UP TO NEW YORK—RIGHT?

BECAUSE YOU'D NEVER ASK ME TO GIVE UP SOMETHIN' THAT'S AS IMPORTANT TO ME AS MY SINGIN' IS—RIGHT?

ESPECIALLY SINCE YOU DON'T HAVE ANYTHING THAT'S ALL THAT IMPORTANT TO YOU!

THE PROBLEM I'M HAVIN' WITH THAT PLAN IS: AM I GONNA BE ABLE TO FIND WORK THERE?

THEY HAVE CARS IN NEW YORK. LOTS OF 'EM! STANDS TO REASON THEY MUST HAVE GAS STATIONS!

THAT'S CRAZY!

NOBODY MOVES TO NEW YORK SO HE CAN WORK IN A GAS STATION!

WE'RE NOT MOVIN' TO NEW YORK FOR YOU, Y'KNOW. WE'RE MOVIN' THERE FOR ME.

THERE'S ANOTHER COMPLICATION I GUESS I SHOULD MENTION.

I THINK I MAY BE IN LOVE WITH LES PEPPER.

DID YOU JUST SAY—??

IT'S PROBABLY STUPID OF ME TO TELL YOU... BUT IT SEEMS BETTER TO GET EVERY-THING OUT IN THE OPEN.

HE AN' I SPENT LAST NIGHT TOGETHER AT THE MELODY MOTEL.

I'M NOT IN LOVE WITH HIM THE WAY I'M IN LOVE WITH YOU, Y'UNDERSTAND. IT'S A WHOLE OTHER—— WHAT'S MAKIN' YOU LAUGH?

I WENT TO BED WITH RILEY LAST NIGHT.

I WAS WITH HIM WHEN YOU PHONED.

I'M NOT REALLY LAUGHIN'. THIS IS ALL JUST SO—

YOU... AN' **RILEY**...?

YEAH.

WE'RE GETTIN' EVERYTHING OUT IN THE **OPEN** TONIGHT— REMEMBER? WE'RE BEIN' **'EXPERIMENTAL.'**

WHAT ABOUT **MAVIS?**

SHE AN' **SAMMY** WERE AWAY AT SOME **MOVIE** WHEN I DROPPED BY.

AN' THERE'S NO REASON SHE SHOULD EVER HAVE TO **KNOW** ABOUT IT.

IT'S NEVER HAPPENED **BEFORE** AN' IT'S **NOT** GONNA HAPPEN **AGAIN.**

GINGER... WHY'D YOU HAVE TO GO AN' **DO** THAT?

IT WASN'T SOME **PLAN** I HAD.

I WENT THERE ON **IMPULSE,** LOOKIN' FOR **COMPANY.** I FELT **BLUE.**

EVERYBODY WAS **OUT** EXCEPT FOR RILEY, AN'...WELL...IT **HAPPENED.**

I **WANTED** IT TO HAPPEN, ACTUALLY. I WANTED TO FEEL A **STRAIGHT** MAN HOLDIN' ME FOR A CHANGE... TELLIN' ME I'M **SEXY.**

I'M **SORRY** IF THAT HURTS YOUR **FEELINGS.**

DID YOU TALK TO RILEY ABOUT...UH...THE **FIX** WE'VE GOT OURSELVES IN?

NO.

WE DIDN'T GET THAT MUCH **TALKIN'** DONE BEFORE THE **OTHER** MOOD SET IN.

I HAVEN'T TALKED ABOUT IT YET TO **ANY-BODY** BUT **YOU** AN' **ANNA DELLYNE.**

AN' YOU DIDN'T SAY ANYTHING ABOUT ME BEIN'—

NO, TOLAND! I DIDN'T TELL HIM ABOUT YOUR AWFUL SECR—**STOP** LOOKIN' LIKE A **WHIPPED PUPPY!**

YOU HAVE NO IDEA HOW **UNATTRACTIVE** THAT EXPRESSION **IS** ON A MAN!

YOU WERE OUT WARMIN' THE BEDSPRINGS WITH **LES** LAST NIGHT. WHAT'VE **YOU** GOT TO COMPLAIN ABOUT?

RILEY'S MY **BEST** FRIEND!

AN' **LES** IS ONE OF **MY** BEST FRIENDS!

SO IS **MAVIS**!

AN' **SAMMY**!

WE'RE **ALL** OF US 'BEST FRIENDS' AROUND HERE!

I'M GOIN' **IN**.

GINGER— **WAIT**.

DO YOU **MIND** IF I...?

IT'S TOO **SOON** BY A **LONG** SHOT TO FEEL ANYTHING **KICKIN'**.

I KNOW. HE PROBABLY HASN'T EVEN FIGURED OUT FOR **HIMSELF** YET THAT HE **EXISTS**! OR **SHE** EXISTS.

STILL—

GO AHEAD AN' **FEEL**. WHOEVER'S **IN** THERE IS YOURS, **TOO**.

WHAT IT **REMINDS** ME OF IS TIMES I'VE LAID ON THE **GROUND** AT NIGHT, LOOKIN' UP AT THE **STARS** AN' WONDERIN' IF THERE ARE ANY **LITTLE GREEN PEOPLE** FROM **OTHER PLANETS** UP THERE.

COULD BE YOU'RE LOOKIN' ONE OF 'EM RIGHT IN THE **EYE**—BUT HE'S SO **FAR AWAY** AN' **TINY**, THERE'S NO WAY OF **KNOWIN'**.

COMIN' FROM THE TWO OF **US**, THIS ONE MIGHT JUST AS **WELL** BE FROM ANOTHER PLANET!

WE'RE A **PAIR**, ALL RIGHT!

Chapter 18

THE NEXT DAY WAS A **FRIDAY,** I REMEMBER.

I WAS SITTING IN SOME MUSTY **OFFICE** WAITING FOR A **JOB INTERVIEW...**

...WHEN ALL OF A SUDDEN VARIOUS **NEURONS** FROM ASSORTED SECTORS OF MY **BRAIN** OPENED **FIRE** ON EACH OTHER...

...AND I KNEW THAT LES WAS **RIGHT:** I **WASN'T** IN LOVE WITH HIM.

LIFE

NOT **HIM** IN **PARTICULAR!**

SOME **EMOTIONS** I DIDN'T **UNDERSTAND** TOOK HOLD OF ME...

MR. POLK...?

...AND I **BOLTED** OUT THE **DOOR.**

THE **MAGAZINE** I'D BEEN LEAFING THROUGH HAD HAD A PHOTOGRAPH OF **SAL MINEO** IN IT.

WHICH REMINDED ME OF THE NIGHT I'D GONE TO SEE **'REBEL WITHOUT A CAUSE'** A FEW YEARS BACK...

...AND COME HOME UNABLE TO THINK ABOUT **ANYTHING** EXCEPT WANTING TO HOLD JAMES DEAN'S DARK-EYED FRIEND IN MY **ARMS** AND **COMFORT** HIM.

IT COULDN'T BE **'LOVE'** I FELT, COULD IT? NOT FOR A **MOVIE ACTOR** I WAS NEVER GONNA BE WITHIN A **THOUSAND MILES** OF... AND NOT WITH **LES PEPPER,** EITHER!

'LOVE' HAD TO BE SOMETHING **ELSE!**

SOMETHING YOU COULD FIT INTO **SONG** LYRICS AND **DANCE** TO!

WHAT I WAS FEELING WAS A YEARNING **ACHE** THAT HAD TO DO WITH **MORE** THAN SOME **ONE GUY** I'D HAD MY ARMS AROUND IN A **MOTEL.**

I SAT ON MY **CAR FENDER** AND WATCHED THE RUSH HOUR **TRAFFIC** BUILD.

A PERSON COULD **HOP** RIGHT OUT INTO THE **MIDDLE** OF IT IF HE WANTED TO.

ONE WELL-TIMED **CARTWHEEL** AND IT'D BE **HELLO-O-O, OBLIVION!**

I WASN'T LOOKING **FORWARD** TO DRIVING BACK TO THE **WHEELERY.**

NOTHING THERE WAS THE WAY IT **USED** TO BE ANYMORE.

SINCE **WEDNESDAY**, RILEY AND I HAD BEEN **DODGING** EACH OTHER'S **GLANCES** WHEN WE PASSED.

AND THERE WERE **OTHER** TENSIONS BUILDING AS **WELL**...

...TENSIONS THAT DIDN'T INVOLVE **ME**.

NOONE, KICK THE **REST** OF YER USED CLOTHES BEHIND MY CHAIR IF YA **GOTTA**, BUT **NOT** YER FUCKIN' **UNDERWEAR**!

SAMMY'S **PRESENCE** IN OUR HOUSEHOLD WAS SEEMING LESS AND LESS **TEMPORARY** BY THE **DAY**.

A NUMBER OF HIS OLD **GUITAR STUDENTS** HAD COME KNOCKING AT THE DOOR ONCE THE **DUST** HAD SETTLED FROM THE **DIXIE PATRIOT'S** ATTACK.

EVEN **CLAYFIELD** HAD ITS SOCIAL CIRCLES WHERE A GOOD MUSIC TEACHER'S **PROWESS** COULD OUTWEIGH HIS STATUS AS A **QUEER**!

BEFORE **LONG**, SAMMY WAS FANTASIZING ABOUT SAVING UP FOR AN **ORGAN** TO PUT IN THE CORNER.

IT'S MY AREA OF GREATEST **EXPERTISE**.

I COULD **DOUBLE** MY **STUDENT LOAD** IN A **MONTH**.

AREN'T ORGANS **EXPENSIVE**, SAMMY...?

THE **EDGE** THAT WOULD CREEP INTO RILEY'S VOICE WHEN SAMMY TALKED LIKE THAT **SCARED** ME.

I GET **MORE'N** ENOUGH **ORGAN NOISE** TO SUIT ME WALKIN' PAST THE **METHODIST CHURCH** ON SUNDAYS.

Chuckle!

OR MAYBE I WAS JUST SPOOKED BY THE WAY **EVERYTHING** THAT HAD SEEMED **STABLE** IN MY LIFE WAS COMING **UNHINGED** ALL AT **ONCE**.

SOME **VOICE** FROM A CORNER OF MY BRAIN WAS **REMINDING** ME THAT THE WHEELERY WASN'T LIKELY TO **KEEP ON** BEING **HOME** FOR ME **FOREVER**.

ON **SATURDAY** GINGER BIT THE **BULLET** AND TELEPHONED HER **PARENTS** IN OHIO TO TELL THEM SHE WAS **PREGNANT**.

SHE USED THE **PAY PHONE** IN A **LAUNDROMAT** SEVERAL MILES FROM THE COLLEGE, NOT WANTING ANY **DORMMATES** TO WANDER BY UNEXPECTEDLY.

SHE ASKED ME TO STAY **NEXT** TO HER FOR **MORAL SUPPORT**.

FROM WHAT I COULD TELL OF THE CONVERSATION'S **DRIFT**, THEY WEREN'T GIVING HER AS **HARD** A TIME AS YOU MIGHT HAVE **EXPECTED**.

Ker-Chunk!
Ker-Chunk!
Ker-Chunk!

DAD WANTS TO **SPEAK** TO YOU.

ME?! YOU **TOLD** HIM I WAS **HERE?!**

HE **GUESSED**.

H'LO, MR. RAINES. UH...

HELLO, TOLAND. IT'S GOOD TO **TALK** TO YOU AT **LAST.** GINGER'S TOLD US A LOT **ABOUT** YOU, SON, AND YOU'VE ALWAYS SOUNDED LIKE A **RESPONSIBLE** KIND OF FELLOW WHO'D WANT TO DO THE **RIGHT** THING....

Ker-Chunk!
Ker-Chunk!!

CONSIDERING THE **CIRCUMSTANCES**, I GIVE THE OL' GUY CREDIT FOR **FORBEARANCE** ABOVE AND BEYOND THE CALL OF **DUTY**!

YESSIR.

YESSIR.

THAT SOUNDS GOOD TO **ME**, SIR.

HE SAID THAT HE AND GINGER'S MOTHER WOULD MAKE A **TRIP SOUTH** VERY SHORTLY SO THAT WE COULD ALL **STRATEGIZE** TOGETHER ABOUT WHAT TO DO **NEXT**.

THEN ON **MONDAY**, AS IF THINGS HADN'T BEEN **STIRRED UP** ENOUGH YET, MY **SISTER** HAD HER **BRAINSTORM.**

MELANIE! ORLEY! WHAT A NICE SURPRISE!

DIDN'T MY BROTHER TELL YOU TO EXPECT US?

WE'RE A SURPRISE?

UH... NO.

≈Sigh!≈ TYPICAL!

I TALKED TO HIM EARLIER TODAY AN' SAID WE'D BE COMIN' OVER TONIGHT WITH SOMETHIN' **IMPORTANT** TO DISCUSS.

I TOLD HIM TO PRY HIS **GIRLFRIEND** AWAY FROM HER BOOKS AN' GET **HER** OVER HERE, **TOO.** I NEED TO TALK TO **BOTH** OF 'EM.

WELL, COME ON INSIDE. THEY'RE NOT **HERE** YET, BUT CHANCES ARE THEY'RE ON THEIR **WAY.**

YOU CAN KEEP ME **COMPANY** WHILE I FINISH DRYIN' SOME **DISHES.**

RILEY! SAMMY! SAY HELLO TO MELANIE AN' ORLEY.

HI, ORLEY.

HI, MELANIE.

DON'T EXPECT **THOSE TWO** TO SHOW ANY **MANNERS!** THEY'RE TOO WRAPPED UP IN THEIR **CHESS GAME!**

WHAT'S THE **CHURCH-MUSIC GUY** DOIN' HERE?

SAMMY'S BEEN LIVIN' HERE AT THE **WHEELERY** SINCE THAT **DIXIE PATRIOT** STORY LOST HIM HIS **JOB.**

ORLEY, DON'T GET US SIDETRACKED ONTO SAMMY NOONE.

I WANNA HEAR WHAT MAVIS THINKS OF OUR PLAN.

Y'SEE, MAVIS, **ORLEY** AN' I HAVE BEEN WRACKIN' OUR BRAINS FOR **DAYS,** TRYIN' TO THINK WHAT TOLAND AN' GINGER CAN **DO** ABOUT THE **BABY,** AN'—

ABOUT THE...

!

YOU DIDN'T KNOW...?

RILEY! SAMMY! TOLAND AN' GINGER ARE GONNA HAVE A **BABY!!**

TOLAND... I'M **SORRY!**

IT NEVER **OCCURRED** TO ME THAT YOU HADN'T **TOLD** THE FOLKS **HERE!**

NOW IN **NINE** OUT OF **TEN** CLAYFIELD HOMES, AN ANNOUNCEMENT LIKE **MELANIE'S** MIGHT HAVE BEEN GREETED WITH **DISAPPROVAL** OR **DISMAY.**

BUT THE **WHEELERY** CROWD HAD **NEVER** BEEN YOUR **AVERAGE BIBLE-BELT BUNCH!** IN FACT...

...EVERYONE'S FIRST REACTION WAS SO **CELEBRATORY,** YOU'D THINK CONCEIVING A **BABY** OUT OF **WEDLOCK** WAS AKIN TO WINNING THE **IRISH SWEEPSTAKES!**

I DID NOTICE **GINGER** AND **RILEY** SHOOTING QUICK **LOOKS** AT EACH OTHER...

...AND I **WONDERED** WHAT THE TWO OF 'EM WERE **THINKING.**

SO...WHAT DOES THIS **MEAN,** EXACTLY?

DO Y'ALL PLAN TO GET **MARRIED?**

WELL-L-L...

OF **COURSE** THEY'LL GET **MARRIED!**

THAT'S WHAT YOU **DO** WHEN A BABY'S ON THE WAY.

SOMETIMES EVEN **BEFORE** THAT!

BUT IT **WON'T** BE JUST **THEIR** BABY!

WE'RE ALL OF US KINDA LIKE ONE **FAMILY.** IT'LL BE **EVERYBODY'S** BABY!

WHY ISN'T IT THAT **SIMPLE?**

IT'S NOT THAT **SIMPLE,** SAMMY.

LISTEN, FOLKS, LET'S DON'T OVERLOOK THE **POSSIBILITY** THAT GINGER AN' MY BROTHER MIGHT HAVE **PROBLEMS** THAT'D MAKE IT **NOT** SO **SMART** FOR THEM TO GET MARRIED.

UH... MELANIE...

...IF THERE **ARE,** THEY CAN FILL THE REST OF US IN **IF** THEY WANT TO, **WHEN** THEY WANT TO. IT'S NONE OF OUR **BUSINESS,** IS WHAT I'M SAYIN'!

I'M **NOT** SAYIN' THERE **ARE** ANY SUCH PROBLEMS. MAYBE THERE **ARE,** MAYBE THERE **AREN'T!**...

MELANIE...

NOW DON'T **INTERRUPT** ME! THERE'S A **POINT** I'M WORKIN' MY WAY AROUND TO!

154

Y'SEE, **ORLEY** AN' **I** ARE HERE WITH A **PROPOSAL** FOR YOU.

IN A **NUTSHELL:** ORLEY AN' I WANT TO **ADOPT** THE BABY **OURSELVES.**

IF YOU TWO COULD JUST SEE YOUR WAY **CLEAR** TO...

PLEASE SAY **YES.**

YOUR FIRST INSTINCT WAS **RIGHT**, MELANIE...

...IT **WOULD'VE** BEEN BETTER TO ASK US IN **PRIVATE.**

WE **PROBABLY** SHOULD TELL IT TO GINGER AN' TOLAND IN **PRIVATE.**

BUT SINCE Y'ALL ARE ALL STANDIN' THERE **LOOKIN'** AT US **ANYWAY,** WE MIGHT AS WELL JUST COME ON **OUT** WITH IT!

I SUGGESTED THAT MELANIE AND ORLEY AND GINGER AND I ADJOURN TO THE **PORCH,** WHERE WE COULD **BACK UP,** TAKE A **DEEP BREATH,** AND TALK THINGS THROUGH **CALMLY.**

GINGER WAS **TOUCHED** BY MELANIE'S OFFER...

&

...AND SHE **KNEW** HOW MUCH MY SISTER WANTED TO BE A **MOM.**

SHE WASN'T SURE HOW **UNEASY** IT WOULD MAKE HER, THOUGH, TO KNOW THAT THE **BABY** SHE'D CARRIED WAS GROWING UP SO CLOSE AT **HAND.**

I ADMIT I'VE **THOUGHT** ABOUT SIGNIN' THE BABY OVER TO AN **ADOPTION AGENCY.**

I'VE SPENT TIME **IMAGININ'** MYSELF DOIN' IT... AN' IT SEEMS LIKE — AS **HARD** AS THE SEPARATION WOULD **BE** — IT'D ONLY BE HAPPENIN' TO US **ONCE.**

YOU SIGN THE **PAPERS** AN' THAT'S **IT!** YOUR HEART GETS TORN UP **ONE TIME.**

BUT IF THE BABY WAS WITH **YOU...** WHAT WOULD THAT BE **LIKE?**

HOW COULD I KEEP MYSELF FROM **MEDDLIN'** IF I KNEW THAT THE BABY I'D CARRIED WAS RIGHT THERE AT **YOUR** HOUSE... **DAY** AFTER **DAY... YEAR** AFTER **YEAR?**

TRYIN' **NOT** TO MEDDLE WOULD BE LIKE BEIN' CUT OFF FROM MY BABY **OVER** AN' **OVER** AGAIN.

WE **WOULDN'T** BE TRYIN' TO FREEZE YOU OR TOLAND **OUT,** GINGER.

IT'S SOMETHIN' THE **FOUR** OF US COULD WORK **OUT.**

ORLEY AN' I CAN **HANDLE** SOME OUTSIDE MEDDLIN' FROM 'AUNT GINGER' AN' 'UNCLE TOLAND'!

IT'S PROBABLY **LESS MEDDLIN'** THAN **MAMA** AN' **DADDY** WOULD BE DOIN' IF **THEY** WERE STILL ALIVE.

MELANIE WOULDN'T TURN US **LOOSE** UNTIL WE'D **PROMISED** TO GIVE SERIOUS **THOUGHT** TO HER PROPOSAL.

WE MUST'VE STARTED **KEEPING** OUR PROMISE RIGHT **OFF**, SINCE NEITHER OF US SPOKE A **WORD** DURING OUR DRIVE BACK TO **WESTHILLS**.

I'M JUST NOT **SURE**...

IT'S **TOUGH**.

WE'LL TALK.

YEAH.

WHERE'S **SAMMY**?

OUT BY THE **TREE HOUSE**.

WHAT'S HE DOIN' **THERE**?

COMMUNIN' WITH **NATURE**, I GUESS.

GOT THE KID **RAFFLED OFF** YET?

YOU DON'T **LIKE** MELANIE'S IDEA ABOUT HER AN' ORLEY ADOPTIN' THE BABY?

YOU DON'T KNOW HOW **LUCKY** YOU ARE, TOLAND.

BABIES JUST **FALL** INTO THE **LAPS** OF YOU STRAIGHT GUYS, WHETHER YOU **WANT** 'EM OR **NOT**!

I'VE ALWAYS WISHED **I** COULD RAISE A KID.

I'D WORK SO **HARD** TO DO IT **RIGHT**. I REALLY **WOULD**.

Chapter 19

MAVIS HAD GROWN UP IN RIDGELINE, **TOO.**

THAT'S HOW SHE KNEW **SAMMY.**

SO WHEN SHE HEARD THAT SAMMY AND I WERE DRIVING **UP** THERE, SHE ASKED IF SHE COULD COME **ALONG.**

RILEY WASN'T **THRILLED** ABOUT GETTING **LEFT BEHIND** FOR THE DAY, BUT HE WASN'T INCLINED TO MAKE THE **TRIP,** EITHER.

SPENDIN' ALL OF THAT **WEEKEND TIME** COOPED UP IN A **CAR** JUST DOESN'T SUIT MY **MOOD** SOMEHOW.

HE **REALLY** BRISTLED WHEN MAVIS SUGGESTED TAKING **LOCO** ALONG.

YOU HAVEN'T HAD A GOOD **CAR RIDE** IN A **LONG** TIME, HAVE YOU, LOCO?

OH, YA **DON'T!**

SAMMY AN' TOLAND ARE **ALREADY** STEALIN' MY **GIRLFRIEND** ON SATURDAY.

THEY **CAN'T** HAVE MY DAMN **DOG, TOO!**

NOW, DON'T **SULK,** RILEY!

I **TOLD** YOU SAMMY'S **PROMISED** TO GET US **HOME** IN TIME FOR YOU AN' ME TO HIT A **DOUBLE-FEATURE** THAT NIGHT AT THE **DRIVE-IN.**

LOCO **LOVES** THE **DRIVE-IN.** HE CAN COME **WITH** US.

YEAH, **LOCO** CAN KEEP TRACK OF WHAT'S **HAPPENIN'** ON THE **SCREEN** WHILE **YOU** TWO **SMOOCH** IT UP!

I ASKED **GINGER** IF SHE WANTED TO COME TO RIDGELINE. SHE TURNED **GREEN** AT THE PROSPECT.

A **LONG CAR TRIP** STARTIN' **EARLY** IN THE **MORNIN'?**

I DON-N-N'T **THINK** SO, HON!

BESIDES, I'VE GOT A **TERM PAPER** TO OUTLINE.

IT **HAUNTED** HER LATER THAT SHE'D MISSED **OUT** ON SPENDING THAT SATURDAY WITH SAMMY, GIVEN WHAT ENDED UP **HAPPENING** BEFORE SUNDAY'S **SUN** CAME UP.

I **REMEMBER** THAT SATURDAY MORNING FOR THE CRISP, TENACIOUS BED OF **FROST** THAT JUST DIDN'T SEEM TO WANNA GIVE **GROUND** TO THE **SUN.**

YOU HAD TO **ADMIRE** THE WAY IT WAS TRYING TO MAKE SOMETHING **PRETTY** OUT OF THE PATCHES OF **STUBBLY GRASS** WE CALLED A **LAWN.**

I WAS ON THE PORCH SIPPING **COFFEE** WHEN **RILEY** CAME AMBLING OUT TO **JOIN** ME.

THAT **SURPRISED** ME. RILEY AND I HADN'T EXCHANGED AN UNAWKWARD **WORD** SINCE THE NIGHT HE WENT TO BED WITH **GINGER.**

SO... Y'GOT THE PLACE TO **YOURSELF** TODAY.

THINKIN' ABOUT INVITIN' **GINGER** OVER?

BROACHING **DELICATE SUBJECTS** IN THE **CLUMSIEST** WAY **POSSIBLE** IS KIND OF A **SPECIALTY** OF MINE.

GINGER'S MADE IT **CLEAR** THAT WHAT HAPPENED LAST WEEK WAS A **ONE-TIME THING.**

AN' **YOU'RE** OF THE SAME **MIND?**

ARE YOU TRYIN' TO LAY SOME **CLAIM** ON HER, BY ANY **CHANCE...?**

...'CAUSE I **HAVEN'T** NOTICED **YOU** OUT SHOPPIN' FOR **WEDDING RINGS** LATELY!

SHITFIRE, RILEY! **YOU** AIN'T EXACTLY A **WALKIN' ADVERTISEMENT** FOR THE INSTITUTION OF **MARRIAGE!**

WHAT WOULD YOUR HERO **HUGH HEFNER** THINK ABOUT YOU LOOKIN' DOWN YOUR **NOSE** AT ME FOR NOT RACIN' TO THE **ALTAR?**

IF IT'S A **WEDDING RING** THAT MAKES THE DIFFERENCE, I GUESS I WOULDN'T BE OUT OF LINE ASKIN' **MAVIS** FOR A ROLL IN THE HAY!

'SCUSE ME IF I DON'T LOSE SLEEP WORRYIN' ABOUT **THAT,** PAL.

I **KNOW** WHERE I STAND WITH **MAVIS.**

LOOK, I DON'T **LIKE** THE WORD **MARRIAGE.** I'VE NEVER MADE ANY **BONES** ABOUT THAT. MAVIS FEELS THE **SAME.**

BUT I AIN'T **HUGH HEFNER** AN' MAVIS AIN'T NOBODY'S **'BUNNY'!**

AN' NEITHER IS **GINGER...** Y'KNOW?

SHE'S A **FREE AGENT.** SHE CAN MAKE HER **OWN DECISIONS,** AS I SEE IT.

BUT THAT DOESN'T MEAN I'VE GOT ANY **INTENTION** OF COMIN' **BETWEEN** THE TWO OF YOU.

'SPECIALLY WITH GINGER **PREGNANT**. **THAT** GOT SPRUNG ON ME OUTA **LEFT FIELD**!

OF COURSE, YOU AN' I **BOTH** KNOW THAT YOU CAN GET **BACK** AT ME IF YOU'RE SO INCLINED BY TELLIN' **MAVIS** ABOUT—

♪O.K.♪ TOLAND!

SAMMY AN' I ARE **READY** TO **GO**! *Yurf!*

NO, **NO**, LOCO. **WE GO**! **YOU** DON'T **GO** NOW! **YOU** GO LATER!

Woof! Woof!

OOPS! I ALMOST FORGOT MY **ENVELOPE**.

WHAT'S **IN** THAT PRECIOUS ENVELOPE OF YOURS **ANYWAY**?

YOU'LL SEE.

IT'S MY **SHOW-AN'-TELL**!

I WON'T SPILL ANY BEANS TO **MAVIS**. IT'S NOT MY **PLACE** TO.

'BYE, RILEY.

WE'LL SEE YOU **LATE** THIS **AFTERNOON**.

TURN ON THE **RADIO**. I WANT **MUSIC**!

♪Walk Right In! Sit right down! Daddy, let your mind roll on!♪

Burma Shave

SAMMY HADN'T GIVEN HIS FOLKS A **WORD** OF **WARNING** THAT HE WAS ABOUT TO PAY THEM A **VISIT**.

HE DIDN'T WANT TO GIVE 'EM TIME TO DIG THE **BARBED WIRE** AND **LAND MINES** OUT OF STORAGE, HE SAID.

DINAH!

MISTER **SAMMY**! I DON'T **BELIEVE** WHAT I'M **SEEIN'**!

YOU COME HERE RIGHT THIS **MINUTE** AN' GIVE ME A **HUG**!

I HAVEN'T SEEN **YOU** SINCE— WELL... NEVER MIND ABOUT ALL **THAT.**

THIS IS MY PAL **TOLAND**... AN' YOU REMEMBER **MAVIS.**

H'LO.

LEMME RUN TELL YOUR **FOLKS** THAT YOU'RE HERE—

NOW DON'T TRY **PRETENDIN'** THAT THEY'LL BE **GLAD** TO **SEE** ME.

I'LL JUST DASH IN AN' **SURPRISE** 'EM. SHH! IT'LL BE **FUN!**

BUT—

YOO-HOO! ANYBODY **HOME?**

SAMMY?

HIYA, RACHEL. WHERE'S **DADDY?**

YOUR **FATHER?** YOU CAN'T—

NEVER MIND...I'M SURE I CAN **FIND** HIM!

I KNOW ALL HIS FAVORITE **PLACES.**

BUT YOU MUSTN'T— **SAMMY!**

HE'S EVEN **SICKER** THAN YOU **REMEMBER.**

SAMMY! COME **BACK** HERE!

EARL! COME HELP!

EARL!

HEY, WHAT ARE WE IN THE **MIDDLE** OF?!

AH.

HI, DADDY.

CUTHEL NOONE DIDN'T MOVE A **MUSCLE** AT THE SIGHT OF HIS SON **BARGING** THROUGH THE BIG **DOORWAY** AND **STALKING** TOWARD HIM.

HE **COULDN'T** MOVE A MUSCLE!

SAMMY HADN'T BEEN **KIDDING** ABOUT THE **EXTENT** OF HIS FATHER'S **PARALYSIS.**

THE OLD MAN WAS **DEFENSELESS.**

SAMMY!

DON'T HURT HIM!

GET AWAY FROM HIM, SAMMY!

I'M WARNIN' YOU, CUZ: WE'LL CALL THE POLICE IF WE HAVE TO—

BACK OFF, EARL'!

BACK OFF OR I DUMP HIM!

UNH!

BACK OFF AN' HE'LL BE SAFE.

SAMMY... DON'T!

I JUST WANNA TALK TO HIM.

SAMMY— SHOW SOME COMPASSION... PLEASE!

Chapter 20

THEN WE MOVED ON TO **OTHER** SUBJECTS AND I LOST TRACK OF **TIME** ...TIL **MAVIS** BROKE IN.

WHEN WE GOT BACK TO THE **WHEELERY,** I TELEPHONED **GINGER** AND TOLD HER ALL ABOUT OUR WEIRD TRIP TO **RIDGELINE.**

TOLAND, I'M **SORRY...** I'VE JUST **GOTTA** INTERRUPT YOU.

HOLD **ON** A SEC, GINGER. **MAVIS** WANTS SOMETHIN'.

BE 'A HONEY AN' GO **LOOK IN** ON **SAMMY.** I'D DO IT, BUT I'VE GOT **SUPPER** COMIN' OFF THE STOVE.

WHY? WHAT'S WITH **SAMMY?**

HE'S BEEN HITTIN' THE **BOTTLE** SO HARD SINCE WE GOT HOME, IT'S **WORRYIN'** ME.

REALLY? I THOUGHT HE WAS IN A **GREAT** MOOD.

MAYBE HE'S JUST **CELEBRATIN'.**

COULD **BE...** BUT IT DOESN'T HAVE THAT **FEEL** TO ME.

I'VE GOTTA **GO,** GINGER.

YOU'RE LOOKIN' DOWNRIGHT **STONKERED,** FELLA.

SHOULD YOU MAYBE SLOW **DOWN...?**

JUST **WINDIN'** DOWN FROM A **THRILL-PACKED DAY!**

I HOPE YOU FEEL **GOOD** ABOUT TALKIN' TO YOUR **DAD** TODAY. WHATEVER **COMES** OF IT, YOU **NEEDED** TO GET THAT STUFF OFF YOUR **CHEST.**

MAVIS AN' I WERE **PROUD** OF YOU.

YOU **WERE?**

WHAT A **COINCIDENCE!** **I** WAS PROUD OF MYSELF, **TOO!**

THE **ONLY** THING THAT WOULD'VE MADE ME **PROUDER** WOULD BE IF I'D **DRIBBLED** THE OL' BASTARD AROUND THE ROOM LIKE A **BASKETBALL** AN' **DROP-KICKED** HIM OUT THE **WINDOW!**

BUT IF I'D DONE **THAT,** HE MIGHT NOT'VE GIVEN ME MY **HAMMOND!**

I THINK I'M GONNA PUT IT **RIGHT...** OVER. THERE....

LOOK, IT'S **SUPPERTIME.** THINK YOU CAN WOBBLE YOUR WAY TO THE **KITCHEN?**

SAMMY MADE IT TO THE **TABLE** AND MANAGED TO STAY PRETTY NEAR **VERTICAL**, GIVE OR TAKE A **FEW** DEGREES...

...BUT WITH HIM **RAVING** AND **FLAILING** THE WHOLE TIME, IT WAS ONE OF THE **LEAST RELAXING** MEALS IN HUMAN **HISTORY.**

YOU COULD **SEE** THAT **RILEY** WAS GETTING MORE AND MORE **PISSED.**

EVENTUALLY SAMMY MADE **ONE** TOO MANY **FLIPPANT REMARKS** ABOUT CUTHEL'S **IMMOBILITY** AND RILEY'S **TEMPER** SNAPPED.

THIS IS ALL GETTIN' TO BE **JUST** A BIT **MUCH!**

THE MAN IS **PARALYZED!**

THAT **AIN'T** NO FUCKIN' **JOKE!**

YOU **EXPECT** THE **REST** OF US TO SIT AROUND AN' **DESPISE** YOUR **FATHER** RIGHT **ALONG** WITH YOU, BUT— **MY GOD,** SAMMY!...

...BASTARD OR **NOT,** IT SOUNDS LIKE THE GUY'S BEIN' PUT THROUGH A PRETTY HEFTY **WRINGER** FOR HIS **SINS!**

NOT HEFTY ENOUGH TO SUIT **ME!**

WELL, **LET'S** JUST MAKE SAMMY NOONE **JUDGE** OF THE **UNIVERSE,** THEN!

HOW WOULD **YOU** LIKE TO GET STUCK IN A BODY LIKE YOUR OL' MAN'S?

tap, tap.

IT COULD **HAPPEN.** SOME DISEASES GET **INHERITED.**

AN' HERE COMES SOME **WILD MAN** STORMIN' INTO YOUR HOUSE, SCREAMIN' 'BOUT WHAT A **SHITHEAD** YOU ARE!

Y'GOT NO **WAY** TO SAY YOU'RE **SORRY!** Y'GOT NO WAY TO GIVE HIM THE **FINGER!**

YOU'RE **WAY** PAST BEIN' ABLE TO MAKE **AMENDS** FOR PAST **FAILINGS!**

DAMN IF I CAN'T MUSTER SOME **SYMPATHY** FOR A MAN IN THAT **FIX!**

Y'KNOW, I **WASN'T** JUST SOME **STRAY PSYCHO** BARGIN' IN ON HIM TODAY!

I'M HIS **SON!** ...AN' I'VE GOT AMPLE **CAUSE** TO BE MAD AT HIM!

THE MOVIE STARTS **SOON**, MAVE.

AN' AT THE TIME THAT HE **SHAFTED** ME, HE COULD WIGGLE MOST ANY **PART** OF HIMSELF THAT HE **WANTED** TO!

COULD WE CHANGE THE **SUBJECT**, PLEASE...?

LET **ME** DO THE **DISHES** FOR YOU, MAVIS. SOUNDS LIKE RILEY'S **RESTLESS** TO GET TO THE **DRIVE-IN**.

JUST PILE 'EM IN THE **SINK**. I'LL WASH 'EM **TOMORROW**.

I'D **RATHER** YOU KEEP AN EYE ON **YOU-KNOW-WHO** THIS EVENIN'.

TOLE AN' I CAN PUT ON SOME FRILLY **APRONS** AN' DO THE DISHES **TOGETHER**, MAVIS!

DON'T YOU GO WITHIN A **MILE** OF THAT DINNERWARE, HON. WE CAN'T AFFORD THE **BREAKAGE!**

THE HEAD OF THE HOUSEHOLD HATH **SPOKEN**, SAMMY!

VEDDY WELL.

AT YOUR **INSISTENCE**, I SHALL **FOR-SWEAR** ALL HOUSEWORK.

OOPS! ALMOST KNOCKED THAT **OVER**, DIDN'T I?

Bonk!

LET'S HIT THE **ROAD!**

C'MON, LOCO!

LEMME GRAB MY **COAT**.

Yurf!

I **HATE** TO ASK YOU TO STAY AN' **BABYSIT** WITH HIM, BUT—

I DON'T MIND.

C'MON, **EASE UP** ON THE **BOOZE**, BUDDY.

YOU'RE STEWED ENOUGH FOR **FIVE** PEOPLE.

I'VE **TRIED** SOBER! IT DOESN'T **SUFFICE!**

ARE YOU **DEPRESSED?**

JUST **REFLECTIN'** ON THE DAY'S EVENTS.

IT'S **DEGRADIN',** TOLE!...

...OR MAYBE Y'DIDN'T **NOTICE...**

...HAVIN' TO **BEG** MY OWN **FATHER** FOR A LITTLE **RESPECT!**

WHY DID I PUT MYSELF **THROUGH** THAT?

WHY IS IT THAT THE **ONLY** WAY I COULD GET HIM TO **LOOK** ME IN THE **EYE** WAS BY WAITIN' 'TIL HE WAS TOO **INCAPACITATED** TO LOOK ANYWHERE **ELSE?**

STILL, WASN'T THAT A **LUMINOUS SPARKLE** I BROUGHT TO HIS EYE WHEN I WAVED THAT **NEWS-PAPER** HEADLINE IN HIS FACE? WHAT A **CHOICE PAGE** FOR MY **MEMORY BOOK!**

O.K., SO NOW YOU'VE **FACED** HIM **DOWN.**

YOU'VE **HAD** YOUR **SAY.**

MAYBE HE'LL BE **WILLIN'** TO HELP YOU **OUT...** MAYBE HE **WON'T.** (HERE, LEMME HAVE A **SWIG** O' THAT....)

SUPPOSE HE'S **NOT** WILLIN'? CAN YOU JUST **ACCEPT** THAT, LEAVE THE FUCKER **BEHIND,** AN' GO **ON** WITH YOUR LIFE?

SURE!

OH, **NATURALLY** THERE'D BE A FEW **LOOSE ENDS** TO TIE UP...

...LIKE **MURDERING** HIM. BUT BEYOND **THAT,** I EXPECT A FULL AN' COMPLETE **RECOVERY.**

IN FACT, EVEN AS WE **SPEAK** I FEEL MY SPIRITS **BOUNCIN' BACK** FROM THE PIT OF **DESPONDENCY!**

I FEEL **EXPANSIVE...** AN' **ADORABLE...** LIKE I COULD MAKE GREAT **LOVE** WITH SOMEONE TONIGHT!

HOW **ABOUT** IT?

WHAT? WITH ME??

COME ON, TOLAND. IT'LL FEEL GREAT!

BE EXPERIMENTAL. TRY A KISS. I PROMISE YOU IT'LL BE SUPER!

NOT A GOOD IDEA, PAL!

C'MON.

IT'S A GOOD TIME TO PLAY.

NOBODY'S HERE.

JUST A KISS, FOR STARTERS.

HEY! SAMMY!

THAT'S ENOUGH!

I'M SERIOUS!

STOP IT!

JESUS!

Sigh!... IT'D BE REALLY NICE TO MAKE LOVE WITH SOMEONE TONIGHT. SOMEONE WHO'S A FRIEND.

IT'D BE JUST LOVELY.

BUT I WAS JUST **TEASIN'** YOU. I **COULDN'T** HAVE SEX WITH YOU TONIGHT **ANYWAY.**

I'M **WAY** TOO **DRUNK.**

MY **WEEWEE'S** ALL **LIMP.**

BUT Y'KNOW, TOLAND... IT'S **NOT** LIKE YOUR **FLESH** WOULD FALL OFF YOUR BONES IF YOU **DID** MAKE LOVE TO ME.

IT MIGHT NOT BE WHAT YOU **DREAM** OF, BUT IT'D PROBABLY BE A LOT MORE **AGREEABLE** THAN YOU **THINK.**

DON'T **LOWER** YOURSELF, SAMMY.

MAKE LOVE WITH PEOPLE WHO **WANT** TO MAKE LOVE WITH **YOU.**

I THINK IT'S **YOU** WHO'S WORRIED ABOUT **'LOWERING'** HIMSELF.

I THINK THAT, AS MUCH AS YOU MAY **LIKE** ME AS A **PERSON,** YOU THINK THAT IT WOULD **'LOWER'** YOU TO MAKE **LOVE** TO ME...

BECAUSE IN YOUR HEART OF **HEARTS,** YOU THINK THAT **STRAIGHT** PEOPLE LIKE **YOU** ARE **BETTER** THAN **GAY** PEOPLE LIKE ME.

UH...

IT'S O.K., TOLAND. IT MEANS A **LOT** THAT YOU **LIKE** ME.

ANYWAY, **LES** LOVES ME. HE'S TOLD ME ANY **NUMBER** OF TIMES.

SO I'M **NOT** BEREFT OF **SUITORS.**

OH, **LOOK** WHAT FELL OUT OF YOUR **POCKET!**

YOUR **CAR KEYS!** SA-Y-Y!...I KNOW A **FUN** THING TO DO!

SAMMY, **GIVE** ME THOSE.

LET'S GO FOR A **DRIVE.** THERE'S SOMETHIN' I WANNA **SHOW** YOU.

FELLA, **YOU'RE** NOT IN SHAPE TO GO **ANYWHERE!**

DO **YOU** WANNA DO THE **DRIVIN'** OR SHALL **I?**

AGAINST MY BETTER **JUDGMENT,** I AGREED TO DRIVE SAMMY TO **WHEREVER** IT WAS HE WANTED TO **GO...**

...WHICH HE INSISTED ON BEING **SECRETIVE** ABOUT.

I WAS HOPING THE CHILLY NIGHT **AIR** WOULD SOBER HIM **UP.**

SEE THAT **HOUSE** THIS SIDE OF THE **FORK?** PARK BY THE **DRIVEWAY.**

I DIDN'T KNOW HOW FAR **GONE** HE WAS.

GOOD! THE **LIGHTS** ARE ON. SOMEBODY'S **HOME.**

WHO **IS** IT WE'RE DROPPIN' **IN** ON?

DAMNED IF **I** KNOW!

ALL **I** KNOW IS: THIS IS WHERE THE **DIXIE PATRIOT** GETS PUT TOGETHER.

WHAT??

LES SHOWED IT TO ME ONE TIME.

I'VE DECIDED TO FOLLOW **MAVIS'S** EXCELLENT **SUGGESTION.**

SAMMY! GET BACK IN THE **CAR!**

Ding, Dong!

YES?

HOLLIS! A **MAN'S** HERE ASKIN' ABOUT THE **PAPER!**

MA'AM, I'M TOLD THIS IS WHERE THE **DIXIE PATRIOT** GETS EDITED. IS THAT **RIGHT?**

I **APOLOGIZE** FOR BOTHERIN' YOU ON A **WEEK-END,** BUT Y'SEE...

...I'M THE **PERVERT** WHO USED TO BE IN THE EMPLOY OF THAT **RACEMIXIN'** CHURCH Y'ALL LIKE TO WRITE ABOUT.

REMEMBER? YOU RAN A **PICTURE** OF ME ON THE **FRONT PAGE.**

Groan!

IT WAS A REAL **NIFTY PHOTO...**

AN' IT MADE ME WONDER IF I COULD ORDER A FEW **DUPLICATE PRINTS** OF IT FOR MY **FRIENDS** AN' **LOVED ONES.**

HOLLIS!

WE'RE COMIN'! WHO'D HE SAY HE WAS?

IT'S THE **FAG** FROM TRINITY.

YOU'RE KIDDIN'!

WE'RE **LEAVIN',** FOLKS! DON'T GIVE THIS CRAZY SON OF A BITCH A **SECOND THOUGHT!**

LESSEE... I'LL NEED ONE FOR MY **DADDY...** AN' ONE FOR MY **CHARMIN'** STEPMOTHER, **RACHEL...**

...AN' ONE FOR MY FAVORITE **NEGRO, LESTER...**

...AN' ONE FOR —

OH, **LOOK!**

LOOK WHO'S **IN** THERE!

IT'S MY FAVORITE **LAW ENFORCEMENT OFFICIAL!**

WHEN WE GOT **HOME**, I SET ABOUT CONFISCATING EVERY DROP OF **ALCOHOL** ON THE **PREMISES**...

* DON'T PUT YOURSELF **OUT** SO, TOLAND. *

...EXCEPT FOR THE '**RUBBING**' KIND WE DOUSED ON SAMMY'S **SCRAPES**.

I SHOVED THE JUMBLE OF **CANS** AND **BOTTLES** UNDER MY BED, SO SAMMY COULDN'T GET **AT** 'EM EVEN AFTER I'D GONE TO **SLEEP**.

* YOU'RE SUCH A **BUSY BEE**! *

THAT DONE, I **COLLAPSED**... STARED AT THE **CEILING**...

...AND WENT **NUMB**.

MY MIND **DRIFTED** AND **SPUN**...

...'TIL I HEARD A **NOISE**...

...WHICH I TOOK TO BE SAMMY **BARFING** OUT IN THE **YARD**.

SAMMY...?

I WALKED OUT THE **BACK DOOR** TO MAKE SURE HE FELT **STEADY** ENOUGH TO GET BACK **INSIDE**.

AND THAT'S ALL I **REMEMBER**.

KRAK

Chapter 21

SOMETIME LATER I PICKED MY SWOLLEN **FACE** UP OUT OF THE **DIRT**.

A **HEADACHE** WAS DRUMMING ON THE INSIDE OF MY SKULL, MIXED WITH FAMILIAR **VOICES** AND A RELENTLESS **DOG'S BARK**.

WHEN THE ONE **EYE** THAT I COULD GET TO OPEN HAD STOPPED **PULSING** ENOUGH TO **FOCUS**, I REALIZED THAT SOMETHING **SPOOKY** WAS GOING ON.

BEAMS OF **LIGHT** WERE SHOOTING THROUGH THE NIGHT INTO THE **WOODS** BEHIND THE **WHEELERY**.

SCOPING OUT THE **SOURCE** OF THE LIGHT DIDN'T MAKE THINGS ANY **LESS** SPOOKY!

RILEY'S **STUDEBAKER** WAS IDLING IN THE DRIVEWAY WITHOUT A SOUL **IN** IT—BUT WITH ITS **HEADLIGHTS** SHINING **BRIGHT**.

THEN I **TURNED** AND SAW THAT THE HEADLIGHT BEAMS WERE AIMED AT THE **CLEARING** NEXT TO THE **TREE HOUSE**...

...AND AT **MAVIS** AND **RILEY**.

THEY **GESTURED** AND **YELLED** AT ME KIND OF **CRAZILY**...

...BUT I COULDN'T MAKE ANY OF THEIR **WORDS** FIT **TOGETHER**.

THEY SURE SUCCEEDED IN **ALARMING** ME, THOUGH, AND I RAN TO SEE WHAT WAS **WRONG**.

THE **CLOSER** I GOT, THE MORE **AGITATED** THEY SEEMED TO BECOME...

...AND BEFORE I COULD MAKE OUT WHAT THEY WERE TRYING TO **WARN** ME ABOUT...

...I BLUNDERED **INTO** IT **FULL FORCE**...

...AND WENT **SPRAWLING**.

BUMP!

BOTH YOUR HOUSEMATES SAID HE LOOKED **DEPRESSED** WHEN THEY LEFT FOR THE MOVIES.

THEY SAID HE'D BEEN **DRINKIN'** PRETTY HEAVY.

THAT WAS SOME **FIGHT** HE HAD WITH HIS FOLKS IN **RIDGE-LINE**, WOULDN'T Y'SAY?

I WOULDN'T CALL IT A '**FIGHT**'!

ARE YOU AWARE THAT HIS **STEP-MOTHER** SWORE OUT A **COMPLAINT** AGAINST HIM EARLIER IN THE DAY?

SHE **DID**?

YEP. FOR **ASSAULT.**

NO. NOBODY **TOLD** ME.

BUT YOU'RE ON THE WRONG **TRACK.** WHOEVER KILLED **SAMMY** KNOCKED **ME** OUT COLD WHILE HE WAS **AT** IT.

DID YOU **SEE** WHO HIT YOU?

NO.

SO IT **COULD'VE** BEEN MR. NOONE **HIMSELF**?

THAT'S **RIDICULOUS!** HE WAS MY **FRIEND!**

Scratch, scratch!

WE'RE **NOT** SAYIN' THAT'S WHAT **HAPPENED.**

IT'S OUR **JOB** TO EXPLORE ALL THE **ALTERNA-TIVES.**

WE LOOK AT **EVERY** ANGLE.

MAYBE HE'D **DECIDED** WHAT HE WAS GONNA **DO** AN' DIDN'T WANT **INTERFERENCE** FROM **YOU.**

WHEN YOU'RE DEALIN' WITH **HOMOSEXUALS,** YOU'RE **NOT** DEALIN' WITH THE MOST **STABLE** CRITTERS AROUND!

Chuckle!

SO WHAT DO YOU THINK ABOUT THAT **NOTE** HE LEFT BEHIND?

SAMMY DIDN'T **WRITE** THAT.

A FEW HOURS **EARLIER** HE WAS USIN' THOSE **SAME WORDS** TO DESCRIBE HIMSELF TO HIS **FATHER,** ACCORDIN' TO MAVIS GREEN.

Y'SEE, HOMOSEXUALS CARRY AROUND ALL SORTS OF **GUILT** ABOUT THESE **SICK DRIVES** OF THEIRS.

Chapter 22

MAVIS PUT OUT SOME **FEELERS** AMONG PEOPLE SHE STILL KNEW BACK **HOME** ABOUT US MAYBE **ATTENDING.**

SAMMY'S **FOLKS** GAVE HIM ABOUT AS **INCONSPICUOUS** A FUNERAL UP IN RIDGELINE AS THEY COULD **MANAGE** AND STILL HAVE IT BE IN A **CHURCH.**

THE WORD SHE GOT **BACK** WAS THAT ANY OF SAMMY'S **CLAYFIELD COHORTS** WOULD BE EMPHATICALLY **UNWELCOME** AT THE **SERVICE.**

IN FACT, THEY'D BE FORCIBLY **STOPPED** AT THE CHURCH **DOOR** IF THEY **CAME.**

THAT LEFT **WAY** TOO MUCH **FREE-FLOATING GRIEF** FOR THOSE OF US WHO'D ACTUALLY **CARED** ABOUT SAMMY TO HANDLE **INDIVIDUALLY...**

ALLEYSAX

...SO MABEL, MARGE AND EFFIE DECIDED THEY'D THROW A **PARTY** AT **ALLEYSAX** WHERE WE COULD ALL **REMEMBER** SAMMY—AND SAY **GOODBYE** TO HIM—**TOGETHER.**

GINGER WAS **TENSE** DURING THE DRIVE OUT TO ALLEYSAX. SHE'D HAD SO LITTLE TO **SAY** TO ME SINCE SAMMY WAS KILLED, IT WAS **UNNERVING.**

I SUSPECTED SHE WAS ONE BIG **EXPLOSION** JUST WAITING TO GET **TRIGGERED**, BUT I COULDN'T FIGURE OUT ANY GRACEFUL WAY TO STAY OUT OF **SHRAPNEL** RANGE.

LOOK, GINGER! **SHILOH'S** OUT OF THE **HOSPITAL!**

SHILOH! WE DIDN'T KNOW YOU WERE OUT OF **BED** YET!

HIYA, MACON. **HI,** ROSE.

HI, LOTTIE. I'M **TOLAND POLK.** REMEMBER **ME?** WE MET OUT AT **RATTLER HILL.**

HELLO.

TOLE... GIN... I... UH...

SHILOH'S **BETTER** THAN HE **WAS,** BUT — UMM —

THE **DOCTORS** THOUGHT IT'D BOOST HIS **SPIRITS** IF WE BROUGHT HIM OUT TONIGHT TO HEAR HIS **FREEDOM CHORUS** SING.

I'M **GLAD** I'M GLAD YOU COULD **COME** TONIGHT, SHILOH.

I'M GONNA BE SINGIN', **TOO.**

I... UH... GOOD.

IT'S **HARD,** SEEIN' SHILOH LIKE THAT, **ISN'T** IT?

I **PROMISED** I'D SING SOMETHIN'... BUT MY **THROAT** FEELS LIKE IT'S GOT A **LOG** STUCK IN IT.

I'M SO **MAD**... AT **EVERYBODY** AN' **EVERYTHING.**

SOUNDS LIKE THAT INCLUDES **ME.**

YES, GOD DAMMIT! I'M **FURIOUS** AT YOU!

WHY COULDN'T YOU HAVE TAKEN **CARE** OF SAMMY?

HOW COULD YOU LET HIM **OUT** OF THE **HOUSE** WHEN HE WAS **DRUNK** AN' **CRAZY** LIKE THAT?

WHATEVER'S BEEN MAKIN' YOU **THINK** — EVEN FOR A **MINUTE** — THAT YOU'RE **FIT** TO LOOK AFTER A **BABY** WHEN YOU COULDN'T EVEN TAKE CARE OF...?

THAT'S NOT FAIR!

I DON'T **FEEL** LIKE BEIN' **FAIR!**

I JUST FEEL LIKE **SCREAMIN'** MY **HEAD** OFF!

I DON'T THINK ANYBODY'S GONNA BE **FAULTED** FOR LETTIN' OUT A **SCREAM** OR TWO **TONIGHT!**

SAMMY **LOVED** YOU, Y'KNOW.

AN' I **LET HIM DOWN?**

THAT'S THE **NEXT** THING YOU WANNA SAY, **ISN'T** IT?

165

AN' I'VE LET **YOU** DOWN BY BEIN' A **FAGGOT**, AN'...

AN' **BOTH** OF US ARE LETTIN' **THIS** LITTLE ONE DOWN.

WELL...DON'T FORGET ABOUT MELANIE AN' ORLEY'S **ADOPTION** OFFER.

PEACHY!

YOU FEEL JUST **FINE—DON'T** YOU?—ABOUT OUR CHILD PICKIN' UP EVERY **BIGOT'S NOTION** THAT ORLEY CAN COME **UP** WITH!

AW, **C'MON!** ORLEY'S NOT **THAT** BAD!

INSIDE THE **HALL** SOMEBODY WAS **SPEAKING** INTO THE **MICROPHONE.**

I CONTEMPLATED THE **PASSION** IN HIS VOICE AS IT SWUNG BACK AND FORTH BETWEEN **SADNESS** AND **OUTRAGE** THAT **GOOD PEOPLE** LIKE **SAMMY** WERE GETTING **SLAUGHTERED** FOR NO **REASON.**

I WONDERED HOW MANY PEOPLE IN THERE WERE SECRETLY MAD AT **ME** OVER MY **OWN** SCREW-UP, THE WAY **GINGER** WAS.

TOLAND??

HOW COME YOU'RE SITTIN' OUT **HERE?** THE **FREEDOM CHORUS** IS FIXIN' TO PERFORM.

This little light of mine...

IT WAS **GOOD** THAT I LET MARGE HERD ME **INSIDE** TO HEAR THE KIDS **SING.**

IT PUT ME IN THE MIND OF **NOBLER** THINGS THAN MY **OWN** PUNY STATUS AS A **MISFIT** AND SCOUNDREL.

...I'm gonna Let it Shine!...

THEN **GINGER** STEPPED ONTO THE PLATFORM.

SAMMY **LIKED** THIS OLD SONG ABOUT **GRIEF** FOR A **FALLEN SOLDIER.**

SHE'D SURE AS HELL DISLODGED THAT **LOG** FROM HER THROAT!

♪ We shall meet... But we shall miss him... ♪

I COULD ALMOST FEEL **SAMMY** STANDING BEHIND ME, BREATHING PLAYFULLY INTO MY **COLLAR** THE WAY HE HAD BACK WHEN **SHILOH** WAS **WHOLE** AND SINGING **DUETS** WITH GINGER AT THE **MELODY MOTEL.**

AND I FOUND MYSELF **MARVELING** OVER HOW SOMEONE WHO'D JUST **PINNED** ME LIKE A **WORM** ON A **FISHHOOK** COULD BE UP THERE SO SOON **AFTERWARDS,** EFFORT-LESSLY SOOTHING A **ROOMFUL** OF **WOUNDS...**

...INCLUDING **MINE!**

♪ ..There will be one Vacant Chair... ♪

I STOOD IN THE ALLEY'S AX SHADOWS FEELING A KIND OF **AWE** AT MY OWN **INEPTITUDE.**

FOR ALL WE'D **BEEN** THROUGH, GINGER WAS STILL LIKE A TRICKY **PICTURE PUZZLE** FRESH OUT OF THE **BOX.**

♪ We shall linger to caress him... ♪

PATCHES OF **BLUE SKY** OVER **HERE!**

FRAGMENTS OF **STORM CLOUDS** OVER **THERE!**

NOT ONLY HAD I SCORED **ZERO** THUS FAR AT FITTING THE PIECES **TOGETHER...**

...BUT IT WAS **DAWNING** ON ME THAT, JUST **POSSIBLY,** I NEVER **WOULD.**

♪ ..while we breathe.. ♪   ♪ ..our evening prayer... ♪

WHENEVER I TRY TO SORT IT ALL **OUT...**

...I KEEP REMEMBERING A **DIFFERENT,** MORE **RECENT** OCCASION...DURING THE EARLY **REAGAN** YEARS... WHEN I SAW GINGER SING.

I WAS ON THE **ROAD** AND, PURELY BY **CHANCE,** I SPOTTED HER **NAME** ON A **POSTER.**

WELL, WHADDAYA KNOW!

Ginger Raines in CONCERT — BENEFIT PERFORMANCE for the UNITED FARM WORKERS

I CALLED FROM A **PAY PHONE** AND RESERVED MY **TICKET.**

HER SINGING WAS AS **IRRESISTIBLE** AS IT HAD BEEN TWENTY YEARS **BEFORE.**

♪ It's a mighty long row that these poor hands have hoed... ♪

THE AUDIENCE WAS IN **LOVE** WITH HER. **I** WAS, TOO.

WHEN THE CONCERT WAS **DONE** I BUTTONHOLED AN **USHER,** EXPLAINED THAT I WAS AN **OLD FRIEND** OF GINGER'S, AND ASKED IF I COULD SAY **HI** TO HER.

HE LED ME DOWN A BACKSTAGE **CORRIDOR** AND POINTED TO HER **DRESSING ROOM.**

I WALKED TOWARD THE HALF-OPEN **DOOR** ...THEN **HESITATED.**

HER **BACK** WAS TO ME. SHE WAS **GIGGLING** AT SOME **JOKE** THAT HAD JUST BEEN CRACKED BY ONE OF THE **STAGEHANDS**.

CONSIDERING THE **MEMORIES** WE SHARED, I WAS SURE I COULD COAX A REFLEXIVE **SMILE** AND **EMBRACE** OUT OF HER BY SIMPLY **STEPPING** INTO THE **LIGHT**.

I DIDN'T **DO** IT, THOUGH.

I SAVORED THE SOUND OF HER **BANTER** FOR A FEW SECONDS, THEN TURNED AND WALKED BACK OUT ONTO THE **SIDEWALK**.

STAGE ENTRANCE

SOMEHOW I **KNEW** THAT— **SMILE** OR **NO** SMILE—IF I STEPPED INTO THAT ROOM WITH GINGER, THERE WOULD BE A **CHASM** BETWEEN US BEYOND **IGNORING**.

AND THE **PARADOX** OF IT IS **THIS**:

IN A **SPOTLIGHT**, WITH A FEW **DOZEN** (OR A **HUNDRED** OR A **THOUSAND**) **OTHER** AUDIENCE MEMBERS **ALONG** FOR THE **RIDE**...

...How noble our brother fell...

...SHE'LL **ALWAYS** BE ABLE TO STRETCH OUT THOSE SOFT **ARMS** OF HERS AND **DRAW** ME RIGHT **IN**...

...AS IF **NOTHING** ABOUT OUR LOVE WAS **COMPLICATED** AND **EVERYTHING** ABOUT OUR TIME TOGETHER WAS **ETERNAL**.

ESMERELDUS IS COMIN' UP HERE NOW. SHE'S GOT **ANOTHER** SONG FOR YOU THAT WAS A FAVORITE OF SAMMY'S.

GINGER, YOUR **PIPES** GIVE ME PALPITA- TIONS!

Squeeze!

click!

LISTEN, I CAN'T GO **ON** UNTIL **I SAY** SOMETHIN' TO Y'ALL ... AN' TO **SAMMY**, TOO.

IT'S ABOUT A **SACRIFICE** I'M PREPARED TO MAKE.

AN' SAMMY, DON'T THINK I CAN'T **FEEL** YOU UP THERE **FIDGETIN'** AN' **TWIDDLIN'** YOUR FLUFFY NEW **WINGS** AN' WONDERIN' WHEN THE **HELL** THIS QUEEN IS GONNA GET **ON** WITH HER **ACT!**

BUT I'M THINKIN' THAT I MAY HAFTA **DISAPPOINT** YOU.

Y'SEE, EVEN THOUGH I'VE **ALREADY** GONE TO THE TROUBLE OF PUTTIN' ON MY **WIG** AN' ALL OF THIS GORGEOUS **MAKEUP**...

...AN' EVEN THOUGH GOD **KNOWS** THAT NOBODY'S MORE INCLINED TO **HOG** A SPOT- LIGHT THAN **I** AM...

...WE ALL KNOW THAT THE **LADY** WHO'LL **OWN** THIS SONG **FOREVER** IS RIGHT HERE **WITH** US IN THIS **ROOM**.

EVERYBODY **KNOWS** WHO I'M **TALKIN'** ABOUT.

IF **SHE'D** BE WILLIN' TO COME UP HERE AN' PERFORM THIS SONG **INSTEAD** OF ME...

...**SHE** WOULDN'T EVEN HAVE TO **LIP-SYNC!**

COME ON AN' **DO** IT, ANNA DELLYNE. EVERY-BODY WOULD **LOVE** FOR YOU TO.

PLEASE —

— **YOU** GO AHEAD AN' HAVE **FUN** WITH IT, ESMERELDUS. I'LL STAND **BACK**.

O.K., HONEY.

EFFIE, STRIKE UP THE **BAND!**

♪ Got a feeling there's a Secret in the Air... ♪

♪ Nods and whispers among my sisters here and there... ♪

Awkward pauses... Eyes averted... Little warnings, oddly worded... ♪

♪ Can the truth be all that hard to bear...? ♪

AND THEN CAME THE TIME WHEN SEVERAL OF SAMMY'S **FRIENDS** WERE SLATED TO SHARE **PERSONAL REMINISCENCES** ABOUT HIM.

OTHERS WENT **AHEAD** OF ME.

IT WAS **HOPELESS** TRYING TO LISTEN TO WHAT **THEY** WERE SAYING WITH MY **OWN** TURN COMING UP.

WHEN MY TIME CAME TO **SPEAK**, I SURPRISED MYSELF BY WINDING MY WAY FAIRLY **ARTICULATELY** THROUGH THE **ANECDOTES** I'D MAPPED OUT IN MY HEAD **BEFOREHAND**.

I WON'T BOTHER **REPEATING** 'EM **NOW**.

MOST OF 'EM I'VE TOLD YOU ABOUT **ALREADY**.

ONCE I'D **FINISHED**, THE **CORRECT** THING TO DO, OBVIOUSLY, WOULD'VE BEEN TO TURN AND STEP **DOWN** FROM THE **PLATFORM**.

BUT TO MY **EMBARRASSMENT**, SOME **WEIRDNESS** TOOK HOLD OF ME.

I COULDN'T GET MYSELF TO STOP LOOKING AT ALL THE **FACES**.

I FELL SILENT AND JUST **STOOD** THERE – **FROZEN**!

AND WITH EVERY **SECOND** THAT TICKED BY, I BECAME MORE **AWARE** OF HOW THOROUGHLY EVERYONE **ELSE** HAD FALLEN SILENT, **TOO**.

AND I WAS AWARE THAT THE **AMPS** WERE GIVING OFF A LOW **HUM**.

AND I WAS AWARE OF THE **CHILLINESS** OF THE STEEL **MIKE STAND** MY FIST WAS CLUTCHING.

AND I WONDERED IF I WAS GOING TO PASS **OUT**...

...'CAUSE ALL OF THE **FACES** I WAS LOOKING DOWN AT WERE BEGINNING TO DROP **AWAY**...

...LIKE THEY WERE SPIRALING HEADLONG DOWN A WEIRDLY LIT **SHAFT** THAT I WAS IN SOME **DANGER** OF TOPPLING INTO **MYSELF**!

EXCEPT FOR **SHILOH**.

FOR **SOME** REASON MY **EYES** LOCKED ONTO **SHILOH'S** EYES...

...AND IT CAME **BACK** TO ME, WHAT HAD **PUT** HIM IN THAT **WHEEL- CHAIR**...

...AND I IMAGINED THE **EXPLOSION** AT THE **MELODY MOTEL**...

...AND WHAT IT MUST'VE BEEN LIKE TO **BE** SHILOH...

...AND SEE A FLAMING TORNADO OF **SHATTERED BEAMS** AND **CONCRETE** BLASTING TOWARD ME...

...AND THEN I WAS ON THE **BACK** STEPS OF THE **WHEELERY** AGAIN...

...WATCHING **HARD STEEL** WHIZ OUT OF **BLACKNESS**.

...AND ALONG WITH THE PAIN RICOCHETING THROUGH MY HEAD, THERE WERE NOISES:

THE MUFFLED, THRASHING SOUNDS OF SAMMY BEING WRESTLED INTO THE WOODS.

AND THEN SOMETHING REALLY BIZARRE TOOK OVER...

...AND IT WAS LIKE I WAS SAMMY...

...AND I WAS FEELING WHAT SAMMY FELT...

...AND STRANGE MEN'S HANDS WERE ALL OVER ME, DRAGGING ME SOMEWHERE THAT I DIDN'T WANNA GO.

AND I HEARD A SCREAM TRYING TO BREAK OUT OF MY THROAT...

...BUT A CALLUSED HAND HAD CLAMPED ITSELF ACROSS MY FACE AND THE SCREAM WAS AS TRAPPED AS I WAS.

AND I KNEW THAT I MIGHT VERY WELL BE ABOUT TO DIE...

...AND I VERY STRONGLY DIDN'T WANT TO.

AND I WENT CRAZY... FLAILING AND TWISTING IN EVERY DIRECTION.

MY FOOT WAS SQUIRMING THIS WAY AND THAT, DESPERATELY SEARCHING FOR AN INCH OR TWO OF SOLID GROUND THAT I COULD USE FOR LEVERAGE.

BUT THERE WAS NOTHING TO PUSH AGAINST BUT HANDS AND EMPTY AIR.

AND I WAS SO TEARY-EYED, THE FACES AROUND ME WERE NOTHING BUT DARK, WATERY BLURS...

...BUT I COULD SEE THEY HADN'T BOTHERED TO BRING THEIR WHITE HOODS.

FOR A SECOND THEY LOST THEIR GRIP AND DROPPED ME, AND I GOT A MOUTHFUL OF DRY LEAVES.

AND THEN I WAS BEING HOISTED SOMEWHERE... AND THERE WAS A WRENCHING JOLT TO MY GUT WHEN SOMEBODY'S FOOTING SLIPPED...

...AND A FORKED TWIG DUG INTO THE SORE PLACE WHERE MY WRIST WAS BANDAGED...

...AND A SPLINTER FROM RILEY'S TREE HOUSE SLID INTO ME LIKE A NEEDLE...

...AND I FELT THE ROUGH LOOP OF ROPE BEING SHOVED DOWN OVER MY FACE...

...AND THEN SOME HANDS SHIFTED MY WEIGHT AROUND SO THAT I LOST TRACK OF WHAT WAS UP OR DOWN...

...AND THEN THE HANDS WEREN'T HOLDING ONTO ME ANYMORE...AND I WAS FALLING....

AND MY **HEAD** JERKED **UP** LIKE IT WAS ABOUT TO **DETACH**...

...AND A FEROCIOUS **FIRE** RIPPED THROUGH MY NECK LIKE THE **CLAWS** OF AN **ANIMAL**...

...AND I COULDN'T EVEN MANAGE A **GASP** OF **DISCONTENT**.

AND THEN...

A SOUNDLESS BOLT OF **LIGHTNING** PLOWED THROUGH THE WRITHING, PROTESTING **WEIGHT** OF ME...

...AND THEN I WAS MADE ONLY OF **AIR**... ...**LIGHT**... ...AND A **QUESTION**.

AND THE QUESTION WAS:

WHY WAS **TOLAND** LYING FLAT IN THE **DIRT** BY THE WHEELERY'S **BACK STEPS**, **UNCONSCIOUS** BUT **ALIVE**...

...AND WHY WAS **I, SAMMY NOONE**, SUDDENLY TEN GALAXIES **AWAY**?

WAS IT BECAUSE I WAS A...

NIGGER LOVING QUEER

...WHILE **TOLAND POLK**, THOUGH REPUTEDLY A 'NIGGER LOVER' AS **WELL**, DIDN'T APPEAR TO BE A 'QUEER' ONE?

ANOTHER NIGHT THAT MIGHT NOT HAVE MADE A **DIFFERENCE**...

THAT ONE STILL OUT **COLD**...?

AIN'T MOVED A **MUSCLE**.

...BUT **TONIGHT**, JUST **POSSIBLY**, IT **HAD**.

AND AFTER A TIME I WAS **TOLAND** AGAIN, STANDING BY THE MICROPHONE AT **ALLEYSAX**.

AND LIKE A **FOOL** I WAS UP THERE **SOBBING** IN FRONT OF **EVERYBODY.**

I **DOUBT** ANYBODY THOUGHT **LESS** OF ME FOR IT, OF COURSE.

IT **WAS** A NIGHT FOR **GRIEVING,** AFTER ALL.

BUT I DIDN'T **DARE** LEAVE PEOPLE THINKING THAT MY TEARS HAD BEEN FLOWING FOR A MURDERED FRIEND AND NOTHING **MORE.**

'CAUSE I **KNEW** THAT, IF I **DIDN'T** SAY THE WORDS **RIGHT THEN**—

—(AND I'M TALKING ABOUT THE REALLY **FRIGHTENING** WORDS THAT ALL THE **HABITS** OF A **LIFETIME** WERE **SCREAMING** AT ME TO HOLD **BACK** AND LEAVE **UNSAID**)—

—I MIGHT JUST **CONTINUE** ON MY COWARD'S WAY THE **NEXT** DAY AND THE **NEXT**... AND THE DAY AFTER **THAT**...

...AND **ALL** THE DAYS **THEREAFTER.**

SO I **SAID** THE **WORDS.**

AND THERE WERE **LOTS** OF THEM!

I **KNOW** THAT I DID 'CAUSE I CAN STILL REMEMBER THE STAMMERING, GULPING **SOUND** OF THEM TUMBLING OUT OF MY **MOUTH.**

AND I'LL BE **DAMNED** IF I CAN RECALL WHAT ANY OF THEM **WERE** IN **PARTICULAR** —EXCEPT FOR THESE **FOUR:**

IT COULD'VE BEEN **ME.**

AND I **REALIZED** AS I **SPOKE** THOSE FOUR WORDS THAT I WAS SAYING THEM TO **SHILOH** MORE THAN TO ANYONE **ELSE.**

I KNEW I'D FIND **UNDERSTANDING** IN SHILOH'S **EYES.**

EVENTUALLY A POINT CAME WHEN I KNEW I WAS **DONE** TALKING.

I'D **SAID** WHAT NEEDED **SAYING.**

AND PART OF ME WAS **EMBARRASSED** BY THE **WETNESS** OF MY **CHEEKS** AND BY THE EMOTIONAL **EXCESSES** I KNEW I'D PROBABLY COMMITTED...

...BUT **ANOTHER** PART OF ME WAS LEFT WITH AN ALMOST GIDDY **SERENITY.**

IN THE DAYS THAT **FOLLOWED,** THE DELICATE SUBJECT OF MY ALLEY-SAX **OUTBURST** GOT **RAISED** A FEW TIMES BY FRIENDS WHO'D **WITNESSED** IT.

I DIDN'T **SAY** TOO MUCH, FIGURING THAT THE MORE I WENT **INTO** IT, THE **CRAZIER** I'D SEEM.

I'M **STILL** NOT A HUNDRED PERCENT **SURE** WHAT REALLY **HAPPENED** THAT NIGHT...

...BUT THE **CLEAR EFFECT** OF IT WAS TO PUT TO **REST** ANY **MISIMPRESSIONS** I'D FOSTERED THAT **TOLAND POLK** WAS ANY **STRAIGHTER** THAN **SAMMY NOONE** HAD BEEN!

SAY IT **ONCE** IN **PUBLIC** AND THE **GRAPEVINE'LL** TAKE IT FROM **THERE!**

193

THE **SKY** DIDN'T FALL BECAUSE OF WHAT I DID AT ALLEYSAX... BUT THERE WERE **CONSEQUENCES.**

DON'T WASTE TIME LOOKIN' FOR **ORLEY,** KIDS. HE DON'T **LIVE** HERE ANYMORE.

I KICKED HIM **OUT** LAST **WEEKEND.**

LORD FORGIVE ME, I'M GONNA BE THE FIRST **DIVORCED WOMAN** IN OUR **FAMILY!**

MELANIE HAD INVITED ME AND GINGER OVER FOR **HOME COOKING...**

...BUT WHEN WE **GOT** THERE, SHE WAS SUCH AN EMOTIONAL **BASKET CASE** THAT WE DAMN NEAR FORGOT TO **EAT!**

YOU'VE NEVER **TALKED** ABOUT THINGS BEIN' **ROCKY** BETWEEN YOU AN' ORLEY, SIS.

OH, THERE'VE BEEN **STORM CLOUDS** BUILDIN', BUT I HAVEN'T WANTED TO **ADMIT** IT.

THEN ALL **HELL** BROKE LOOSE WHEN I GOT BACK FROM SAMMY'S **MEMORIAL PARTY** SATURDAY NIGHT...

...WHICH **ORLEY** COULDN'T BE BOTHERED TO EVEN **ATTEND,** OF COURSE!

I **TOLD** HIM ALL ABOUT WHAT YOU **SAID,** TOLAND, WHILE YOU WERE UP THERE AT THE **MICROPHONE.**

I THOUGHT HE'D FIND IT **MOVING,** LIKE **I** DID.

BUT HE WENT **OFF** ON A WHOLE OTHER **TACK....**

THAT **DOES** IT, MEL!

YOU CAN JUST **SHELVE** THOSE **PLANS** OF YOURS ABOUT YOU AN' ME TAKIN' YOUR BROTHER'S **BABY** INTO THE HOUSE!

AN' **WHY** IS **THAT,** PRAY TELL?

'CAUSE IT'S **UNNATURAL** AN' IT GIVES ME THE **CREEPS!**

IF A **QUEER'S BABY** DON'T QUALIFY AS SOME KINDA **DEVIL'S SPAWN,** I DON'T KNOW WHAT **DOES!**

I BLEW MY **TOP** WHEN HE SAID THAT, AN' WE STARTED **ARGUIN'** LIKE WE'VE **NEVER** ARGUED **BEFORE.**

AN' IN THE **MIDDLE** OF IT ALL, HE SAID THIS AWFUL **OTHER** THING!

I DIDN'T EVEN **REALIZE** AT FIRST HOW **MAD** HE'D MADE ME BY **SAYIN'** IT...

...BUT SOMEWHERE DOWN **INSIDE** OF ME, A LI'L **TIME BOMB** STARTED **TICKIN'.**

WHAT WAS IT HE **SAID,** HON?

LOOK, I SHOULDN'T OF EVEN BROUGHT IT **UP.** 'CAUSE I HAVE NO **INTENTION** OF **REPEATIN'** IT TO YOU.

IT WAS BAD ENOUGH TO FREEZE THE **BLOOD** IN MY **VEINS.** THAT'S **ALL** YOU NEED TO **KNOW.**

I WALKED OUT BACK AN' **CRIED** ON THE **PATIO** FOR A WHILE.

THEN I **CAME BACK** AN' LET HIM **HAVE** IT!

ORLEY, I HEAR THEY RENT **FURNISHED ROOMS** REAL **CHEAP** DOWNTOWN AT THE **CLAYFIELD LODGE.**

I SUGGEST YOU GO AN' CHECK **INTO** ONE OF 'EM IF YOU WANNA **WAKE UP** TOMORROW MORNIN' WITH THE SAME' NUMBER OF **BODY PARTS** YOU WENT TO **SLEEP** WITH!

WELL...IT'S A MOVE I'D NEVER EXPECTED YOU'D **MAKE,** SIS, BUT I CAN'T HONESTLY SAY THAT—

DON'T YOU UNDERSTAND WHAT THIS **MEANS,** LI'L BROTHER?

I'M **NOT** GONNA BE ABLE TO **ADOPT** YOUR **BABY.**

I'D MESS UP SO BAD IF I TRIED TO RAISE A BABY ON MY **OWN.** I JUST **KNOW** I WOULD!

BEIN' ENGAGED OR MARRIED TO **ORLEY** IS ALL I'VE **KNOWN** SINCE **HIGH SCHOOL.** WHO **KNOWS** WHAT KIND OF **FUTURE** I'M GONNA HAVE **NOW?**

OH, **DRAT!** ≥Sniff!≤ I FEEL LIKE THE WORST **DOUBLE-CROSSER** IN THE **WORLD!** ≥choke!≤

THERE WASN'T ANY WAY OF **PREDICTIN'** THAT THINGS WOULD TURN **OUT** THIS WAY, MELANIE.

I'M GLAD **GINGER** WAS CAPABLE OF MUSTERING SOME WORDS OF **COMFORT** FOR MY SISTER, 'CAUSE MY **OWN** BRAIN HAD SPUN RIGHT OFF INTO THE **OZONE.**

COULD BE YOU WERE BEIN' **FOOLHARDY** AS MUCH AS **GOOD-HEARTED** WHEN YOU **MADE** THE OFFER IN THE **FIRST** PLACE.

BUT I **DID** MAKE THE OFFER...AN' IT WAS BECAUSE I **WANTED** TO.

I WOULD'VE **LOVED** MOTHERIN' A CHILD THAT CAME FROM **YOU** TWO.

AN' WHAT I **HATE MOST** IS NOT BEIN' **WISE** ENOUGH TO **ADVISE** YOU ABOUT WHAT TO **DO** NOW.

I'VE GOT NO **RIGHT** TO EVEN OPEN MY **MOUTH,** CONSIDERIN' HOW I'VE LET Y'ALL **DOWN!**

BUT I STILL CAN'T **STOP** MYSELF FROM **BEGGIN'** YOU, PLEASE...

...FIND **SOME** WAY TO HANDLE THINGS WITHOUT **ABORTIN'** THAT PRECIOUS **GIFT** THAT'S **INSIDE** OF YOU.

KNOWIN' THE TWO OF **YOU,** I FEEL SO **CERTAIN** IT'LL GROW UP TO BE SOMEBODY REALLY **SPECIAL.**

I DON'T KNOW WHAT WAS GOING ON IN **GINGER'S** HEAD...

...BUT ALL **I** COULD THINK ABOUT WAS AN IMAGINARY **KID**...

...HOPSCOTCHING ACROSS THE SURFACE OF IMAGINARY **WATERS** TOWARD A **FAR SHORE** I WAS NEVER LIKELY TO **SEE**.

I KEPT MY **CURIOSITY** IN **CHECK** ABOUT THE **'OTHER THING'** THAT ORLEY HAD SAID TO MELANIE, FIGURING THAT **SIS** WOULD FILL ME IN ONCE SHE FELT **CALMER**.

BUT I WAS NEVER ABLE TO WHEEDLE IT **OUT** OF HER.

AS FOR **ORLEY**, HE DROPPED OUT OF **SIGHT** SO FAST, I NEVER GOT A CHANCE TO FAKE ANY EXPRESSIONS OF **REGRET**.

WHEN **MONTHS** AND THEN **YEARS** PASSED WITH NONE OF US HEARING A **WORD** FROM HIM, I STOPPED EXPECTING I'D EVER LAY **EYES** ON THE GUY **AGAIN**.

BUT DAMNED IF OUR **PATHS** DIDN'T CROSS FIVE YEARS **LATER**, IN SAN FRANCISCO'S **GOLDEN GATE PARK**.

A CO-WORKER AT THE **BUS STATION** SAID HE SPENT A FEW DAYS FEELING **SORRY** FOR HIMSELF, THEN WALKED OFF THE **JOB** AND SPLIT FOR **PARTS UNKNOWN**.

HEY! **TOLAND POLK!**

AND **THAT** WAS WHEN THE MYSTERY ABOUT WHAT **ELSE** HE'D TOLD MELANIE FINALLY GOT CLEARED **UP**.

UH...DO I **KNOW** YOU, MAN?

I'D TURNED INTO A MORE OR LESS STANDARD-ISSUE **HIPPIE** BY THEN...

YOU **MIGHT**. I USED TO BE **MARRIED** TO YOUR **SISTER**.

ORLEY??!

Chuckle!

...AND **ORLEY'D** GONE THROUGH A FEW CHANGES OF HIS **OWN!**

I LOOK **DIFFERENT**, DON'T I?

FAR FUCKIN' OUT!

THAT WAS THE **SIXTIES** COUNTER-CULTURE FOR YA!

EVERY TIME YA **BLINKED**, ANOTHER HUNDRED **YOUNG REPUBLICANS'D** BE BLOSSOMING INTO LONG-HAIRED **'FREAKS'!**

SIT **DOWN**, BUDDY...WE'VE GOTTA CATCH **UP**! ARE YOU **LIVIN'** IN **SAN FRANCISCO** NOW?

NOPE. I'M JUST HERE P-PICKIN' UP SOME **STUFF** I'M S'POSED TO DELIVER TO A **CHICK** IN **BOSTON**.

IT WAS SUCH A **TRIP** TO SEE ORLEY LOOKING LIKE HALF THE **POTHEADS** I'D SHARED A **BONG** WITH, MY IMMEDIATE INCLINATION WAS TO LET **BYGONES** BE **BYGONES**.

HOW'S **MELANIE**?

SHE'S COOL. SHE WENT BACK TO **SCHOOL** FOR A WHILE.

SHE WAS WELL RID OF **ME**—TH-THAT'S FOR **SURE**!

ARE YOU AN' **GINGER** STILL TOGETHER?

NAH, SHE AN' I WENT OUR SEPARATE **WAYS**.

I **KEEP UP** WITH HER SOME FROM **NEWSPAPER WRITE-UPS**.

I READ **SOMEWHERE** THAT SHE MIGHT CUT A **RECORD**.

YOU'RE STILL **GAY**, THEN?

UH... YEAH.

LAST I **CHECKED**!

Y'KNOW, I'VE SEEN LOTS **MORE** OF THE **WORLD** SINCE YOU KNEW ME, TOLAND. I'VE GOT SEVERAL HOMOSEXUAL **F-FRIENDS** NOW, IF YOU CAN **BELIEVE** IT.

I MEAN, I'M **WAY** MORE **T-TOLERANT** THAN I USED TO BE.

HE WAS **ALSO** WAY MORE **JITTERY** THAN HE USED TO BE, THANKS TO SOME **CHEMICAL** OR OTHER THAT HE'D APPARENTLY HAD FOR **BREAKFAST**.

UH...IF IT'S NOT TOO P-**PERSONAL** A THING TO BRING **UP**...WASN'T GINGER **PREGNANT** AROUND THE TIME THAT ~~

IT WAS A **GIRL**. WE GAVE HER UP TO BE **ADOPTED**.

GINGER CHECKED INTO THE **HANNAH BAY HOME** IN **WILLOWVILLE**.

THEY TOOK GOOD **CARE** OF HER AN', Y'KNOW, HELPED WITH THE **PAPERWORK**.

THEY LET ME COME **SEE** THE BABY ONCE, A FEW WEEKS AFTER SHE WAS **BORN**.

I GOT TO **HOLD** HER AN' **EVERYTHING**!

BUT THEN IT WAS **GOODBYE FOREVER**.

THAT'S THE WAY ADOPTION **WORKS**.

WOW, ORLEY! I'M MAKIN' YA **CRY**!

NAW, MAN...I'M MAKIN' **MYSELF** CRY!

LISTEN, TOLAND, Y'GOTTA B-**BEAR** WITH ME—*DIG*?—WHILE I SAY SOMETHIN' **HARD**.

I'VE ALWAYS **KNOWN** THAT SOMETIME, SOMEPLACE, I MIGHT RUN INTO YOU **AGAIN**...

...AN' I'VE ALWAYS KNOWN THAT IF I **DID**, THERE WAS SOMETHIN' I'D HAFTA B-BITE THE BULLET AN' **TELL** YA.

TOLAND... IT WAS **ME** THAT MURDERED SAMMY NOONE.

YOU **WHAT??**

NOW DON'T GET ME **WRONG**.

I WASN'T PART OF THE GANG THAT **HUNG** HIM! NO **WAY!**

BUT THERE **WAS** SOMETHIN' I **DID** ....

JESUS! AM I GONNA HAVE THE **B-BALLS** TO ACTUALLY **TELL** YOU THIS...?

REMEMBER THE N-NIGHT WHEN THEY RAN **FILM** OF SAMMY ON THE **TV NEWS** AN' HE WAS BAD-MOUTHIN' **SUTTON CHOPPER?**

WELL, WATCHIN' THAT MADE ME SO **MAD,** I COULDN'T **SEE** STRAIGHT!

AN' WHAT **I DID** WAS, I WAITED 'TIL **MELANIE** LEFT THE R-ROOM...AN' THEN I TELEPHONED THE **DIXIE PATRIOT.**

I TOLD WHOEVER CAME ON THE **L-LINE** THAT THE **RACE-MIXER** WHO'D JUST B-BEEN ON TV WAS AS **QUEER** AS A **THREE-DOLLAR BILL**...

...AN' THAT THEY COULD FIND HIM PLAYIN' THE **ORGAN** EVERY S-SUNDAY AT **TRINITY EPISCOPAL.**

I KNEW IT'D DRIVE 'EM **C-CRAZY** TO HEAR THAT.

I CAN'T PLAY **INNO-CENT.**

IT WAS A PURE ACT OF **MEANNESS** TOWARD SAMMY...'CAUSE OF THE **PREJUDICES** I HAD.

AN' MY **CONSCIENCE** TELLS ME THAT IF I **HADN'T** MADE THAT CALL, SAMMY MIGHT'VE SLIPPED BY AS JUST ONE MORE STRAY **'T-TRAITOR'** TO THE **WHITE RACE'** FOR THE REDNECKS TO **C-CURSE** AT AN' THEN **FORGET.**

BUT WITH ME PUTTIN' OUT THE **W-WORD** THAT HE WAS A **QUEER** AN' A LOCAL **CH-CHURCH ORGANIST** TO **BOOT**...

...WELL, IT DON'T TAKE A **G-GENIUS** TO KNOW HOW **THAT'D** STICK IN THEIR CRAWS!

SO IT WAS **ME** THAT MADE SAMMY A **TARGET,** Y'SEE?

THERE'S NO **SEPARATIN'** WHAT **I** DID FROM WHAT HAPPENED **LATER.**

THE **GUILT** I FEEL, TOLAND...IT'S J-JUST **TERRIBLE!**

WELL, I'VE **TOLD** YA NOW.

GIMME CREDIT FOR EITHER **G-GUTS** OR **STUPIDITY!**

I KNOW IT'S **ASKIN'** TOO MUCH FOR YOU NOT TO **H-HATE** ME, BUT—

YOU'RE **RIGHT,** ORLEY. I'M NOT **SAINT** ENOUGH NOT TO HATE YOU.

I **LOVED** SAMMY. HE WAS A GOOD **FRIEND** AN' HE MADE ME **BRAVER** THAN I WOULD'VE BEEN **OTHER-WISE.**

I DUNNO IF I'LL END UP HATIN' YOU OVER THE LONG HAUL. IT'LL TAKE ME A **WHILE** TO WORK THAT **OUT.**

...BUT 'TIL FURTHER **NOTICE**...

...IF YOU EVER HAPPEN TO SPOT ME IN A **CROWD** AGAIN, THE WAY Y'DID **TODAY**—DO ME A **FAVOR**, O.K.?

DON'T BOTHER COMIN' OVER TO SAY **HELLO.**

DEAL?

DEAL.

SO **WHY** DID I COME DOWN SO **HARD** ON ORLEY?

THE DUDE WAS ANGLING FOR **FORGIVENESS**, FOR CHRIST'S SAKE! **HARLAND PEPPER** WOULD'VE AT **LEAST** OFFERED SOME **GENEROSITY** OF **SPIRIT!**

I MEAN, IT WASN'T **ORLEY** THAT SLID A NOOSE AROUND SAMMY'S NECK.

HE'D JUST BEHAVED LIKE A GARDEN-VARIETY BIGOT **ASSHOLE.**

AND FRANKLY, WHO OF US **HASN'T**, ONCE OR TWICE IN OUR LIVES?

LOOKING AT IT IN **RETROSPECT**, IT'S PLAIN THAT I WASN'T GIVING THE BASTARD ANY **QUARTER** BECAUSE WHAT HE'D **SAID** TO ME HAD HIT **WAY** TOO CLOSE TO **HOME!**

Y'SEE, I'D KNOWN FOR YEARS THAT **I** WAS **REALLY** THE ONE WHO'D MURDERED SAMMY NOONE.

IF I HADN'T BEEN TOO **CHICKENSHIT** TO LET HIM KNOW THAT **I** WAS AS GAY AS **HE** WAS...

...IF I'D ONLY BEEN WILLING TO **KISS** AND **HOLD** HIM WHEN HE **NEEDED** ME TO...

HOW **ABOUT** IT?

...WHETHER OR **NOT** EITHER OF OUR **DICKS** GOT HARD...

...THEN WE JUST MIGHT'VE STAYED **HOME** THAT NIGHT...

...AND THE **DIXIE PATRIOT** WOULDN'T HAVE HAD ITS **DELIBERATIONS** DISTURBED...

...AND THE WORLD OUT-SIDE THE **WHEELERY** MIGHT'VE GONE ON ITS MERRY **WAY**...

...WITHOUT BEING **REMINDED** OF THE **FAGGOT** WHO'D ONCE POPPED UP ON THE **SIX O'CLOCK NEWS**...

...JUST **BEGGING** FOR SOME FINE **TOWNS-MEN** TO DROP BY AND **HANG** HIM.

I WALKED THROUGH THE SAN FRANCISCO HILLS FOR **HOURS** AFTER LEAVING ORLEY...

...WHILE **SCENES** AND **EMOTIONS** FROM MY CLAYFIELD DAYS FLASHED **BACK** AT ME IN MORE **DETAIL** THAN I WOULD'VE EVER THOUGHT **POSSIBLE.**

I'D LOGGED A LOT OF **MILES** SINCE THEN...

...BUT IT WAS STILL A REAL QUICK **TRIP** BACK TO **KENNEDYTIME.**

199

KENNEDYTIME WAS STILL A **FRESH** ENOUGH MEMORY TO HAVE SOME **STING** IN IT THE DAY I DROVE TO **WILLOWVILLE** TO SEE MY **DAUGHTER** FOR THE FIRST AND LAST TIME.

AND **BELIEVE** ME—THAT WAS A TRIP THAT HAD MORE THAN A **LITTLE** STING OF ITS **OWN!**

I'M **SURE** I HEARD HIM **STIRRIN' AROUND** UPSTAIRS, TOLAND. WOULD YOU LIKE SOME **COFFEE** WHILE YOU WAIT?

MAMA, DID I HEAR **TOLE** DRIVE UP?

WHEN I CONFIDED TO **LES** WHAT THE TRIP WAS **FOR,** HE DECIDED I SHOULD HAVE **COMPANY** ON THE DRIVE.

WE AGREED THAT I'D PICK HIM UP AROUND **TEN** IN THE **MORNING** AT HIS **FOLKS'** HOUSE, WHERE HE WAS STAYING WHILE HE WAS 'BETWEEN **APARTMENTS,'** AS HE PUT IT.

NATURALLY, HE OVER-SLEPT...

...BUT I DIDN'T MIND THE **DELAY,** SINCE IT GAVE ME TIME TO VISIT WITH **ANNA DELLYNE,** WHICH WAS **ALWAYS** A PLEASURE.

WE'RE OUT ON THE BACK **STOOP,** LES.

NOW DON'T YOU BOYS **FORGET** TO GIVE GINGER AN' THE BABY A **KISS** FROM HARLAND AN' ME.

NOT MUCH USE IN SAYIN' THAT TO **ME,** MAMA!

THE HANNAH BAY FOLKS WON'T BE LETTIN' **ME** THROUGH THE **DOOR!**

IT'S ONLY THE BABIES' **BLOOD RELATIVES** THAT HAVE VISITIN' PRIVILEGES AT **THIS** STAGE OF THE GAME.

WELL... MAYBE **HANNAH BAY** KNOWS **BEST.**

I GUESS YOU'LL HAVE TO DO **KISSIN' DUTY** FOR **ALL** OF US, TOLAND.

I COULDN'T HELP **NOTICING** HOW **DIFFERENT** IT WAS SHARING A CAR RIDE WITH LES **THAT** DAY COMPARED TO THE NIGHT WE'D DRIVEN TO **ALLEYSAX** TOGETHER.

HE WASN'T SLUMPING WAY DOWN IN HIS **SEAT** ANYMORE.

WHICH WAS **PRAISEWORTHY** AND **STRONG**... SO I'M **EMBARRASSED** TO ADMIT HOW **NERVOUS** IT MADE ME!

I MADE A **REMARK** ABOUT IT AND HE SAID:

MY **SLUMPIN' DAYS** ARE **OVER!**

HE DIDN'T **ELABORATE** AND I DIDN'T **PRESS.**

THE **TIMING** OF THAT AND **OTHER** CHANGES IN LES MADE ME WONDER IF ANY OF IT WAS CONNECTED TO SAMMY'S **MURDER.** IT WAS AS IF LES HAD TAKEN A PERSONAL **VOW** OF **RECKLESSNESS** IN SAMMY'S **HONOR!**

LOOK. SOME **COPS** AHEAD.

HE ALL BUT GAVE ME **HEART FAILURE** BY COOLLY STARING DOWN SOME **COUNTY PATROLMEN** THAT CRUISED BY.

I OFTEN **THINK** ABOUT LES AND WONDER IF THAT EXTRA COCKINESS **SERVED** HIM WELL IN THE YEARS AFTER I LOST **TOUCH** WITH HIM.

I COULD NEVER **FORGET** THAT IT WAS ON THE **HEELS** OF OUR WILLOWVILLE TRIP THAT THE BODIES OF **CHANEY, GOODMAN,** AND **SCHWERNER** GOT DUG OUT OF A MISSISSIPPI **DAM**...

...WHICH LED ME TO REFLECT ON THE **PRICE** THAT CAN GET EXACTED WHEN YOU LOOK BIGOTRY TOO **SQUARELY** IN THE **EYE.**

THEY'RE NOT TURNIN' **AROUND,** ARE THEY?

NAH... THEY JUST **SLOWED UP** FOR A MINUTE.

OF COURSE, THE **FLIP** SIDE OF THAT COIN IS THE PRICE THAT GETS PAID WHEN YOU **DON'T!**

WHAT? ARE YOU **SCARED** O' THOSE **CRACKERS?**

Y'BET YER **ASS** I AM.

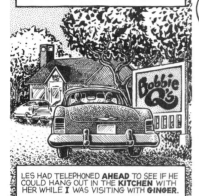

THERE WAS A ROADSIDE **DINER** THAT RAEBURN'S **SISTER** COOKED FOR, SITUATED A MILE OR SO UP THE **HIGHWAY** FROM THE **UNWED MOTHERS' HOME** I WAS GOING TO.

Bobbie Q's

LES HAD TELEPHONED **AHEAD** TO SEE IF HE COULD HANG OUT IN THE **KITCHEN** WITH HER WHILE **I** WAS VISITING WITH **GINGER.**

WELL... BEAR **UP,** MAN.

AN' TELL GINGER THAT ALL THE **PEPPERS** SAY HI.

THE HANNAH BAY HOME

TOLAND! WE'RE GLAD YOU COULD **COME.**

BY THAT POINT I'D HAD **SEVERAL** ENCOUNTERS WITH GINGER'S PARENTS, DURING WHICH WE'D TALKED NERVOUSLY THROUGH THE WORST OF THE **SPECULATIONS** THEY'D HAD ABOUT **ME** AND THE WORST OF THE **FEARS** I'D HAD ABOUT **THEM.**

ON BALANCE, **THEY** SEEMED AS RELIEVED NOT TO HAVE THEIR DAUGHTER SUCKED INTO ANY **DUBIOUS NUPTIALS** AS **I** WAS NOT TO HAVE THE MATTER SETTLED BY **SHOTGUN!**

MR. POLK, I'M **IVY** McGINNIS.

SHALL I TAKE YOU TO **GINGER** AND THE **BABY?**

H'LO.

LOOK AT HER, TOLAND. CAN YOU **BELIEVE** IT?

AM I ALLOWED TO **HOLD** HER?

Whew! THIS IS **REALLY** SOMETHIN' ELSE!

ARE YOU **PLEASED** TO SEE YOUR DAUGHTER, MR. POLK?

MOST **DEFINITELY**, MA'AM. I JUST WISH IT WAS UNDER DIFFERENT **CIRCUMSTANCES**.

I NAMED HER **MELANIE**.

YEAH? I KNOW SOME-BODY WHO'LL LOVE **THAT**!

IT'LL GET **CHANGED** ONCE SHE'S BEEN **ADOPTED**, PROBABLY... BUT IT FELT NICE WRITIN' THAT DOWN ON THE **FORM**.

I'LL SLIP INTO MY **OFFICE** SO YOU TWO CAN **VISIT**.

THANKS.

THANKS, IVY.

SHE'S SO **TINY**, GINGER... I'M SCARED I'LL **BREAK** HER! WHAT IF SHE STARTS **CRYIN'**?

I'LL TAKE HER **BACK** IF SHE GETS **RESTLESS**. GO AHEAD AN' SIT **DOWN**.

SO WE HAD THE **VISIT** I'D DRIVEN TO **WILLOWVILLE** FOR. WE TALKED ABOUT WHAT OUR **FRIENDS** WERE UP TO AND WHAT MIGHT LIE IN **STORE** FOR **HER** AND FOR **ME**.

WHAT I REMEMBER **MOST** IS HOW **HARD** WE BOTH WORKED TO IGNORE THE SHADOW OF **FINALITY** THAT DIMMED EVERY CORNER OF THE **ROOM**.

GINGER SAID SHE'D DECIDED **AGAINST** GOING BACK TO **CLAY-FIELD**. SHE FELT READY TO HEAD **NORTH** AND SEE WHAT **NEW YORK** HAD TO OFFER.

I DIDN'T **ARGUE**. IT WAS ALL GROUND THAT WE'D COVERED **BEFORE**.

AT **ONE** POINT I FOUND MYSELF DESCRIBING THE CONVERSATION THAT I'D HAD WITH **ANNA DELLYNE** EARLIER THAT DAY.

YOU MAKE **TOO MUCH** OF IT, HONEY.

I KNOW IT'S **HARD** FOR YOU TO UNDERSTAND WHY I WON'T **SING** IN **PUBLIC**.

NOT MY OLD SONGS FROM THE **CLUBS**, I MEAN.

I GUESS YOU LOOK ON SHOW BUSINESS AS BEIN' SO **GLAMOROUS**, YOU CAN'T **BELIEVE** IT'S NOT STILL IN MY **BLOOD** SOME-WHERE!

IT'S NOT **SHOW BUSINESS** I'M TALKIN' ABOUT. IT'S SINGIN' HERE IN **CLAYFIELD**.

YOU COULD GIVE SO MANY PEOPLE AROUND HERE SUCH A **KICK**!

YOU **USED** TO THINK THEY WERE **GOOD** SONGS. DO YA **NOT** THINK SO **NOW**?

NO... THEY'LL **ALWAYS** BE GOOD.

DO YA THINK THEY'RE **SINFUL**? IS IT 'CAUSE YOU'RE A **PREACHER'S WIFE** NOW?

NOW LOOK **HERE**! — I **HAVEN'T** TURNED INTO SUCH A **PRISSY** OL' PREACHER'S WIFE THAT I'D CALL THOSE SONGS **SINFUL**!

SIN'S **NOT** THAT **SIMPLE**!

 IT'S 'CAUSE I'M A **COWARD**, HONEY. I'M A PLAIN OL' **SCAREDY CAT**!

 IT'S NOTHIN' **NEW**. MY NERVES WERE ALREADY GETTIN' **SHAKY** WHEN MY '**CAREER**' WAS JUST BREAKIN' OUT OF THE **STARTIN'** GATE.

THERE I **WAS** — IN THE MIDDLE OF A HORSE RACE WHERE **AMBITION** AN' A TOUGH **HIDE** COUNTED FOR **EVERYTHING**!

MY HIDE'S NOT THAT **TOUGH**, TOLAND... AN' EVERYBODY **ELSE** ALWAYS HAD MORE AMBITION ABOUT MY SINGIN' THAN **I** DID.

 I GOT TALKED INTO CUTTIN' THOSE **TRACKS** THAT YOU'VE HEARD.

BUT WITH SO MANY PEOPLE ALL **OVER** ME, PUSHIN' AN' **PULLIN**'...

(MOST OF 'EM WITH THE **BEST** OF **INTENTIONS**...

...A FEW **OTHERS** NOT SO **MUCH** SO)...

...IT **TOOK** ME A WHILE TO SIT DOWN AN' REALLY **LISTEN** TO THE MUSIC **QUIETLY**, ALL BY **MYSELF**.

 ONCE I **DID**, I KNEW IT WAS ALL **OVER**.

BUT YOU SOUND **GREAT** ON THOSE RECORDINGS! EVERYBODY THINKS SO!

 BUT Y'SEE, **OTHER** PEOPLE DON'T **HEAR** WHAT **I** HEAR WHEN THOSE RECORDS ARE PLAYIN'.

 I HEAR THE VOICE OF A **CHILD** WHO'S ALL DOLLED UP IN A GROWNUP'S SLINKY **GOWN** BUT WHO'S **TERRIFIED** DOWN TO THE **PIT** OF HER **SOUL**.

SHE DOESN'T KNOW WHO SHE **IS**, AN' THERE'S NOBODY SHE CAN **TRUST** TO **TELL** HER.

 I HEAR EVERY **BIT** OF IT IN HER **VOICE**, TOLAND...HOW SHE'S LET HERSELF GET HUSTLED INTO A WORLD THAT'S ALL **WRONG** FOR HER...

...'CAUSE SHE'S ALWAYS DONE WHAT **OTHER** PEOPLE SAID SHE WAS S'POSED TO DO.

 WHEN I GET UP IN **FRONT** OF PEOPLE AN' SING THOSE **SONGS**...IT JUST BRINGS IT ALL **BACK** TO ME.

I'VE GOTTEN REAL **LILY-LIVERED** ABOUT **ENDURIN'** THOSE FEELINGS.

 I STILL LOVE THE MUSIC **ITSELF**, YOU UNDERSTAND. JUST DON'T MAKE ME LISTEN TO MY **OWN** VOICE **MAKIN'** IT.

NOT WITH A **CROWD** WATCHIN'.

MORE **COFFEE**?

 NO, THANKS.

MY, MY, **MY**! LOOK AT HARLAND **GO**!

HE **INSISTS** ON MOWIN' THAT GRASS **HIMSELF**, EVEN THOUGH **LES** IS PERFECTLY WILLIN' TO DO THE JOB **FOR** HIM.

HE SAYS HE **ENJOYS** IT. SAYS IT KEEPS HIS **SWEAT GLANDS** IRRIGATED!

I **HAVE** FELT LIKE I'VE KNOWN WHO I WAS SINCE I'VE BEEN BACK IN **CLAYFIELD**, TOLAND.

I **LIKE** BEIN' PART OF HARLAND'S **WORK**.

I'VE **KNOWN** THAT MAN SINCE HE WAS A SMART-ALECKY LITTLE **BUTTERBALL** IN **GRAMMAR** SCHOOL...

...AN' THERE'S HARDLY BEEN A **TIME** IN HIS **LIFE** WHEN HE WASN'T LOCKED ONTO SOME **GOAL** THAT I THOUGHT WAS **ADMIRABLE**.

NOW **LOOK** AT YOU! YOU'RE **DISAPPOINTED** IN ME, **AREN'T** YOU?

I JUST DON'T THINK YOU'RE **RIGHT**, CALLIN' YOURSELF A **COWARD**.

I'M A COWARD IN **SOME** WAYS... BUT IN **OTHER** WAYS, I'M **BRAVE**.

NOBODY'S BRAVE **ALL** THE TIME!

BUT FOR GOODNESS' SAKE, TOLAND— DON'T ACT SO **DEPRIVED!**

IF YOU WANT ME TO **SING** FOR YOU, I'LL **SING** FOR YOU.

JUST COME OVER HERE TO THE **HOUSE** NOW AN' AGAIN WHEN YOU'VE GOT **TIME** TO KILL.

WE'LL COME OUT HERE ON THE **STOOP** AN' YOU CAN WATCH ME SING FOR THOSE **BIRDS** IN THE YARD!

THEY **DON'T** COME TO **REVIEW** ME FOR THE **NEWS-PAPERS!**

THEY DON'T CLUSTER UP IN CHAIRS TO **STARE** AT ME!

AN' THEY DON'T EXPECT ME TO BE **ANYBODY** BESIDES WHO I NATURALLY **AM!**

BE LIKE **THEM**, HONEY, AN' I'LL SING FOR YOU WHENEVER YOU **LIKE**.

I WONDER IF **I'LL** LIKE NEW YORK ANY BETTER THAN **SHE** DID.

YOU'LL **ALWAYS** BE WELCOME TO MAKE YOUR HOME BACK IN **CLAYFIELD**.

YEAH... I'M **SURE** SUTTON CHOPPER'LL ROLL THAT OL' **RED CARPET** RIGHT **OUT** FOR ME!

HERE... **HOLD** HER A MINUTE. I WANNA TAKE HER **PICTURE**.

THERE'S NOT MUCH CHANCE I'LL EVER **SEE** HER **AGAIN**, Y'KNOW.

WOW!

DID IVY EVER GO ON FUCKIN' **RED ALERT** WHEN I PULLED MY **KODAK** OUT!

AM I NOT SUPPOSED TO BRING A **CAMERA** IN HERE?

THE **RULES** SAY YOU CAN'T TAKE A **PHOTOGRAPH** THAT SHOWS MY **FACE**.

THEY'RE PRETTY **PROTECTIVE** OF THE HANNAH BAY GIRLS' **PRIVACY**.

BUT IF I TURN MY **BACK** TO YOU AN' HOLD HER LIKE **THIS**, IT'LL BE O.K.

OH. GOTCHA!

HERE WE GO. LOOK AT **DADDY**, SWEET-HEART....

CLICK!

ANY INTERESTING **MAIL?**

NO **LETTERS**, JUST **BILLS** AND **FUND-RAISERS**.

ENOUGH ALREADY WITH THE DAMNED **SNOW** AND **ICE!**

Brush, brush!

I AM SO **READY** FOR **SPRING!**

YOU **SOUTHERN BOYS** ARE SUCH **DELICATE FLOWERS!**

HOW ABOUT IF I PUT ON SOME WATER FOR **TEA?** WILL **THAT** HELP?

♪ ♪
... But you can't leave me behind. ♪
♪

♪

A C K N O W L E D G M E N T S

S*tuck Rubber Baby* is a work of fiction, not autobiography. Its characters are inventions of mine, and Clayfield is a make-believe city.

That said, it's doubtful I'd have been moved to write and draw this graphic novel if I hadn't come of age in Birmingham, Alabama, during the early '60s. My own experiences as well as those of old friends and new acquaintances who were kind enough to share their memories with me have served as springboards for various incidents in my narrative, as have the news accounts that I and a nation watched together. I'm grateful to the following individuals for setting aside time to tell me tales: Bob Bailey; Irene Beavers; Clyde and Linda Buzzard; Nina Cain; Dr. Dodson Curry; William A. Dry; John Fuller; Harry Garwood; Mary Larsen; Bill Miller; Bertram N. Perry; Cora Pitt; Perry Schwartz; Jim and Eileen Walbert; Jack Williamson; and Thomas E. Wrenn.

Let me emphasize that none of the individuals cited above had any hand in the actual development of my storyline nor any opportunity to evaluate the liberties I've taken in bringing my own point of view to the fictional incidents loosely inspired by their accounts. Any errors of history or perceived wrong-headedness of interpretation should be laid at my door, not theirs.

Others have aided me, too, in varying ways. Much help was provided at the outset by Marvin Whiting, the Birmingham Public Library's distinguished archivist. I have turned for enlightenment on technical points of law to David Fleischer and to David Hansell. Ed Still provided background on the history of Jim Crow laws. John Gillick helped me with guns; Diana Arecco provided architectural reference; and Murdoch Matthew and Gary Gilbert instructed me on Episcopalian matters. Mary McClain, Stephen Solomita, Dennis O'Neil and John Townsend also provided important nuggets of information.

I'm grateful to Harvey Pekar for answering my questions about jazz lore and to Wade Black of Bozart Mountain/Jade Films for letting me photograph his old movie cameras for reference. And it's by the good graces of Morton J. Savada of Records Revisited in Manhattan that Anna Dellyne's record labels and sleeves have a touch of authenticity.

I'm especially indebted to Leonard Shiller of the Antique Auto Association of Brooklyn, Inc., for cheerfully escorting me from garage to garage in his borough as I photographed not only classic cars but also his fascinating cache of gas pumps, washing machines, vacuum cleaners, scooters, bicycles, beverage trucks, fire engines and other collectibles from a bygone era.

I owe thanks to those who admitted me into their private domains so I could snap reference photos of old furniture, appliances, and representative bits of architecture: Arthur Davis and Ellen Elliott; David Nimmons and David Fleischer; Howie Katz; Elyse Taylor and Leonard Shiller; and Tony Ward and Richard Goldstein. And I'm grateful as well for the special contributions of Grady Clarkson, Tim J. Luddy, and David Hutchison.

I want to thank Andrew Helfer and Bronwyn Taggart, respectively the group editor and editor of Paradox Press, for supporting *Stuck Rubber Baby* unwaveringly during its extended incubation and for allowing me great artistic autonomy in its execution. I'm indebted to Mark Nevelow, the founding editor-in-chief of Piranha Press (Paradox's predecessor), who said yes in 1990 to my proposal for a graphic novel embodying themes that might have tempted a less adventurous editor to stand back, and whose subsequent feedback contributed to a sturdier narrative; and to Margaret Clark, Ms. Taggart's predecessor as editor, for her helpfulness while in that position. My agent, Mike Friedrich of Star∗Reach Productions, Inc., has been an effective problem solver and a valued advisor with regard to both pictures and text. And I'm especially grateful to my longtime friend Martha Thomases, publicity manager of DC Comics, for the help she has provided on too many fronts to mention here, as well as for her seminal insistence, in the face of my initial skepticism, that space might exist at the House of Superman for an underground cartoonist's pursuit of a labor of love.

When I started *Stuck Rubber Baby*, I thought I could do it in two years. It took four. Thus was precipitated a personal budgetary crisis of unnerving proportions, one that forced an unwelcome diversion of energy into the search for enough supplemental funds to cover two unanticipated years of full-time drawing.

Accustomed as I am to creating art in relative solitude, it's been disorienting to find myself so dependent on assistance from others. But dependent I've been, and it's with deep gratitude that I catalog here the varied ways that friends and creative colleagues have gone to bat for me during difficult times.

Most of the forms I filled out in applying for foundation grants asked for letters of endorsement from individuals of creative accomplishment. The following people wrote such letters in my behalf: Stephen R. Bissette; Martin Duberman; Will Eisner; Harvey Fierstein; Richard Goldstein; Maurice Horn; Scott McCloud; Ida Panicelli; and Harvey Pekar.

When things seemed most precarious, a fundraising tactic was devised by which individuals could become "sponsors" of this book through the purchase of original artwork from it — at higher than market value and in advance of its even being drawn. In support of this tactic, a letter of endorsement for *Stuck Rubber Baby* was drafted and signed by fifteen writers, artists, film and TV producers, and other cultural leaders. Those who signed that letter were: Michael Feingold; Matt Foreman; David Frankel; Richard Goldstein; Arnie Kantrowitz; Tony Kushner; Harvey Marks; Lawrence D. Mass; Jed Mattes; Armistead Maupin; Michael Musto; Robert Newman; John Scagliotti; Randy Shilts; and John Wessel. Crucial technical tasks related to fundraising were performed by Tony Ward, Jennifer Camper, Robert Hanna, and Suk Choi of Box Graphics, Inc. I appreciate the willingness of Paul Levitz, the executive vice-president and publisher of DC Comics, to sanction the bending of some normal company practices in the assembly of our fundraising prospectus.

I am deeply grateful to the individual sponsors themselves, whose advance purchases of original art from this graphic novel made the completion of *Stuck Rubber Baby* possible. They are:

Fred Adams
Allan Cruse
Kevin Eastman
Richard Goldstein
Tony Kushner
Stanley Reed
Martha Thomases and John R. Tebbel
Bob Wingate

Additional support for this project was provided by:

Joan Cullman
Glenn Izutsu
Chopeta Lyons
The Anderson Prize Foundation

Let me finish by thanking Ed Sedarbaum, my companion of sixteen years, for his unshakable belief in me and in the merits of this graphic novel; for the concrete help he offered when practical problems loomed; and for the encouragement and thoughtful feedback he has provided as successive chapters have been offered for his assessment.

Howard Cruse
July 1995

Howard Cruse, creator of *Barefootz* and *Wendel* and the founding editor of *Gay Comix*, is an Alabama preacher's kid who counted *The Baptist Student* among his cartoon markets while still in high school. Since then his comic strips and cartoon illustrations have appeared in dozens of national magazines, underground comic books, and anthologies as well as in four book collections of his own. Since 1979 he has shared his life in New York City with book editor and political activist Ed Sedarbaum.